An Artful Seduction

Infamous Somertons

Infamous Somertons

TINA GABRIELLE

This book is a work of fiction. Names, characters, places, and incidents are the product of the author's imagination or are used fictitiously. Any resemblance to actual events, locales, or persons, living or dead, is coincidental.

Copyright © 2016 by Tina Sickler. All rights reserved, including the right to reproduce, distribute, or transmit in any form or by any means. For information regarding subsidiary rights, please contact the Publisher.

Entangled Publishing, LLC
2614 South Timberline Road
Suite 109
Fort Collins, CO 80525
Visit our website at www.entangledpublishing.com.

Scandalous is an imprint of Entangled Publishing, LLC.

Edited by Alycia Tornetta
Cover design by Erin Dameron-Hill
Cover art by Period Images

Manufactured in the United States of America

ISBN 978-1-68281-231-0

First Edition June 2016

For my father, who taught me to work hard and reach for my dreams.
I miss you every day.

Chapter One

JANUARY 15, 1815
THE ESTATE SALE OF THE LATE VISCOUNT BARTHOLOMEW TUTTON
TUTTON HOUSE, MAYFAIR

The first time he saw her, he knew she was going to be trouble. Grayson Montgomery, the Earl of Huntingdon, considered himself an excellent judge of character. Only once had he been wrong, and he'd paid the price.

The lady wove through the crush of well-dressed attendees in the late viscount's elegant library. His eyes were drawn to her ebony curls, full lips, and the lush curve of her breasts. There was no denying that she was a beautiful woman, but hers was a deceiving beauty, and he suspected that many men missed the sharp intelligence in her green gaze.

"From what I have discovered, Eliza Somerton is a respectable proprietor of a small print shop near Bruton Street," Thomas Begley leaned close to whisper.

Grayson glanced at the short, portly man beside him, the Duke of Desford's man of affairs who had sought him out a week ago.

"She is the lady in question," Grayson said. "Her father was Jonathan Miller, the most infamous art forger in London. She will know where to begin."

Begley pushed his spectacles farther up the bridge of his nose. "Still, I—"

Grayson frowned. "You asked for my assistance, correct?"

Begley's head bobbed up and down. "Yes, my lord. His Grace was most insistent on seeking your help in finding the stolen Rembrandt. The painting was to be loaned to a museum and cost the duke a small fortune. His Grace abhors losing money."

Grayson didn't care about the duke's financial loss. His Grace was, after all, one of the richest men in England. Rather, Grayson's motives for agreeing to aid him were twofold. Yes, he wanted the priceless painting returned to the museum for the public's enjoyment. But there was also the issue of Jonathan Miller. The infamous "forger of the *ton*" had fooled the best art critics, auctioneers, and buyers.

Five years ago, Grayson had been one of them.

Grayson nodded in greeting at several passersby, recognizing many of the wealthy collectors, museum curators, and titled nobility who gazed at the soon-to-be auctioned items with an avaricious intensity that marked them as fervent art collectors.

Priceless oils, watercolors, and tapestries hung on the walls. Shelves crowded with Greek pottery, Roman busts, and delicately carved ivory trinket boxes displayed the late viscount's expensive, eclectic taste for fine art.

Despite the vast array of art spread out before him, Grayson's gaze was fixed on Eliza Somerton as she moved among the crowd. She carried herself—regally, almost haughtily—as if she belonged with the throng of rich, influential collectors that graced the library.

Of course, he mused. *Her father was the best charlatan in the country.*

"Her father's been missing for years," Begley said, interrupting Grayson's thoughts.

"She knows where he is. It shouldn't be difficult to discover the truth."

"But the stolen artwork is not a forgery," Begley protested.

"No matter. Jonathan Miller knew every immoral art broker in London who could fence a stolen or forged painting. I plan to use the daughter to find the father."

Eliza Somerton halted in front of a reprint of a fourteenth-century engraving of *I Modi*. Although the erotic piece was merely a reprint, the detail was exquisite—the naked couple, Paris and Oenone, in the throes of passion, limbs entwined, lips meshed, man atop woman.

Mrs. Somerton's eyes widened, her red lips softened a degree as she gazed at the engraving. If she was embarrassed by the erotic nature of the work, she did not show it. A moment later a man bumped into her shoulder and her genuine look of pleasure was broken, replaced by a facade of indifference.

Grayson's opinion shifted. For those few seconds he saw what only a true connoisseur could recognize. She was an art lover herself.

Interesting.

She continued on, stopping before an oil of a landscape, the colors of the artist a masterful blending of vibrant green forest and subtle blue-gray sky. She glanced about as if she were looking for an acquaintance, but she remained in front of the painting, leaning close every few moments as if to study the brushstrokes or the artist's signature in the lower corner.

Clearly she was interested. But why? The painting was a small find in the viscount's vast collection.

What was the lady up to?

"I'm going to speak with her," Grayson said.

Begley's eyes widened behind thick spectacles in alarm. "Here? Now?"

"Yes."

"But the auction is about to commence."

"It's perfect timing, then."

A tall, bald man with a striped waistcoat walked to a podium in front of the room. "Ladies and gentlemen! If you would please take your seats, the auction will begin."

The chairs were three rows deep, jammed next to each other, and swiftly occupied. Grayson quickly took a seat beside Eliza Somerton. She glanced at him sidelong, thick, black lashes lowering as she clutched her reticule in her lap and avoided direct eye contact with him.

"Are you interested in anything in particular?" he asked, his tone light.

She looked up at him then. This close, she was even more striking than from across the room. Her green eyes were tip-tilted at the corners, and her skin was flawless and smooth. How did a criminal like Miller have such an exquisite daughter?

"An experienced bidder never asks what another plans to bid on," she said.

"You're afraid I'll drive up the price?"

"Perhaps."

"Perhaps I'm merely curious."

"I don't think so. I recognize you," she said.

"Oh?" He masked his surprise.

"You are one of London's most prominent art critics and active collectors, Lord Huntingdon."

"I fear you have me at a disadvantage, Lady…"

"Mrs. Somerton."

"Ah, you're a widow, then?" he said.

"What makes you believe I'm a widow?"

"If I were your husband, I wouldn't let you out of my

sight, let alone permit you to speak to me."

She hesitated a moment, then shrugged. "Then it's fortunate indeed that you are not my husband."

She remained cool and composed and he had a sudden urge to unnerve her, to test her mettle and see exactly what he was up against.

He dipped his head close to hers and lowered his voice. "I saw you looking at the *I Modi* engraving. I find the position of the couple most inspiring."

She arched a delicate eyebrow. "Truly? You look like a man who would find such an ordinary position quite droll."

His heart hammered as erotic images instantly came to mind. Images of her naked in his bed, not with her beneath him, but with her on top, those lush breasts bouncing as she rode him.

By God, she was a saucy piece. The conversation was entirely improper. Certainly nothing he would dare speak to a lady. *But she isn't a lady*, he reminded himself. She was Jonathan Miller's daughter.

A moment later the auction began. An assistant brought forth the first item—a bronze bowl from the late Middle Ages. Eliza Somerton turned in her seat and faced the podium, and within seconds appeared immersed in the dynamics of the sale, her eyes lighting with excitement when a notable piece was sold. Her easy dismissal irked him. He was not a man accustomed to women ignoring him.

As the auction progressed, Grayson bid on a few watercolors, but purposely did not offer the winning bid on any of them. The rhythmic pattern of the auctioneer calling out the bids was swift and precise. The *I Modi* engraving was brought forth and sold for an astonishing one thousand pounds. She never placed a bid.

"Next we have the 1640 oil *Landscape with Peasants,* painted by the Flemish artist Jan Wildens," the auctioneer announced as the painting was carried to the front of the room and presented for bidding.

Grayson noted that it was the landscape that had previously captured Mrs. Somerton's interest. She sat slightly forward in her seat, and bit her bottom lip.

Ah, perhaps she wouldn't make a masterful card player after all.

The auctioneer cleared his throat. "We shall start the bid at twenty pounds."

Eliza Somerton raised a gloved hand.

The bidding continued, increasing by increments of five pounds, until the price was up to forty pounds. Grayson waited until two bidders remained—Eliza and an aging gentleman in the front row. When the bid reached fifty pounds, only the lady's hand remained raised.

"Going once, twice…"

Grayson raised his hand. "One hundred pounds."

Gasping, Eliza whirled to face him fully.

His lips curled in a mocking smile.

She lowered her hand, and the auctioneer rambled on, "Sold for one hundred pounds!"

Her eyes flashed emerald fire. "Why? Just to flaunt your wealth over a woman?"

"I desired it."

"You're lying."

"When I see something I want, I won't allow anything to stand in my way of possessing it."

Her lips parted slightly, then closed. "I don't suppose you'll agree to sell it in the future?"

His gaze traveled over her face, feature by feature, then roamed to the bodice of her gown and lingered on her breasts before meeting her eyes. He smiled suggestively. "Everything has its price, Mrs. Somerton, don't you agree?"

If her eyes had flashed fire before, they were absolutely

murderous now. She stood abruptly, knocking her chair over in the process. "Enjoy your acquisition, my lord."

Several people eyed him. Ignoring them all, he leaned back in his seat.

Mr. Begley rushed over. "Well? What did Mrs. Somerton say? Did she tell you where to find her father?"

"Not yet. But I have something she wants, and I expect a visit from her very soon."

・・・

Eliza Somerton burst into the Peacock Print Shop, making the bells chime nosily above the door. Her younger sister, Amelia, stood behind the counter, holding a lithograph in one hand and a wood frame in another.

"I lost the Wildens painting," Eliza said without preamble.

Amelia's blue eyes grew wide. "What do you mean?"

"There was a man…Lord Huntingdon. He outbid me."

Amelia gasped, and the frame clattered on the counter. "Lord Huntingdon? The art critic and collector?"

"He's nothing but trouble."

"Are you certain the painting was the one?"

Eliza's voice was shakier than she would have liked. "I studied it as best as I could, and I'm fairly certain. It's yours, not father's."

"Lud! And Lord Huntingdon purchased it?"

"Yes."

Amelia's brow creased, and she pushed a wayward auburn curl over her shoulder. "Perhaps he'll never know. Didn't he acquire one of father's paintings in the past believing it to be authentic?"

Eliza's stomach sank. "Huntingdon was the worst. His reputation was damaged after it was discovered that he had purchased one of father's forgeries. He was the lead man who rallied the magistrate to press charges."

Amelia came around the counter. "You look tired. Come and rest." Her sister said as she led Eliza to a striped settee in front of the window.

Amelia sat beside Eliza. "Please don't worry. Perhaps Huntingdon will remain a priggish, ignorant aristocrat and hang the painting in his home for the next thirty years and no one will be the wiser."

Eliza bit her bottom lip. "He didn't strike me as priggish."

The man struck her as imposing, demanding…virile. From the moment he had strolled over to occupy the seat beside her at the auction she had taken notice. He was tall and lean and moved with an athlete's grace. His eyes were dark as his hair, which he wore roguishly longer than fashion dictated to brush his collar. His features were bold — nose and chin ruggedly chiseled, making him strikingly handsome rather than pretty.

And the way he had looked at her…dear lord, like he wanted to strip her naked and lick every inch of her flesh. No decent gentleman should look at a lady that way. It had taken all her self-control to act the cool, indifferent widow in Lord Huntington's presence.

"We can't afford a scandal," Eliza said. "We've worked so hard to keep the business."

Eliza scanned the shop, noting the original paintings on the walls, the racks of prints before the settee, and the shelves of artistic decorative items. "There's hope that you and Chloe can both make successful matches."

Amelia rolled her eyes. "Marriage is not on our minds."

The curtain to the back workroom was suddenly swept aside, and Eliza's youngest sister rushed forward to hug her. Chloe smelled like wildflowers and her blond curls bounced with exuberance.

"I made my first sale today! A piece of pottery to the son

of a stockbroker. Nathan's young and handsome with fair hair, warm brown eyes, and—" Chloe halted in mid-sentence after finally noticing Eliza and Amelia's grave expressions. "What's amiss, Liza?"

Amelia spoke up first. "Eliza was outbid on the Wildens painting by an earl."

Chloe shrugged. "So?"

Eliza's brow creased as she gazed at her sisters. Three years younger than Eliza, Amelia was twenty-one, and Chloe was only eighteen. Eliza wanted a better life for them—not to live in fear of their father's sins.

"The Earl of Huntingdon happens to be a renowned art critic," Eliza said.

"You two worry for naught," Chloe insisted. "No one will ever learn that it's a forgery. Amelia's work is impeccable, even better than father's."

"But it's a risk!" Eliza said, unable to hide the fear from her voice.

Chloe's eyes lit with excitement. "Was your earl handsome? I daresay life has been boring around here."

"Chloe! Did you hear what Eliza said?" Amelia admonished. "An art critic outbid Eliza."

Chloe sighed dreamily. "Maybe he thought you were beautiful and he wanted to introduce himself."

Eliza thought of Huntington's hot gaze when he spoke of the erotic *I Modi* engraving. "He didn't act like a suitor."

To the contrary, he'd acted like a man who desired a wild, lustful night with an experienced courtesan.

Perhaps another time, long ago, Eliza would have been thrilled to attract the attention of such a handsome man. An earl, no less! But that time had passed, and she'd learned the hard way that men couldn't be trusted.

Chloe folded her arms across her chest. "How would you know how a suitor should behave, Lizzie? It's been so long since you've had one."

Eliza threw her hands up in exasperation and turned to Amelia. "Tell her. Chloe thinks about nothing but men. Tell her Huntingdon could ruin us. Ruin this." she waved her hand around the shop. "And then where would we be? On the streets or on the way to the poorhouse?"

Silence reigned, then Amelia spoke. "By how much did Huntingdon outbid you?"

"By too much."

As it stood, the fifty pounds she had intended to spend on the Jan Wilden's forgery was close to their entire savings. But it would have been worth it.

The alternative was unthinkable.

Amelia took a deep breath. "I can finish another, you know. We can sell it and disappear—"

Eliza shook her head. "No! I refuse to follow in Father's footsteps."

"But we've done it before," Amelia argued.

"Once and never again," Eliza swore.

One week after their father had disappeared they were forced to leave their modest town home. They were left with little money—just enough to rent the shop and the small rooms above where they'd lived and to buy food to last them through the winter. Eliza had been in a panic. They hadn't the money to heat their living space and Chloe, then only twelve, had developed a lingering cough.

Since that frightening winter, the thought of using Amelia's skill to masterfully forge paintings had always been in the back of Eliza's mind, but she had feared the worst.

Arrest. Imprisonment. Deportment.

Amelia twisted her hands in her lap. "What do you think we should do, Eliza?"

Eliza hesitated, then worked to keep all expression from her voice. "I have to get the painting back before Lord

Huntingdon discovers the truth."

Amelia looked at her as if she had lost her mind. "You can't be serious? It's too risky."

"He doesn't know who I am," Eliza pointed out.

"What if he suspects you?" Amelia countered.

Eliza stood and stiffened her spine with resolve. "He won't. My acting skills have been honed over the past five years."

Chloe's nose crinkled. "You are overreacting, Lizzie. The dead viscount had that painting for years and no one suspected a thing. What makes you think anyone will now?"

Because of him. There had been something sinister in Huntingdon's jet eyes. Something that raised the hair on her nape. He was not a man to be trifled with, but to be taken seriously.

Her future course of action was clear. The truth must never come out, no matter the price.

Chapter Two

Eliza stared at the white stone walls of the imposing mansion in Mayfair. She clutched her cloak with one hand, held a leather satchel with the other, and drew a deep breath.

I can do this, she thought. *I've fooled many men over the years.*

She proceeded to the front door and lifted the heavy brass knocker. A moment later, a somber-faced butler opened the door and stared down at her.

"Mrs. Eliza Somerton to see Lord Huntingdon."

"His lordship is not receiving calls this afternoon," he said coolly.

Eliza handed him an embossed card. "This is my establishment. Lord Huntingdon expressed an interest in some rare prints to add to his collection," she said with just the right note of impatience. "I assure you he will want to see me."

The man's mouth thinned with displeasure, but he nodded curtly and opened the door wide for her to pass.

Eliza stepped inside a grand vestibule with black and

white marble tile, crystal chandeliers, and a winding staircase with a gilded balustrade. A footman immediately appeared to take her cloak.

Eliza followed the butler down the hall. Opening a door, he motioned for her to enter. "Wait here while I advise his lordship of your presence."

Eliza entered a drawing room and surveyed her surroundings. It was decorated in shades of blue, with striped azure silk drapes, an Oriental carpet, and Roman inspired settees. Eliza hadn't set foot in such an elegant room since she was a child and her father had visited a duke intent on commissioning his portrait.

She felt dwarfed by the tall frescoed ceiling, but it was the gilt-framed artwork on the walls that caught her breath. Works by sporting artists George Stubbs and James Ward were displayed for her perusal. She walked close, marveling at the meticulous detail of hunting dogs and muscled prized stallions with glistening coats. She wondered if Huntingdon had a private gallery in his mansion and if the treasures displayed here were but a sampling of his collection.

"Do you like what you see?"

She spun around at a masculine voice. Huntingdon stood in the doorway—tall, broad, and compellingly male. Her heart started to pound. Goodness! In the afternoon sunlight from the drawing room windows, he was even more handsome than at the auction. He was dressed in a meticulously tailored jacket of navy superfine, buff-colored trousers, and shiny black Hessians. His dark hair curled around his collar, and he appeared to be a gentleman of fashion that matched the artwork in his drawing room.

But Eliza wasn't fooled. There was a predatory gleam in his dark eyes that simmered beneath his polished veneer.

How long had he stood there observing her?

"I was told you weren't receiving," she said.

"I wasn't. Until Hutchins informed me I was to buy artwork from you." His tone held a note of challenge.

She forced herself to smile, all the while wondering if he would have her thrown out.

But the earl strolled into the room and held up her card. "The Peacock Print Shop. What precisely do you sell?"

"Paintings, engravings, and decorative items. Work from aspiring, local artists."

"You compete with Ackerman's in the Strand?"

"Not its clientele. Our customers are well-to-do merchants who wish to own a piece of art, but not pay Ackerman's exorbitant prices," she said.

"Fascinating."

She looked at the frames on the drawing room wall and struggled to maintain an even, conciliatory tone. "I don't see the Jan Wildens painting that you purchased at the Tutton auction."

An appealing smile curved his lips. "Ah, I knew there must be more to your visit than you led my butler to believe, Mrs. Somerton. For a moment, I thought you liked me."

Could he tell she found him attractive? She struggled to calm her racing heart and gave him a pointed look. "Let us speak plainly, my lord. I don't believe you truly desire the Wildens painting."

He tsked. "Untrue. I plan on hanging it in my private gallery. Would you like a tour?"

She'd love one. She could spend hours in a museum if she were not a struggling tradeswoman. "Thank you, but no. I truly am here on business."

"Business?" He arched a dark eyebrow as if the mere thought of a woman visiting for business purposes was ludicrous.

"Yes. I have a proposition for you."

He walked closer, his smooth movements reminding her

of a jungle cat. "A proposition? What an interesting choice of words."

Her pulse skittered alarmingly at his nearness. "A business offer, my lord."

"You have my interest." He gestured toward a pale gold settee. "Please sit, Mrs. Somerton. If we are to discuss your offer, let's be comfortable."

He ignored a nearby armchair and sat beside her on the settee. Leaning against the cushions, he stretched his long legs, his polished Hessians shining in the sunlight streaming from the windows.

Eliza was not easily intimidated. She was no longer a young girl straight from the schoolroom, but a woman who worked for her living. But Lord Huntingdon was an imposing man…a big man. Everything about him was alarming, from his height of over six feet, to his broad shoulders, and his chiseled features. He was rumored to be immensely wealthy, a much sought-after bachelor who could be charming when it served him, and highly intelligent.

It was the last trait that concerned her.

"It's not every day a beautiful lady visits with a business proposal."

His voice, deep and sensual, sent a ripple of awareness through her.

She took a breath. "It should come as no surprise to you that I want the Jan Wildens painting."

"It's not for sale."

She placed her leather case on a dainty end table and withdrew an engraving. "I plan to sweeten the deal. As I stated, I sell works from aspiring, local artists. They are exquisite pieces. As an influential art critic and enthusiastic collector, I'm sure you will be interested."

Just as she thought, his curiosity was piqued at the mention of the artwork. The engraving was of a religious scene, Madonna with child, and the work painstaking and impressive. The artist, an unknown laborer, displayed his work at Eliza's shop. Once sold, they would split the earnings.

Huntingdon sat forward and studied the piece. "The detail is quite astonishing for a new artist."

Hope blossomed in her chest. "You can have it plus the fifty pounds I had planned to pay at the auction in exchange for the Wildens painting."

Pushing the engraving aside, his dark eyes studied her intently. "It's not enough."

Her heart sank.

Then he leaned close, very close, until she could feel his warm breath on her cheek. Her pulse quickened and a disturbing tingling began in the pit of her stomach. She'd been wrong about his eyes, she realized. They weren't black, but a rich, coffee brown.

"There are other types of beauty," he said, "living beauty which I crave."

Her heart thundered at his outrageous words. "How dare you! I'm not for sale, my lord."

"Ah, but you are, Mrs. Somerton. You are very much for sale, and I—"

She came to her senses and reached up to slap him. But he was too quick, grasping her wrist before she made contact with his cheek.

His eyes narrowed. "The Jan Wildens oil is a forgery, albeit a meticulous and frighteningly good one," he said, his voice cold and exact.

A cold knot formed in her stomach. "I don't know what you're—"

"You're very good. At first I thought it was your father's work, but the brushwork is slightly different, the signature not a perfect match. You were taught well. I'm not surprised since you're Jonathan Miller's daughter."

He knows!

She felt as if her breath was cut off. He thought she had created the forgery. She'd go to her grave before she confessed it was Amelia's work.

Her voice wavered. "You can't prove it."

"I am an expert."

"You were wrong before, as I recall," she said sharply.

She could have bit her tongue the moment the words left her lips. His face hardened like granite at the mention of the past when he had been fooled by her father.

His fingers tensed on her wrist. "I lost my credibility as a critic at the Royal Academy because of your father. It took me years to earn back my reputation. Jonathan Miller was never found and tried for his crimes."

She was right; Huntington thirsted for revenge. She'd come here to prevent disaster, but had caused it instead. She suppressed the panic rising in her chest. She couldn't give in to it now, not when she needed all her wits about her to survive.

He released her wrist suddenly. "Your choice of artwork to forge is interesting. The Flemish painter Jan Wildens—an artist who often painted backgrounds for the popular Peter Paul Rubens."

"I'm duly impressed by your artistic knowledge."

He ignored her sarcasm. "Wildens is someone your father would have chosen. Miller never copied the masters, but less acknowledged artists, oftentimes a master's students or assistants. That way the history of a painting's ownership was much more ambiguous and could be concocted by a crafty and shrewd art broker."

It was true. Amelia had followed her father's reasoning when she'd chosen to forge Jan Wildens.

Despite her inner turmoil, Eliza lifted her chin and boldly met his gaze. "Since you're certain of your opinion, I shall see myself out—"

"Oh no, you won't. You've come to bargain, remember?"

"I have nothing you want."

He gave her body a raking gaze. "To the contrary, I like what I see."

An alarming heat curled low in her belly. Could she do it? Trade her body for the painting…for their survival?

Yes, if it means protecting Amelia and Chloe.

She swallowed hard and looked into his eyes. "Just what are you proposing?"

His mouth twisted wryly. "As tempting as I find the offer, Mrs. Somerton. I've never forced a woman into my bed. I've never had the need."

She felt her face grow hot with humiliation. Had she misinterpreted so badly? "Then what do you want?"

"A painting has been stolen. Rembrandt's 1624 early self-portrait, *Artist in his Studio.* The owner has requested my aid."

A Rembrandt! It would be priceless! "I don't know anything about it. I swear to you," she said.

"I'm not accusing you of the theft."

"Then what?"

"Where is your father?"

Her father? He believed her father had stolen the Rembrandt? "He's gone."

"He's dead, then?"

"No. Just gone. He left five years ago after…after he was accused." She wanted to say by *him*, but she held her tongue this time.

"He left you alone? And your two sisters?"

She shouldn't be surprised that he knew about Amelia and Chloe. He was too intelligent and ruthless not to have done his research. "We opened the print shop."

He watched her intently, his brow furrowing. "He left you without funds and protection? It must have been difficult for you."

He had no idea. She had spent countless sleepless nights worrying whether they would survive.

The well-rehearsed lie came smoothly to her lips. "You misunderstand. Mr. Somerton opened the shop after we married."

"And after your husband's passing? You continue to run the shop alone and support your sisters?"

Her chin thrust forward in defiance. "We manage."

His frown deepened. "So Jonathan Miller is gone and you don't know where he is?"

"I swear."

"Then *you* must help me find the Rembrandt."

She blinked in astonishment. "Me?"

"You are the oldest. You will recall where to find the immoral and corrupt brokers who can fence a stolen painting of such notoriety."

Her mind whirled with the possibilities. Perhaps not all was lost. She no longer maintained contact with her father's underworld acquaintances. She knew a few of their names, of course, as they were regular guests growing up under her father's roof.

But could she find them?

"If I help you, will you promise to return the Wildens painting?" she asked.

"Why do you want it back so badly?"

"I am a respectable shopkeeper now. I do not want to spend time in Newgate for past mistakes."

"The painting is yours if you keep your end of the bargain," he said.

Her hands twisted her skirts. "What if I help you and you fail to recover the stolen Rembrandt?"

"I'll return your forgery to you nonetheless."

"What about my father? Is this just a farce to find him?" she asked.

"It is not. The Rembrandt is my utmost concern."

She felt impaled by his steady gaze, but she refused to look away. Instead she searched his face for signs that he was lying. A moment passed, then two, before she nodded. "Then I'll agree to those terms."

Eliza stood and held out her hand.

He rose and took her hand in his larger one. "I've never shaken a woman's hand before." His palm was warm through her glove and she suppressed a shiver as his thumb traveled over the satin.

"There's always a first," she said.

"I know of a better way to seal the bargain."

He stepped close, and her stomach dropped. Was he truly going to kiss her? And why did that thought fill her with a strange anticipation rather than panic?

His sensuous lips curled in a smile as if he knew the effect he had on her senses. His arrogance was enough to fight the devastating pull of attraction. She was no longer a young, innocent girl. If he was trying to intimidate her, then he would quickly learn that she was a woman who was accustomed to fighting for her very survival.

She eyed him warily. "You said your interests lay elsewhere, Lord Huntingdon."

He arched a dark eyebrow. "I never said I didn't find you attractive, Mrs. Somerton. To the contrary, I find your questionable roots quite stirring. I've never kissed a forger before."

"Don't call me that," she said tersely. "I'm a shopkeeper now."

"No matter. In case you plan on reneging on our bargain, you should know there is nothing stopping me from calling the constable and handing over your forgery," he warned.

She glared at him. "I'll keep my end of the bargain. But remember this: Our arrangement does not include a liaison."

He chuckled and released her hand. "Don't fret. I'll keep my distance." Walking to the drawing room door, he held it open for her. "Expect me at your shop at ten o'clock tomorrow morning. Have a name for me."

She halted halfway to the door. "Tomorrow? So soon?"

His mouth quirked with humor, and he nodded. "Time is of the essence. If the Rembrandt is to be recovered, we must act swiftly."

...

Clutching her leather case, Eliza departed Huntingdon's mansion. Her nerves were wound as tightly as clock springs. It wasn't only because of the arrangement she'd just struck with the earl, but because of her unexpected physical response to him. When he'd held her hand and stepped close to kiss her, her heart lurched and her knees grew weak. She shook her head at her foolishness. An attraction to the Earl of Huntingdon was dangerous—certainly something she couldn't risk.

At least the visit wasn't an entire failure. Huntingdon knew about the forgery, but he'd offered her a deal, and if she played her part well, she'd get the forgery back. Her goals would be achieved: the print shop would survive and her sisters would be protected. As for how she would find her father's old acquaintances, she didn't know. But she'd think of something…she always did.

The hackney had remained just as Eliza had instructed. The driver was standing outside, and he opened the door as she approached. "I have your guest, Miss."

"Guest?" Eliza frowned as she stepped inside the cab.

"Hello!"

Eliza was startled to see a smiling, young girl sitting on the opposite bench seat. She was pretty with curly, dark hair and brown eyes. Eliza guessed she was no more than fifteen.

"Hello," Eliza said. "Are you in the right conveyance?"

"Oh, pardon. I'm Sara, Huntingdon's sister. I saw you come into the house to visit my brother."

Eliza was surprised to find Huntingdon's sister sitting across from her. "How old are you, Sara?"

"I'm thirteen."

"I see. Does Lord Huntingdon know you're here?"

Sara shook her head, and her curls bounced on her shoulders. "Of course not. He's too busy with the artists to find time for me."

Eliza felt sad for the girl. Huntingdon's reputation in the art world was considerable and she could only assume he spent little time at home.

"Well, it's nice to meet you, Lady Sara. I have two sisters of my own," Eliza said.

Sara's brown eyes widened. "Really? I'd love a sister, but my parents died in a carriage accident when I was young."

"I'm sorry. My parents died also." Or at least her mother had when Eliza was five. Her father had abandoned them, but if she shared Amelia's opinion, then he was dead to them as well.

"I just had to meet you. You see, ladies don't visit Grayson. Well, no ladies other than Lady Kinsdale, and I don't even consider her a lady." Sara wrinkled her nose as if she'd just smelled something foul.

"Goodness. That doesn't sound very nice."

"It's true. Lady Kinsdale — or Leticia, which she insisted Grayson and I call her — often visited him late in the evening, even though I wasn't supposed to know about *those* visits. I never liked her. She's quite full of herself and cold. She may call herself a lady, but she doesn't act like one."

Eliza stifled a laugh. Sara was so refreshingly honest, she couldn't help herself.

"You're friendly and kind," Sara said.

"How do you know that? We just met," Eliza pointed out.

Sara raised her chin. "You haven't scolded me or told me to leave. Lady Kinsdale would have."

Footsteps sounded outside, and seconds later, the door swung open. Huntingdon loomed in the doorway. Tall and muscular, his broad shoulders blocked out the sunlight. His frown was focused on his sister. "Go inside," he said tersely.

Sara sat up straight. "But we were just talking—"

"Inside. Now!" he ground out.

Sara grasped her skirts, slid across the seat, and departed from the cab with a huff.

"Good-bye, Sara," Eliza called out.

The girl turned around to give a jaunty wave, then fled into the house.

Eliza almost felt sorry for Huntingdon. He had his hands full with his thirteen-year-old sister. Eliza vividly recalled Amelia and Chloe at that age.

Eliza's sympathy fled as Huntingdon's dark gaze focused on her. "I apologize for her behavior," he said.

"No apologies needed. She's lovely."

A glint of surprise reflected in his eyes. "She's good, just a bit stubborn and willful."

Eliza smiled. "I deem both admirable character traits in a girl."

He arched a dark eyebrow. "Perhaps for a girl, but not a woman." His look clearly said he thought Eliza possessed both traits in ample abundance.

She opened her mouth to argue, but he didn't give her a chance. "Until tomorrow, Mrs. Somerton," he said, and closed the door.

Chapter Three

"You lucky devil, Grayson. Who was the fetching female that I just saw leaving your home?"

Grayson shut the study door and turned to his long-time friend. "What are you doing here, Brandon?"

Brandon St. Clair, the Earl of Vale, leaned against the fireplace mantle. "I stopped by to see if you wanted to go to White's. Kent and Rodale are placing another ridiculous bet on the books about who will be the first to bed the new Drury Lane actress. But just as my carriage pulled up to your front door, I saw your sister dart inside and the dark-haired woman leave in a hackney."

Grayson frowned. He really needed to do something about Sara. But Eliza hadn't minded the girl's meddling. To the contrary, she'd been polite and friendly to his sister.

Don't be fooled, he told himself. *Eliza Somerton comes from unscrupulous stock.*

"Well?" Brandon prodded. "Who's the woman?"

Grayson crossed the study and went to the sideboard. Reaching for a crystal decanter, he poured whiskey into two glasses. He handed one to Brandon.

"She's Jonathan Miller's eldest daughter."

Brandon's jaw dropped. "You're jesting. How on earth did you find her?"

Grayson took a sip of the whiskey. "I didn't. The Duke of Desford's man of affairs located her."

Brandon stared, clearly baffled. "The duke? I don't understand?"

"Thomas Begley—the duke's man—contacted me to request my assistance in finding a piece artwork that was stolen from the duke. A priceless Rembrandt," Grayson said.

"What does that have to do with Jonathan Miller? The criminal hasn't been seen in London in years."

"True. But he knew all the immoral art brokers who could sell stolen and forged artwork. I believe second best to Miller is his offspring. She agreed to aid me."

"In exchange for what?"

"She is to help me find the stolen Rembrandt, and in exchange, I'll return a painting she forged."

Surprise flickered across Brandon's face. "She's an artist?"

"No. She's a forger."

Brandon chuckled and took a sip of his drink. "Go on."

"She was at an auction desperate to reclaim one of her own pieces. She claims she is now the owner of the Peacock Print shop," Grayson explained.

"I take it you don't believe her."

Grayson scoffed. "She's the daughter of the 'forger of the *ton*.' Would you?"

"You think she'll willingly help you find the stolen Rembrandt?"

"If she wants her incriminating painting returned, then she has no choice."

Brandon regarded him thoughtfully. "Don't jest with me, Grayson. Why did you agree to help?"

"Isn't it enough that I prevent a stolen Rembrandt from being squirreled away in a wealthy man's private collection never to be displayed in a museum for the public's enjoyment?"

Brandon chuckled. "No. What else are you after?"

Grayson drained the remainder of his glass in a single swallow and poured himself another. "I want to find her father. See justice served."

"You're still bitter about the past?"

"Miller sold me a forgery and humiliated me amongst my peers. A critic's reputation is everything."

"I take it she believes you just want to find the Rembrandt," Brandon said.

Grayson shrugged. "She asked me if I wanted to find her father, of course. But I told her the stolen painting was my foremost concern."

"Careful, Grayson. You have a vengeful side, and Jonathan Miller's daughter had nothing to do with her father's crime against you years ago."

Grayson shot Brandon a hard stare. "She's hardly an innocent widow. She's a forger…a charlatan, just like her father."

Brandon took another sip of his whiskey. "Perhaps. But she's also a beautiful woman. Well-shaped, too. Even a monk would notice those breasts."

Grayson raised his glass, ignoring the comment as if he hadn't noticed Eliza Somerton's beauty. But the problem was he couldn't stop thinking about her. She had stood in his drawing room minutes before and glared at him with willful defiance and stubbornness. Yes, he'd noticed her beauty *and* her breasts.

Damn. Why couldn't Jonathan Miller's daughter be a homely, chicken-breasted widow?

"Ah, you've noticed, too," Brandon said.

"What warm-blooded man wouldn't?" Grayson snapped.

The truth was that working with Eliza Somerton was going to test his self-restraint, but Grayson's goal was more important than a tempting bit of flesh. After years of wanting justice for Miller's crimes, the perfect opportunity had presented itself. Eliza Somerton was the key to finding her father.

Nothing more.

...

"He wants you to help him find a thief?" Amelia dropped her brush on the workbench and wiped her hands on her apron.

"Not the thief. Just the stolen Rembrandt." Eliza picked up the discarded brush and set it in a glass jar of turpentine. It was full of other brushes waiting to be cleaned.

There, in the back workroom of the shop, canvases leaned in stacks around the perimeter of the room. Chloe was busy organizing shelves lined with art supplies, glass jars, oil paints, and cakes of watercolor. The odor of turpentine and drying paint permeated the space.

Amelia removed the kerchief that covered her hair and tossed it on the table next to a bowl of red and green apples. She had been painting a still life of the bowl of fruit and wore an old gown and paint-stained apron.

"He knows who we are. He wanted to know father's whereabouts, but when that failed, he bargained for me to help him," Eliza said.

"He thinks you know how to reach father's friends?" Amelia said.

"By 'friends' he's referring to the art brokers who sold father's forgeries. It's been years, but I have an idea where to start."

"What if you don't succeed and the Rembrandt is never

recovered?" Amelia said.

"Huntington promised to return the Jan Wildens painting. He knows about you and Chloe, but thankfully, he believes the forgery is my work, not yours," Eliza said.

Amelia frowned. "How is that good? You are not guilty."

"I don't want you or Chloe involved in this mess. You are both beautiful, young ladies and I want you to meet fine men and marry."

Amelia's lips puckered with annoyance. "I don't want to marry now, and Chloe is too young."

Chloe set down a jar and whirled around. "Don't answer for me, Amelia. I want to marry a rich lord of leisure who can afford to buy me a new dress every week."

Amelia rolled her eyes. "Don't be ridiculous, Chloe. Gentlemen of the *ton* marry for title or money or both and we have neither."

"But Papa was a knight," Chloe argued.

"That was before," Amelia admonished.

Eliza watched her sisters. They were so different in their coloring—Amelia with her striking auburn hair and Chloe with her fair beauty. Amelia was the painter in the family and she had the talent and patience to create carefully crafted forgeries. Chloe was impulsive, free-spirited, and obsessed with men, but she was skilled with a burin and engraved her own original landscapes.

Eliza, for all her love of art, had not inherited the ability to create masterpieces, but the shrewdness to run a business and accurately keep the books and account to the last shilling. They often bickered, but each other was all they had left in this world.

And her sisters were her responsibility.

Eliza stepped forward to end the argument. "Huntingdon is coming to the shop tomorrow. Amelia, you must hide all of your questionable work. Only your originals and Chloe's engravings should be displayed in the workshop."

"Where will you take Lord Huntingdon?" Amelia asked.

"I'll reach out to Mr. Cain first," Eliza said.

Amelia looked at her in surprise. "Mr. Cain? That blackguard won't tell you a thing."

"Mr. Cain is as unscrupulous as they come. If he believes there's profit in it for him, he may be tempted to speak. Besides, I need to purchase supplies. You need paint and brushes, and the fancy gilt frames he imports have helped to sell every painting they've framed."

"What if you refuse to help Lord Huntingdon?" Chloe asked.

"He threatened to notify the constable of the forgery."

Chloe's blue eyes widened. "You believe him?"

An image of the earl's face rose in Eliza's mind. Dark and handsome, but also dangerous. If she intended to help him find the stolen Rembrandt, she'd have to be very wary of him. "I have little choice. He's determined and powerful. A volatile combination."

...

Eliza was ready for Lord Huntington the following morning. The little bell above the door rang at exactly ten o'clock and Huntington swept inside with a blast of cold wind that extinguished one of the wall sconces. He was as strikingly attractive as she'd remembered, and his great coat billowed about him.

Eliza moved from behind the counter to greet him. "Good morning, my lord."

His eyes immediately swept the interior of the room, and she knew his dark gaze missed no detail.

"Your print shop is charming, Mrs. Somerton," he said simply.

Eliza had prepared for his visit. The floor was swept, the counter polished with linseed oil until it gleamed in the sunlight from the large front window, paintings hung on the walls, prints were displayed in racks around the room, and most importantly, Amelia's forgeries were well hidden in the back workroom.

She took great pride in the welcoming character of her shop, ensuring it was well lit, comfortably warm during business hours of the winter months, and offering her customers a pleasant experience.

But now with Lord Huntingdon—the important and influential art critic—standing in the center of her shop, studying his surroundings, she felt oddly nervous. She couldn't help but wonder what he thought. She knew the shop didn't compare to the opulence of Ackerman's. Her customers were wealthy merchants, not aristocrats or members of the *beau monde*.

And she certainly never, ever entertained art critics.

She bit her bottom lip as he moved about the room. Sunlight from the window glinted off his dark hair and highlighted his chiseled features. The lighting was one of the reasons she had initially rented the building. The artwork could be displayed in the most favorable natural light. The rent was costly and there had been months she feared they couldn't afford to pay the landlord.

Huntington flipped through several prints on a rack. "I must admit I'm pleasantly surprised. Your establishment is not what I expected."

Looking up, his gaze caught hers and he smiled. There was something lazily seductive in his look, and she felt a flutter of excitement in her stomach.

"Impressive, very impressive, Mrs. Somerton," he said.

Sweet heavens! Was he still speaking of her shop?

Feeling self-conscious, she smoothed the skirts of her

gray alpaca gown. For a brief moment, she wished she was wearing a fine gown like the ladies of his acquaintance, then inwardly shook herself at her folly. The dress she'd worn to the auction and to visit him at his home, had been her finest and a previously owned and made-over gown. But the dresses she wore during working hours were plain, respectable for a shopkeeper, and much less costly. She was no longer in his realm.

"The artists are unknown, but the paintings are of good quality. How do you afford to buy the artwork?" he asked.

"I don't. Local artists need a place to sell their works and agree to display their prints and paintings in my shop. Once a piece sells, we split the profits. It's a mutually beneficial arrangement," she said.

He pointed to Amelia's landscape of Hyde Park. "Did you paint this?" he asked.

The signature in the bottom corner wasn't legible. It was one of Amelia's tricks. Many customers didn't want works of art produced by female artists, and they always assumed the work belonged to a male.

"Yes," she lied.

"What about your sisters? Are they artists as well?"

"Oh, no. They help me with the day-to-day business of the shop. Nothing else."

"Are they present?"

"Of course." Eliza went to the bottom of the stairs leading to their living quarters above the shop and called out their names.

Her sisters came down, exactly as they had rehearsed. Chloe carried a tea tray, with a steaming teapot. Amelia's paint-stained apron was gone, and she had changed into a different dress.

"May I introduce Amelia and Chloe," Eliza said. "I took the liberty of preparing tea."

Lord Huntington bowed gallantly before the two women. "It is a pleasure to meet both of you lovely ladies."

Amelia curtsied properly, but eyed him speculatively.

"Thank you, my lord," Chloe said, her blue eyes widening at the sight of the earl. She curtsied with enthusiasm. "It's a pleasure to have you in our shop." She set the tray down on an end table beside the settee.

"Go on, girls," Eliza said. "There's work to be done in the back room and Lord Huntington and I have business to discuss."

"Thank you for the tea, ladies," Huntingdon said. "Your shop is quite lovely, but pales in comparison to you both."

Amelia tugged on Chloe's sleeve to get her to leave. Chloe tripped as she strained to glance back.

Once they were alone, Eliza motioned for him to join her on the settee, poured the tea, and handed him a cup and saucer.

Dark eyes surveyed her. "Have you learned anything of interest?"

"I doubt you will believe me, but I recall very little of my father's acquaintances."

He sipped his tea. "You're correct. I don't believe you. Have you a name for me?"

She sat forward. She was expecting him to be difficult and was prepared with her answer. "There is a man who owns a warehouse. He knew Father. I buy art supplies from him, and gilt frames for the artwork I display in the shop. He may have information. I shall meet with him and relay anything I learn—"

"I shall accompany you."

"That's not necessary."

"I shall accompany you and question the man," he said firmly.

"You don't trust me?"

He flashed a wolfish grin. "As much as you trust me."

Oh, what she wouldn't give to wipe the smug grin from his lordly face.

"I'm free this morning," he said.

She blinked in surprise. "This morning? But Mr. Cain isn't expecting me."

"You do business with the man, correct?"

She frowned. "Yes, but still—"

"A businessman's first interest is in profit."

She knew what he was thinking, of course. He wanted to take Mr. Cain by surprise. Unnerve the man in the hopes of obtaining information. "Fine," she snapped waspishly. "If you insist, my lord."

"I insist. Fetch your cloak."

Chapter Four

Grayson wasn't certain what he would find when he had first walked into Eliza Somerton's print shop. He'd told her he was impressed and it was the truth. The shop offered quality prints as well as original artwork from local artists. Although the art may not be worthy of gracing the Royal Academy, it was skillful and creative. Eliza explained that Mr. Somerton had opened the establishment, but Grayson had an understanding of the art business and knew it took a significant amount of work to maintain and keep the shop profitable.

Yet he suspected Mrs. Somerton had hardships. The chairs and settee needed refurbishing, the blue curtains were faded from the sunlight, and the counter, though polished to a high shine, was nicked and old. The signs were subtle and her customers would be hard-pressed to notice, but they were perceptible to his discerning eye nonetheless.

So how had Eliza and her sisters managed?

He leaned against the counter and waited for Eliza to fetch her cloak. He was tempted to stroll to the back room. He could learn much more about the business from the back.

But it was his first time here and he didn't want to press his advantage just yet.

Eliza was going to introduce him to Mr. Cain, and he wanted to question the man.

The curtain to the workroom parted, and Eliza came forward. She was dressed entirely in gray, complete with a plain gray bonnet. The fabric was cheap, coarse wool and the dress had a high collar. Her hair was pulled back in a tight bun that was more suitable for an aging governess than for the striking widow he'd first seen at the Tutton auction. Donning a wool cloak the exact unappealing shade as her gown and tying the strings of a bonnet under her chin, she appeared covered from head to toe.

For some reason, he wanted to tear the coarse wool from her shoulders, toss the bonnet aside, and loosen her ebony hair. Jonathan Miller had been knighted before his disgrace, and his daughters should have dressed in fine silks and satins.

"My carriage is ready out front, Mrs. Somerton," he said, motioning to the door.

She hesitated and met his eyes. "I beg you to reconsider. I do think it's best if I go alone."

There was no way he was letting her question Mr. Cain without him, but his curiosity was piqued. There was an air of apprehension about her that was oddly disconcerting. "Why?"

She shrugged her shoulders. "Mr. Cain's warehouse is near the docks, hardly a location for a lofty lord."

He arched a dark brow. "Should I take offense? I've never been called lofty before. And what about you? Is this warehouse a proper location for a lady?"

"I'm a shopkeeper, not a lady. I am accustomed to Mr. Cain and I frequent his warehouse to buy most of my supplies."

"Is there something I should know about this Mr. Cain?"

"He's particular about whom he sells to, my lord. His

prices fluctuate depending on who his customers are. As soon as he learns an earl has frequented his warehouse, his greed will show through."

"I understand your concern, but we are not intending to purchase today."

Her green eyes widened. "Oh, but we must. Mr. Cain is pleasant only when he makes a sale. I thought to purchase some supplies first and then question him."

"All right. If my presence results in an inflated price today, then I shall account for the difference. Does that put your mind at ease?"

She bit her full bottom lip. "I suppose so."

His gaze dropped to her mouth, and he had a maddening urge to kiss her, to lick her delectable bottom lip.

Damnation. Now was not the time. He needed a clear head and all his wits for their trip to the warehouse.

He assisted her into his carriage and told his coachman the address. A cold rain had started and pattered against the roof of the coach. Eliza sat stiffly across from him, her hands folded in her lap while she looked out the window. She was silent and made no effort to strike up a conversation. Just like at the Tutton auction, he found her easy dismissal of him disturbing. His fingers itched to touch her, to thaw the icy exterior and unleash her passionate nature that he suspected she kept well hidden.

Soon the stench of the London docks permeated the coach, and the masts of tall ships loomed in the distance. The carriage swayed on the cobbled street until the view of the river was blocked by immense warehouses situated close together.

Just then, there was a jingle of harness and the carriage jerked to an abrupt stop. Shouts sounded ahead.

"What in the world?" Eliza said.

"Stay here." Grayson opened the door and hopped out.

A brewer's cart had overturned in the road. Barrels of beer scattered across the cobbled road, blocking the path.

Grayson opened the carriage door and spoke to Eliza. "We have to walk the rest of the way."

"Can't we return another time?" she said.

He shook his head. "I can see it from here. It's not far."

His footman rushed forth and handed Grayson a large umbrella. Holding the umbrella above their heads, Grayson shielded Eliza from the pelting rain as she alighted from the carriage and they made their way to the warehouse.

The impressions between the cobblestones were full of muddy puddles of water. She had to stay very close to him in order not to get wet. He was aware of her hip grazing his thigh, and the lavender scent of her perfume coiled about him. He grasped her hand as they rushed inside the warehouse.

Mr. Cain came forth and eyed the pair with interest. At the sight of Eliza, his face broke into a smile. He was of average height and build with a round face and dishwater brown hair. But it was the lascivious gleam in his brown eyes as he spotted Eliza that shouted a warning to Grayson.

"Mrs. Somerton! What an unexpected surprise." Mr. Cain came forward, raised her gloved fingers, and pressed his lips to the back of her hand. "My assistant did not tell me you were to visit today."

"I failed to write in advance, but I'm glad you are present. May I introduce Lord Huntingdon."

Mr. Cain looked up at Grayson and bowed. "A lord in my warehouse. What can I do for you?"

"The previous frames you sold me were stunning. The artwork in them sold twice as quickly as usual. After visiting my shop, Lord Huntington expressed an interest in purchasing similar frames for his own artwork. Do you perchance have more, Mr. Cain?" Eliza asked.

"Of course! I have a new shipment that will undoubtedly

interest you. Please follow me."

They trailed behind Mr. Cain into the cavernous space of the warehouse. Cain held a lamp and led the way past stacks and stacks of crates. A dozen burly men were busy moving the crates and carrying them into the bowels of the building. Sweat beaded off their brows and the stench of the nearby docks, burning oil, dirt, dust, and perspiring workers pervaded the warehouse. Grayson's gaze was drawn to the crates that had been pried open, revealing everything from Chinese vases to Armenian carpets, as well as rare spices, all stuffed in packing straw.

Cain turned right, then left, then right again in the dim warehouse until at last he stopped. Crates and trunks were piled in a haphazard manner, and Grayson wondered how the man kept track of his shipments.

Mr. Cain set his lamp down and pushed aside a loose lid of a crate. Reaching inside, he held up an ornately carved gilt frame. The workmanship was beautiful and Grayson could envision it framing a Thomas Gainsborough portrait hanging in the Royal Academy.

"This just arrived from Italy," Cain said.

Eliza ran her finger down the frame. "It's beautiful."

"It's a sample. The rest of the crate contains exotic wood that a carpenter can carve and use to frame any painting. Feel free to look, my lord. If Mrs. Somerton will accompany me into my office, I can show her my newest shipment of art supplies." Cain offered his arm.

A flicker of unease crossed Eliza's face before a serene smile descended and she placed her hand on Cain's sleeve. "Pardon us for a moment, my lord. We can discuss our business when I return."

Grayson's eyes narrowed as the pair proceeded to the back of the warehouse. The expression on Eliza's face had been unnerving. He wasn't fooled by her masked tolerance.

The place was immense and he would be hard pressed to find them once they disappeared from sight. Dropping the frame back into the straw, he made a quick decision. He followed at a discrete distance, careful to hide behind crates and remain out of sight until he spotted the doorway of a small room. Grayson crouched behind a pile of carpets, and peeked inside.

Eliza stood before Cain as he opened a wood box and withdrew cakes of watercolor. Words were exchanged, but Grayson couldn't make out what they were saying.

Then the pair stepped out of view. A primitive warning sounded in his brain. He drew closer, straining to see and hear.

"I have Asiatic brushes, oil paints, and canvas as well." Cain's voice.

"How much?" Eliza asked.

"Alas, I'm afraid prices have risen since last time."

"The winter has been harsh on business," Eliza said.

"Oh?" Cain said. "That's a shame, Mrs. Somerton. I suppose I can make an exception for you seeing we've known each other for a while now." Cain reached out to stroke Eliza's arm. His eyes roamed her face, then traveled over her form.

Eliza stood rigid, eyes wide, never pushing Cain's hand aside or objecting. "I will pay as soon as business picks up and I sell more artwork."

Cain stepped close. "I suppose you seek the same payment terms as before?"

"Yes, just as before."

"I'm an agreeable businessman. Let me get your supplies for you." Cain reached up high to remove a box from a shelf, and as he lowered his hand he grazed the side of Eliza's breast.

Grayson had seen enough. Clenching his teeth, he burst inside the room. "What the hell are you doing?"

Mr. Cain's jaw dropped. "I was showing her my goods, my lord."

"By God, I bet you were!"

Grayson grabbed Cain by his shirtfront and shoved the man against the wall. "You perverted blackguard. You were molesting her!"

"I wasn't doing anything the lady objected to, my lord. Just ask her."

Eliza's face was ashen. "He…he's right, my lord. All is fine, really. There's no need for your highhanded manner."

Grayson looked at her in astonishment. *His highhanded manner!* Her face was deathly pale and she gripped the wool cloak tightly about her neck. He couldn't believe she didn't put Cain in his place.

Where was her shrewd tongue? Did she sheath it for everyone but him?

Grayson released the man's shirt, but didn't step back.

Cain smirked. "Do you still want the supplies, Mrs. Somerton?"

"Yes, yes!"

"Forget the art supplies, dammit," Grayson growled. "That's not why we're here."

Cain's eyes sharpened. "Ah, I knew there was a reason behind your presence. It's not everyday a lord visits my warehouse."

"You're right," Grayson said tersely. "I want information."

"It's going to cost you, my lord. I'm foremost a businessman."

"It's about my father's friends, Mr. Cain," Eliza said.

"Where is Jonathan Miller?" Grayson demanded.

Cain chuckled. "You think I know?"

"You were his friend," Eliza said.

"I don't know where Jonathan ran off to, and that's the truth," Cain said.

"What about Miller's acquaintances?" Grayson said. "Someone who sold his forgeries for him. An art dealer of sorts."

Cain's eyes glittered with greed. "I can give you a name. For a price, of course."

A muscle ticked in Grayson's jaw. Cain had some kind of hold over Eliza Somerton, and Grayson refused to give the man a shilling. "Your price is your freedom," Grayson said, his tone hard.

"What's that supposed to mean?" Cain said.

"I wonder about the ethics of your business practices, Mr. Cain," Grayson said cynically. "One word from me and your warehouse will be descended upon by a mob of customs officers."

Cain's eyes were filled with contempt. "His name is Dorian Reed, my lord. You'll find him on Filch Street, in the artist's district. He may even know where Jonathan Miller ran off to."

Eliza blinked in surprise. "This man may know where my father is?"

Mr. Cain glanced at Eliza, then turned back to glare at Grayson. "He might. But you'll have to wait to ask him. Reed is out of town until next week. I suggest you take Mrs. Somerton with you. Dorian Reed can smell a trap a mile away."

Grayson's face turned grim. "One more thing. Don't ever touch Mrs. Somerton again."

"The lady and I have a long-established business relationship. Don't we, Mrs. Somerton?"

To Grayson's surprise, Eliza smiled meekly at Cain. "Your frames are beautiful, Mr. Cain. I'll soon be in need of additional supplies. I shall return another time."

Mr. Cain bowed mockingly. "I look forward to it."

Grayson wanted to smash the man in the face. Grasping Eliza's arm, he hauled her out of the warehouse. It was raining hard now and they hurried down the cobbled street in silence. As soon as they came to his waiting carriage, he thrust her inside.

She waited a full minute until the warehouse was out of view before whirling to confront him. "How dare you threaten Mr. Cain!"

He sat back on the padded bench. "The man was touching you. Don't tell me you liked it?"

Her green eyes flashed in anger. "To whom I allow liberties is none of your affair. Your behavior may have cost me my business."

"Your business? Pray tell me how the owner of a warehouse could ruin your print shop?"

"You arrogant swine! You know nothing."

He narrowed his eyes. "Then tell me. What's Cain's hold over you?"

"The shop has not always been profitable. He's the only supplier who permits me to purchase on credit rather than to pay in advance."

He immediately understood. Buying on credit rather than paying up front existed in business. But for a woman, who most likely had trouble paying in a timely manner in the past, it was probably unheard of. The shrewd Mr. Cain understood this and took every advantage with the lovely Mrs. Somerton.

Still a cynical inner voice cut through his thoughts, and he wondered if she was telling the truth. "I find it hard to believe you cannot buy what you need from another," Grayson said. "You were willing to pay fifty pounds for the Wildens painting at the Tutton auction."

Her eyes flashed emerald fire. "That was almost all of our savings, and I had no choice. As you very well know, I could serve time in Newgate for forgery."

Grayson experienced a moment of unease. He never believed Eliza and her sisters were wealthy, but neither did he believe they were desperate for funds.

"Cain would have sold you what you needed today,"

Grayson pointed out.

"Only because of your intimidating presence. But what about when I must return alone?"

His gut clenched at her words. He shouldn't care that she had to return, but he did. Damn it, he did.

He frowned. "I'm sorry. I didn't know."

She turned her head and looked out the window. Her features looked even paler in the dowdy gray gown. Was that why she wore such an unattractive dress? To dissuade Cain's advances? If so, it hadn't worked. The unappealing color could never diminish her natural beauty. And the swell of her breasts could never be hidden, no matter how many layers of cheap wool.

"I'll go back and speak with Cain," he said.

She spun to face him. "No! Please…you have what you wanted. Mr. Cain gave you a name. Leave it be."

His unease increased at the note of pleading in her voice.

Minutes later, the carriage pulled up in front of the Peacock Print Shop. She was reaching for the door handle when he placed a halting hand on her sleeve. "We'll have to visit Dorian Reed next week together."

"As you very well know, I have little choice in the matter." Not waiting for his footman, she opened the door, hopped down, and rushed inside.

...

A tumble of confused thoughts assailed Eliza as she entered the shop. Whether it was over Lord Huntington's behavior with Mr. Cain or the fact that Cain had provided the name of a man who might know Father's whereabouts she didn't know.

Was it possible? Could she find her father after all this time?

She had tried searching for him for a full year after his disappearance. She had looked everywhere—his favorite coffeehouses, the taverns the artists frequented, and the galleries he often visited—but to no avail. She'd spoken with his friends and no one had known where he had gone. Eventually, she ceased looking and focused on making a new life for herself and her sisters.

But now Mr. Cain had given her a name of a man she'd never heard of—one of her father's dealers who had fenced his forged paintings.

Would Dorian Reed know where her father was?

If so, she had to find out the truth.

Eliza wove through the shop in a daze. Chloe was assisting a customer behind the counter. She looked up with a questioning look as Eliza passed. Eliza merely shook her head and gestured that she would speak with her later.

Eliza climbed the stairs that led up to their small living quarters while pondering the dilemma.

If she found Father after all these years, what would she tell him?

That she missed him. That she had struggled after he had left, but had managed to survive. That she longed for the old days when their mother was alive and their future was bright.

Or that she despised him for abandoning them.

By the time Eliza reached the top of the landing, she felt empty and drained. Amelia was in the front room.

"Eliza! You've returned. What occurred at Mr. Cain's warehouse?"

"Mr. Cain provided us with a name."

Amelia looked at her in surprise. "Who?"

Eliza hesitated. How much to tell? Should she confess what she'd learned?

Looking into her sister's blue gaze, Eliza knew she couldn't lie to Amelia. Never Amelia. They'd been through too much together to start keeping secrets from one another.

"Mr. Cain mentioned an art dealer named Dorian Reed who may have something to do with the stolen Rembrandt." Eliza bit her bottom lip before continuing. "It's possible Mr. Reed may know Father's whereabouts."

Amelia frowned. "I've never heard of a Mr. Dorian Reed before."

Eliza walked farther into the room and set her reticule down on an end table. "Neither have I. But we couldn't have known all of Father's contacts. Mr. Reed may know the truth."

"Don't think of it until then," Amelia said, trailing behind.

"Don't you want to know the truth?"

Amelia looked at her gravely. "You mean find out where Father ran off to? Or if he's even alive?"

"Yes."

To Eliza's surprise, Amelia shook her head. "At one time I would have given anything to see him again. But he made his choice. Because of you, we are better off without him."

"Me? Not a day goes by that I don't fear the worst. That the shop will fail, our savings will be depleted, that we'll be sent to the poorhouse."

"You'd never let that happen," Amelia said with conviction.

Eliza sighed. "Oh, Amelia. I wish I had your confidence."

"You want to find Father badly, don't you?"

"I have to know. Is he alive? Sick? Alone?"

"Chloe still cries for him at night. She was so young and innocent when he left. The poor girl doesn't remember Mother," Amelia said.

Eliza shut her eyes in despair. "Sweet Chloe. All she thinks about is men. I fear she's trying to replace Father."

"We must not tell her about Mr. Reed and the possibility of finding Father. There's no sense in giving her false hope."

"I agree."

"You look exhausted. Come sit and I'll make some tea."

Eliza followed Amelia to a small table and sat. She watched as Amelia filled the kettle with water from a pitcher and set it to boil.

Reaching for her shawl, Eliza draped it around her shoulders. Their living quarters were chilly. The winter seemed endless and they were running out of coal. Most of the precious coal they had was used to heat the shop downstairs, rather than their living quarters upstairs.

She rubbed her throbbing temples. The day had been exhausting, first battling Lord Huntingdon and then Mr. Cain. And there was Huntingdon's outburst with Mr. Cain to consider. The earl had been furious with Cain.

Why?

He'd gotten the information he wanted. She admitted she was grateful that he'd hauled Cain off of her. She despised the short man and the way he felt free to molest her person. She put up with his repulsive touch only because she had no choice. Without his business, there would be no supplies for Amelia and Chloe, no frames to sell her prints. So she smiled, allowed his fetid breath to brush her nape, and his wandering hands to touch her.

Amelia handed her a teacup, and Eliza cradled it in her hands. "I'm afraid Mr. Cain will be difficult to deal with on my next visit," Eliza said.

"More than usual?"

Amelia and Chloe had never met Mr. Cain. Eliza had purposely never taken them along. Only Amelia knew of Cain's moods and what Eliza had to endure to do business with the horrid man.

"Lord Huntingdon threatened Mr. Cain in order to get him to speak."

Amelia's face lit up. "Oh, how I wish I was there to see it."

Eliza thought of Huntingdon's intense eyes, his fierce

expression when he'd grabbed Mr. Cain by his shirtfront and thrust him against the wall. He hadn't looked like a civilized lord; he'd looked like a savage ready to tear Cain apart limb by limb.

Eliza shivered. The notion that anyone would fight to defend her honor was somehow…exciting and exhilarating.

It has been so long.

Eliza swallowed. "I only hope I'll be able to smooth Cain's feathers the next time I must conduct business with him."

"You're right," Amelia said. "I hadn't thought of the future. I wish you'd never have to buy from Mr. Cain again."

"That's just wishful thinking. Sooner or later, I must return."

"What about Lord Huntingdon?" Amelia asked. "Should we expect the earl again soon?"

An image of the handsome earl flashed through Eliza's mind. Her attraction was as perilous as it was unwanted, and it was difficult to think straight in his presence. "No, thank heavens. Mr. Reed is out of town until next week. I have a reprieve from Lord Huntingdon until then."

Chapter Five

Grayson couldn't stop thinking about Eliza Somerton. He should be pleased with today's outcome. The inquiry into Jonathan Miller's whereabouts and the stolen Rembrandt was progressing. He had the name of Miller's art dealer. He'd soon know if the painting had already been sold and to whom. Thomas Begley, and in turn the duke, would be satisfied.

But pleased was the last word that could describe Grayson's mood at the moment.

He kept reliving the look of well-masked revulsion on Eliza's face as Cain had touched her. And the anger in her lovely green eyes when Grayson had interfered had been just as jarring. She'd actually been furious that he'd put Cain in his place.

Maddening woman.

Clearly she was in a bad position and that was what had spurred him to act. With a few hastily scribbled notes, he'd reached out to reputable merchants and arranged for Mrs. Somerton to buy her supplies from other sellers. Never again would she have to deal with the likes of the perverted Mr.

Cain.

Grayson had no reason to visit the Peacock Print Shop until Dorian Reed returned to London. But the truth was he wanted to see Eliza again. She was so different from any other woman of his acquaintance—the widows who boldly propositioned him for affairs, the silly young debutants and their ambitious mamas who vied for his attention at society functions, and the seductive courtesans who sought to be his mistress.

He was an earl, a man of wealth and standing who was used to being pursued by women.

But Eliza Somerton wanted nothing to do with him. Or so she wanted him to believe. There was a spark there, a challenge in her exotically slanted green eyes, the pulse at her throat.

Yet, she was an accomplished actress. He recalled her performance at the Tutton auction, where she'd appeared a haughty art connoisseur who blended in with the clientele. Then she'd shown up at his front door, lied to his butler, and attempted to barter for the Jan Wildens painting. And most disturbing of all, she'd sought to appear a widow of loose morals at Mr. Cain's warehouse.

So who was the real Eliza Somerton?

She was a refreshing challenge and he was drawn to her like a hunter pursuing his prey.

Dorian Reed wasn't expected for another week. Grayson should leave Eliza to her business until then. But he didn't want to wait, and the troublesome thought in the back of his mind refused to be stilled.

What if she went back to see Cain before then?

A low knock on his study door disturbed Grayson's thoughts.

Sara stepped inside. "You asked to see me?" Dressed in a light blue morning dress, she looked young and innocent.

Grayson had been her guardian since their parents died in a tragic carriage accident seven years ago. He'd been busy handling the estates after he'd inherited the title and he hadn't spent as much time with Sara as he'd liked. She had grown into a beautiful albeit headstrong and spirited girl.

Heaven help the man who married her.

"Hello, Sara. I want to discuss your behavior the other day. You cannot just climb into strange carriages and speak to—"

Sara's face lit. "Is Lady Eliza visiting again soon?"

"Sara," Grayson snapped. "Are you listening?"

"She's nice. Oh, and I realize she may not be a real lady. She didn't come in a fine carriage like Lady Kinsdale, but Eliza's much kinder and I hope to see her again."

Grayson raised his hand. "Sara, promise me you will not do it again."

She hesitated, then nodded. "I'll try."

"That's not good enough for—"

There was another knock on the study door, and his butler stood in the doorway. "Lord Vale to see you, my lord."

"Please let him in."

Brandon strolled into the room. "Hello, Lady Sara. You look lovely today."

Sara curtsied. "Good afternoon, Lord Vale. I'll leave you to my brother." She turned and bounced out of the study, clearly more than happy to take advantage of Brandon's presence to flee.

Grayson sighed. "Your timing suited her well. I was lecturing her on her unladylike behavior. Sara chose to introduce herself to Eliza Somerton by climbing into her carriage."

Brandon's lips twitched. "Sara's getting older, you know. Soon it will be her coming out, and you'll be sitting through dress fittings."

"God forbid," Grayson said.

Brandon laughed. "Don't think of it just yet. Now are you ready to go to White's? You can easily forget your problems with a good bottle of brandy."

Grayson rose from his desk. "I was looking forward to it, but something else has come up."

A mischievous glint lit Brandon's eye. "Again? Don't tell me, does it have to do with Jonathan Miller's buxom daughter?"

"It does."

"Have you bedded her yet?"

"For God's sake man, is that all you think about?" Grayson glared at his friend.

"Is that a yes?" Brandon said.

"No. It's a no."

"Then enlighten me as to why you're dismissing your best friend?"

"We visited a warehouse yesterday. The owner was a troublesome sort, but he supplied the name of an art dealer who'd sold Miller's forgeries. There is a good chance this dealer may have sold the stolen Rembrandt," Grayson said.

"What about Miller himself?"

"I'm hoping the dealer knows where Miller is, too."

Brandon's face lit. "Then why are we standing here? Let's go question this dealer."

"We? This doesn't involve you. And besides, Dorian Reed is out of town until next week," Grayson said.

"But something else is troubling you."

Grayson let out a sigh. "I need to see Mrs. Somerton again. I left her in a bad position with the warehouse owner. I want to make amends."

Brandon laughed. "Are you actually speaking of Jonathan Miller's daughter?"

"I know," Grayson snapped. "But I didn't realize the

consequences to Eliza or her sisters."

"I'd like to meet her sisters. Are they as comely as Mrs. Somerton?" Brandon asked.

"Truly, Brandon. Do you think of nothing else?" Grayson replied.

Brandon waved a dismissive hand. "We are titled men, Grayson. We must marry out of duty. But when it comes to our mistresses, we have free will."

Grayson understood Brandon's position. As the eldest son of an old aristocratic family that was admired by Society, but was short on blunt, Brandon had to marry an heiress. His grandmother was insisting he honor a betrothal agreement that was made when he was a young boy to the rich Duke of Townsend's daughter.

Grayson himself had inherited a significant amount of his father's debt along with the earldom, but he had managed to pay off what was owed and earn a large fortune by shrewdly investing in the London Stock Exchange. But Brandon was right about their future. Grayson had to marry a respectable, titled lady. He had Sara to consider, and he required his future wife to help launch his sister properly into society.

But his duty had nothing to do with his current feelings for Eliza.

"Do you plan on buying artwork today as well?" Brandon asked.

Grayson shook his head. "I'm not going as a customer. Mrs. Somerton lives above the shop with her sisters. I want to speak with her."

Brandon strode to the door and held it open. "Let's go, then."

• • •

It was snowing when they left Grayson's Mayfair mansion.

The weather was frigid, and snow had just begun to stick to the cobblestones. The wheels of the conveyance crunched across the road. They passed the Bond Street shops, and the normally bustling business district was deserted.

At last they stopped before the Peacock Print Shop. The sign swung on its hinges from a gust of wind. Grayson and Brandon alighted from the coach and Grayson knocked on the shop's door.

A young lady peered out the window. Grayson recognized her as Amelia, the middle of the Somerton sisters. She mouthed the words "We're closed for the day."

Clearly she didn't recognize him. The curled brims of their beaver hats were pulled down to shield their faces from the wind and snow. Grayson took off his hat, shook his head at her, and continued to pound on the door.

The door finally opened and Amelia stared at them, a look of confusion on her face. She wore a faded dress and her auburn hair was tied back with a simple bow. Her blue eyes shone inquiringly as she glanced from Grayson to Brandon.

"Lord Huntingdon! The store is closed for the day."

"I apologize for my unexpected visit. I'd like to speak with your sister."

Amelia's eyes widened. "I'm afraid Eliza's not here."

His immediate thought was where could she have gone in this weather? And had she taken a hackney or walked?

"Do you know when she is expected back?" Grayson asked.

"Soon."

"May we wait inside?"

Amelia hesitated for a moment, a flicker of unease passing over her face before nodding. "Yes, of course." She held the door open wide for the men to pass.

They entered the shop, and Grayson motioned to Brandon. "This is my friend, Lord Vale."

Brandon bowed, his gaze riveted by the lady. "It is a pleasure, Miss Amelia."

Amelia blushed prettily. "May I take your coats?"

Removing their greatcoats, they handed them to Amelia. Grayson immediately noticed it was cold in the shop. Damn frigid, in fact. He glanced at the fireplace in the corner. Two small pieces of coal burned low in the grate. The burlap sack of coal beside it appeared almost empty. A wool shawl was draped around Amelia's slim shoulders and even with the additional layer of clothing, he wondered why she wasn't shivering. The temperature in the shop could not be more than ten degrees warmer than outside.

"It's quite cold in here," Grayson said.

"I apologize, my lord. We limit the coal we use after the shop closes for the day."

Just then, a coughing sound came from upstairs, followed by a hoarse voice. "Is that you with my tonic, Lizzie?"

"Pardon, my lords," Amelia said. "Our sister Chloe is unwell with a cough. Eliza went to the apothecary to procure a tonic." She motioned to the settee the customers often sat on while perusing prints. "Please make yourselves comfortable. Would you like tea?"

"Tea would be lovely," Grayson said.

Grayson turned to Brandon and found him openly staring at Amelia. The lady stole one last look at them before departing.

Grayson punched Brandon in the arm. "That's not what we're here for."

"Blast! Did you have to do that?" Brandon said, rubbing his arm. "There's no crime in looking, is there?"

Grayson ignored him and waited until he heard Amelia's footsteps on the stairs leading up to the living quarters. He then rose and headed for the back of the shop.

"What are you doing?" Brandon asked, trailing behind.

"Just observing."

Grayson parted the curtain leading to the back workroom. Unframed prints and paintings were neatly stacked against the walls. Small collectibles were arranged on a table. An easel with a canvas was situated in the center.

Grayson walked around to study the work in progress. A palette with wet paint and a palette knife for blending oils rested on the corner of the table. A glass jar was crowded with brushes. The distinctive odor of turpentine wafted to him. The unfinished painting was a landscape of oak trees, rolling hills, and a clear-blue sky. A discarded, paint-stained apron was slung across a rickety chair.

Grayson leaned close to the canvas. The paint was wet. He studied the leaves of the trees, which appeared to be moving.

"I'll be damned," Grayson said.

"What?"

"Amelia is the forger of the Jan Wildens painting, *Landscape with Peasants*, not Eliza."

"How can you tell?"

"Eliza said her sisters didn't paint. She lied. We must have interrupted Amelia in her work. The brush strokes, the minute detail of the leaves and the bark. The way the puffs of cloud seem to be moving across the sky. She is very talented. Just like her father."

"She seems so young," Brandon said.

"Eliza's protecting her sister. That's why she so desperately wants to reclaim the forgery."

She lied to me.

He should be angry, but he experienced something else entirely.

Admiration.

She was completely loyal to her sisters. So much so that she would go to prison for a crime she didn't commit. Her family loyalty was foreign to him—so different from his own upbringing and his father who had cared more for his whiskey and his club than for his young son and wife.

He debated whether to tell Eliza he knew her secret. The knowledge was an ace up his sleeve.

Careful not to disturb anything, they returned to the front room and the settee just as Amelia returned carrying a tea tray. She proceeded to serve them tea.

Grayson looked out the window and was alarmed to see the snow was falling heavily now. His need to see Eliza escalated. He was concerned, damn it. They had been in the shop for a half hour now and she had not returned. She would be chilled to the bone.

"Hasn't it been a while since your sister departed?" His tone was harsher than he'd intended.

Amelia glanced up. "She should be back shortly. If you have business elsewhere, I will advise her of your visit."

"No. We'll wait."

He had finished his cup of tea when the store's bell chimed and the door opened.

Grayson was instantly on his feet.

Eliza rushed in shaking off snow from her cloak. She clutched a dark bottle in her right hand. Grayson noticed her thin gloves were soaked. Her fingers would be numb.

"I've returned with the tonic, Chloe!" Eliza called out.

She stopped suddenly as she spotted the men, her green eyes wide. "What are *you* doing here?"

It wasn't the greeting he'd hoped for. But what did he expect? "I came to speak with you, Mrs. Somerton."

Brandon stepped forth and bowed. "As Grayson has forgotten his manners, may I introduce myself. Lord Brandon Vale."

Just then, Chloe started down the stairs, clutching a robe to her chest. Her face was pale and her nose red. She coughed and halted halfway down the stairs when she spotted the crowd. "What have I missed?"

Grayson turned to Eliza. "Is there a place we may speak in private?"

Eliza was clearly taken by surprise. Her eyes darted to the back room, but one glance from Amelia and she'd changed her mind.

"Chloe, have some tea." Eliza handed Amelia the bottle. "Amelia, please give Chloe her tonic."

Eliza then turned to him. "We can speak privately upstairs, my lord." She headed for the stairs, and Grayson followed.

Chapter Six

Eliza was aware of Lord Huntington's every step behind her as she climbed the stairs. She had been freezing, rushing through the snow-covered streets to the apothecary. She had hurried back with the medicine only to find Lord Huntingdon waiting for her.

Her first thought had been shock, followed by the odd flutter of excitement she felt low in her belly. He'd looked so masculine standing in the shop. Then she'd studied him more closely. He'd appeared tired, and fine lines had carved furrows between his brows. Why? Had something transpired?

Their living quarters were modest, with a tiny kitchen and adjoining bedroom. He came forward and she motioned for him to sit at the kitchen table. She was conscious of his gaze as he scanned the space. It wasn't his luxurious Mayfair mansion, but it was their home and it wasn't inherited or given to them. She'd worked hard for what they had and it was a far cry from the poorhouse.

Huntington sat and crossed his legs. He seemed far too large and masculine for the table.

"It's chilly in here," he said.

She detected a hint of censure in his tone, and her lips thinned with irritation. "Is that what you came to tell me?"

"You cease adding coal to the fire after business hours."

"Coal costs money; we must conserve." Her fingers twisted in her skirts.

"What's wrong with Chloe?"

She was startled by the change of subject. "She has a cough."

"Maybe if there were heat in the place she wouldn't be sick," he said.

She stiffened, pride rising to her defense. "Don't you think I've thought the same thing? What would you have us do? Spend all our money on heat and then be out on the street a week later? Would that be better for Chloe?"

"I'm duly reprimanded, Mrs. Somerton."

"Why are you here? Dorian Reed will not be back in town until—"

"It has nothing to do with Reed. I came to apologize. I handled Mr. Cain badly yesterday. When I saw him touch you, I didn't think. I just reacted."

She was truly shocked now. "I...I..."

He pulled out a sheet of foolscap from his jacket pocket. "I've many contacts in the art world. This is a list of reputable merchants who will sell you art supplies and anything else you may need for your shop. They are to deal with you on credit with the understanding that if you do not pay, I will. You need never return to Mr. Cain's warehouse again."

She stared at the paper, afraid to take it and even more afraid not to. "Why? Why would you do this?"

He leaned forward in his chair. "Because I didn't like the way he touched you."

She gasped and stared up at him. The current between them was there again, damn him. Every inch of her body responded to his nearness, his medievally possessive words. She nervously licked her bottom lip, and his gaze dropped to her mouth. Then he reached out and stroked the pad of his thumb across her lip. Her breath hitched, and her insides seemed to melt. It was like lightning during a storm, uncontrollable and forceful, and it frightened her just as much as it enthralled her.

She reached up and touched his wrist. "Don't, my lord,"

"It's Grayson. Call me Grayson." He didn't remove his touch on her mouth. For several heartbeats they stayed like that; his thumb grazing her lip, her fingers on his wrist.

Then he leaned forward in his chair and kissed her. She'd been kissed before, but nothing could compare to Huntingdon's mastery. He was skilled; it was clear in the stroke of his tongue on the soft fullness of her bottom lip. He was patient and calculating. His warm lips lightly brushed hers, back and forth, in a series of slow, shivery kisses. He did not try to ravish her or grope her in an overzealous fashion. Nor did he use brute force to overpower her. He preferred skill and seduction. He devastated her senses with one touch of his mouth.

She sat perched on the edge of her chair as his lips grazed hers over and over. He touched her only with his mouth, and yet liquid heat flooded her limbs, and her nipples tightened and chafed against her chemise. The scent of his shaving soap, sandalwood and cloves, filled her senses. Her eyelids fluttered closed and she leaned closer and parted her lips with a sigh. His tongue slid into her mouth, hot and delicate. Her tongue tentatively followed his. He teased her, gently, seductively, until the kiss sang through her veins.

She fervently wished they weren't sitting, that she was in his arms and pressed against his broad chest. She was so cold and she longed to feel his strength, his glorious heat… feel *him*.

Then he raised his hand and cradled the side of her face like she was made of precious china. The light touch was intimate and nearly her undoing. She moaned, she couldn't help herself, and her fingers slid over his forearm.

He stiffened. Her lashes flew up to see the depths of desire in his dark eyes.

She experienced a shiver of fear and came to her senses. This wasn't a lover's tryst, but a dangerous game, a battle of wills between two combatants. If she showed lust, any weakness, he would seize the advantage between them.

She stood and shook out her skirts in an effort to hide her shaking legs. "This was a mistake. You should leave, my lord."

He pushed his chair back and rose. He was much too close to her, and she had to crane her neck to look up at him. "How long were you married?"

She frowned. "Pardon?"

"How long?"

"Three years," she blurted out. She knew exactly what to say as she had rehearsed the story often enough in the past.

"You kiss like an innocent."

Of all the things she expected him to say after their intimate experience, *that* was not one of them. "Mr. Somerton was older, but we had a satisfying marital relationship."

"How satisfying?"

She must not let him presume or question. "You should leave now," she said curtly.

His face hardened. Gone was the man who had kissed her so seductively and gently mere moments ago. The desire was still written on his face, but there was something else, something more in the depths of his gaze.

Determination. Possessiveness.

Picking up the sheet of paper from the table, he thrust it at her. "Take it. Never go back to see Mr. Cain again."

She'd forgotten all about his list of reputable merchants

eager to do business with her on credit, knowing Lord Huntingdon backed her transactions. Her gaze snapped to his. Oh, how she wished she could rip the paper and throw the pieces at him. But she wanted that list, needed it, and he knew it.

She took the paper and raised her chin. "I'll consider it."

His nostrils flared at her statement. "Dorian Reed returns in five days. I'll send my carriage for you."

Chapter Seven

"Lord Vale is very handsome," Amelia said.

"Pardon?" After Grayson departed, Eliza had tucked Chloe into bed beneath their warmest wool blanket and joined Amelia for tea. Eliza struggled to remember what they had been talking about. She tried to focus her mind on something other than the passionate kiss she'd shared with Huntingdon.

Amelia waited expectantly, teacup in hand. "I said Lord Vale is handsome."

"I didn't notice."

"No doubt since you were consumed with Lord Huntingdon."

Eliza's teacup shook as she placed it on her saucer. "Amelia! I'd hardly call myself consumed."

"Oh? What did you two discuss upstairs then?" Amelia challenged.

Eliza didn't want to talk about what had occurred. How long had it been since he'd kissed her? An hour at most? Her emotions still rioted within her. Her body still trembled. Not from fear, but from something much worse, something as exciting and dangerous as fire to dry kindling.

Desire.

He'd started with a simple kiss, but it had been so easy for him to coax her response. Then his lips and tongue had explored and tasted and she had been hard pressed to stop him. She'd realized for the first time just how potent lust could be and how much power it gave a skilled man.

"Well? Aren't you going to tell me?" Amelia prodded.

Eliza pulled a folded sheet of paper from her skirt pocket and handed it to Amelia. "He gave me this."

Amelia's brow furrowed. "It's a list of names. What is it for?"

"He apologized for his behavior with Mr. Cain. Those are names of suppliers who will sell to me on credit with the earl's financial backing."

Amelia dropped the paper in her lap. "This is wonderful! You never have to deal with the likes of Mr. Cain again."

Eliza chewed her lower lip. "Huntingdon's after something."

"What? He already has your cooperation. Perhaps he's a true gentleman."

"Ha! You sound like Chloe."

Amelia sighed. "Huntingdon's friend seems like a gentleman."

Amelia had a strange dreamy look on her face, one Eliza had never noticed before. Amelia had always been levelheaded and shrewd when it came to men. It was unlike her to overlook social rank and fall prey to a handsome, charming lord.

"You're smitten," Eliza said.

Amelia stiffened. "I'd hardly call it smitten just because I find a man attractive. And I'm *not* Chloe. She's already lost her head and believes she's in love with Lord Huntingdon.

She called him an Adonis."

Eliza rolled her eyes. "Lord help us all."

Amelia handed the list back to Eliza. "Are you going to use this then?"

Eliza shrugged. "I haven't decided. I don't want to be indebted to Huntingdon. As it stands, I must accompany him to see Dorian Reed next week."

Amelia shot her a skeptical look. "I know you, Lizzie. You're thinking about Father and whether Reed knows his whereabouts."

"How can I not?"

"Don't go," Amelia implored. "Sell one of my forgeries. We can leave town."

It always amazed Eliza how Amelia had no qualms about selling forged works. She was like their father in that regard; she'd do what was necessary without fully considering the consequences. Eliza, on the other hand, didn't want to flee London like common criminals.

Where would they go? How long would the money last?

Her sisters stood no chance at a respectable marriage if they took that course of action.

"No, Amelia," Eliza said forcefully. "I'll not live a life like Father. He may have escaped a trial and Newgate, but we may not be so fortunate. I'll not put you and Chloe at risk."

Amelia sat forward in her chair, a look of resolve flashing in her blue eyes. "Use Huntingdon's contacts then. If he hadn't behaved as he had with Mr. Cain, you wouldn't need to go elsewhere."

Eliza forced her confused emotions into order. "I suppose you're right. I'll accept his help just this once. But he's a dangerous man and I'd be a fool to allow myself to be indebted to him."

• • •

After departing the Peacock Print Shop, Grayson and Brandon made their way to White's Club. A porter took their topcoats, gloves, and beaver hats, and they seated themselves in Chippendale chairs at a table in the famous bay window overlooking St. James's Street. Snow fell heavily, covering the vacant street with a white blanket as a waiter arrived and served them brandy. Coal burned brightly in the grate of the ornate fireplace. Candlelight reflected off the deep burgundy paneling and the gilt framed portraits of former Tory club members.

Warmth seeped into Grayson's bones. Such comforts should be satisfying enough, but his thoughts returned to Eliza and her sisters in the cold shop.

"Quite the charming family, don't you agree?" Brandon said.

Grayson turned from the window. "I suppose you could call them charming."

Coarse male laughter sounded from the rear of the club where a few men had ventured out in the weather to engage in a game of hazard. Attendance was sparse tonight, but gamblers could never stay away for long.

"I had no idea Jonathan Miller's daughters were so attractive," Brandon said.

Grayson sipped his brandy. "Why am I not surprised you noticed?"

Brandon lowered his glass. "I think you should leave them be."

Grayson scowled. "Leave them be? It's only the eldest I'm interested in. She's going to lead me to a stolen Rembrandt and her father."

Brandon took on a serious expression, obviously displeased. "They have enough hardship in their life without you bringing back their thief of a father who abandoned them. It's a wonder they've kept their household together thus far."

Guilt pierced Grayson's chest. He didn't want to feel it, but the unwanted emotion was there. His thoughts returned to Eliza and their shared kiss. The sizzling attraction that had been building between them since he'd set eyes on her at the Tutton auction had driven him to kiss her. She'd been tentative at the first touch of their lips, and even stunned by the stroke of his tongue against hers. For all her worldly demeanor as a widow, she'd reacted like it was her first.

Ludicrous.

She'd been married for three years. And she was clearly a woman of passion. Her instinctive response to him had been strong, and it had taken all of his willpower not to sweep her into his lap and ravage her mouth. He'd wanted to press his lips to more of her skin—her nape, her shoulders, her magnificent breasts. He didn't know what was more disturbing, her apparent inexperience or the explosion of lust that had shot straight to his groin.

He inwardly cursed himself. To want any woman so badly was unwise, let alone his enemy's daughter.

He *refused* to succumb to the temptation.

"I'm not a bastard. I realize they're struggling," Grayson said.

"The place was freezing. I wouldn't be surprised if they all came down with colds," Brandon countered.

Grayson was again besieged by remorse. "I'll see that they don't."

"How? She seems too proud to accept your charity."

"She is stubborn," Grayson mumbled. "And too pretty for her own good." He sipped his drink, and the alcohol left a bitter taste in his mouth despite the fine quality of the brandy. "And to think all along that her sister is the artist and forger."

"Leave Amelia out of this," Brandon snapped, drawing the attention of an older gentleman enjoying a plate of roast beef a few tables away.

Grayson's lips curled in a mocking smile. "Don't be so fiercely protective. My arrangement is with Eliza. She has no idea that I'm aware Amelia is the artist and I'm going to keep the knowledge to myself for a while."

Brandon shifted in his seat. "Good. Because I'd like to see Amelia again."

"Don't be an idiot. You need an heiress, remember? The Duke of Townsend's daughter waits."

Brandon narrowed his eyes. "If I didn't know better, Grayson, I'd say you're lusting after Eliza Somerton. How long has it been since your last mistress? Perhaps you need to replace her."

Grayson drained his glass in one swallow, remaining silent. He never lusted after a woman. He was always in control of his emotions, in and out of the bedroom. The only wild passion he experienced was when gazing at expertly executed artwork. Even then, he presented a cool facade as the critic. No one could know the inner euphoria he was experiencing. No one knew his opinions or his thoughts until he decided to express them.

Until I kissed Eliza. He wasn't in complete control then.

Perhaps Brandon was right. It had been four months since Grayson had ended his last relationship—not with a mistress, but with a wealthy widow. She was more than eager in the bedroom, a well-practiced lover, but she had a troublesome tendency to want more—more of his time in and out of bed, which was something he was unwilling to give. So he'd ended it.

Kissing Eliza Somerton in her tiny upstairs kitchen had surprised him. She'd been sweet with simmering passion, and his response had been instant and combustible. She was fresh, exciting…genuine. It was like coming upon a beautiful work by a new artist. His blood would pound and his pulse race with the thrill of discovery.

But the excitement of the first moment rarely lasted. He would soon be distracted by another fine work uncovered in a visit to an artist's studio or masterpiece displayed on a gallery wall.

Eliza was no different. Now that he was no longer in her presence his head was clearer. His strong attraction was simply due to a recent lack of sex. She was a beautiful woman, nothing more. There were scores of attractive females in London who could eagerly satisfy his needs. If he couldn't have Eliza, he could easily find another.

Chapter Eight

The snow continued to fall heavily overnight, finally stopping in the early morning hours. Eliza parted the curtains in the front window of the shop and gazed outside. Snow covered the street, crisp and pristine. The row of small, bow-fronted shops appeared uninhabited, her view of the street far from the usual bustling London business district. Sunlight reflected off the snow-capped church spires in the distance. The effect gave one a feeling of bottomless peace and satisfaction, like gazing at a lovely watercolor.

But no matter how beautiful the snow appeared, the weather was bad for business. The shoppers they relied upon seemed to be hibernating. There hadn't been one customer all day, and she worried about the remainder of the week. No one wanted to buy artwork, prints, or bric-a-brac decorations in such weather. They needed necessities, food and coal. Items Eliza would have to venture out to obtain as well.

Chloe's cough had worsened overnight, and to Eliza's dismay she'd developed a fever. Both Eliza and Amelia were up all night laying cool cloths on Chloe's forehead in an attempt to bring down the fever. They'd given Chloe their warmest blankets and then had huddled together on the same mattress for warmth, until Eliza had broken down and burned their small, precious store of coal. Without customers, there was no reason to keep the shop well heated during the day. And coal wasn't all they needed. They were running low on tonic for Chloe. Eliza knew she'd have to make another trip to the apothecary.

Later that afternoon, Eliza approached their shop with another small bottle of tonic and paused at the sight of the fine coach and matching bays stopped in front. The horses tossed their heads restlessly and snorted, steam curling from their nostrils in the frigid air.

Eliza's pulse quickened with a strange inner excitement. *Grayson.*

Hurrying inside, she scanned the room for the tall, handsome earl. The shop was blessedly warm, heat radiating from the grate in the corner. A burly footman was setting down a heavy burlap sack of coal to the left of the fireplace. Multiple lanterns burned brightly adding a cheerful glow to the prints on the wall.

Amelia rushed forward, her cheeks flushed with excitement. "Look what Huntingdon sent. Warm cloaks for all three of us. Blankets, too. And enough coal to heat the place for at least three months." Amelia thrust a fur-lined cloak at Eliza.

The cloak grazed her cheek, and Eliza gasped. The fur was sable and the softest she'd ever felt. It was too much to comprehend. She thought of the last time Huntingdon was here, when they'd kissed. He'd said the place was freezing.

She removed her own threadbare cloak and went to the radiating grate. Peeling off her wet gloves, she held out her cold hands and tried to calm her racing heart. "What is he thinking?"

Amelia approached. "Perhaps he's simply being nice."

"First the list, now this," Eliza muttered.

"Maybe he's concerned."

"Men aren't intrinsically altruistic, Amelia. They are a self-serving lot," Eliza argued.

Just like Father. The one man they'd believed they could trust above all others—their flesh-and-blood parent—had abandoned them. If her own father was so selfish, how could Eliza trust any man?

Turning from the fire, Eliza spoke to the footman. "Where is his lordship?"

"He's not here, miss. He gave orders to deliver the coal."

She stiffened her spine. "Take it back. We're not in need of his charity."

Amelia groaned behind her.

The footman straightened to his full height. "I have my orders. Lord Huntingdon was most insistent."

"Then will you deliver a note to his lordship?" Eliza asked.

He nodded and Eliza took paper and pen from the counter and hastily scrawled her brief message.

> *Lord Huntingdon,*
> *Thank you for the coal and cloaks, my lord. But as I recall our arrangement did not include gifts of any nature.*
> *Mrs. Somerton*

She sealed the envelope and handed it to the footman.

"Wait!" Amelia cried out. "What about the doctor? You cannot think to send him away. You must do what's best for Chloe."

"What doctor?"

"He arrived shortly after the coach with the coal. He's

upstairs examining Chloe as we speak."

Just then a rotund man wearing thick spectacles and clutching a black bag came down the stairs. "Miss Chloe is resting peacefully now." He handed Eliza a dark bottle. "Cease giving her the tonic from the apothecary and replace it with this instead. If you keep the place warm and have her drink plenty of water, she should recover quickly enough." He proffered a card with his details. "I shall return in two days' time to check on her. If she appears worse, I may be reached at this address."

Eliza glanced down at the card in her hand, then back at the doctor. "Thank you. I'm afraid I will have to pay you for your services over time."

His eyes warmed behind his spectacles. "You misunderstand, Mrs. Somerton. My services were paid in advance by Lord Huntingdon."

Amelia handed the man his hat and coat, and he departed with the footman.

Eliza stood staring at the door, dumbfounded.

Amelia approached and touched her arm. "For the first time in so long it's blessedly warm and the cloaks are wonderful. Don't be a fool, Lizzie. Take what the earl's offering. How else will we get through this horrid winter until a steady business returns?"

Eliza's mind reeled. "I agree we need such things. I'm not a fool. But what does Huntingdon want in exchange?"

...

Grayson's answer to Eliza's note arrived the next day along with a tin of medicinal tea for Chloe.

> *Mrs. Somerton,*
> *I'm perfectly aware of our arrangement; however, you are useless to me if you catch a cold.*

Burn the coal and wear the fur.
Huntingdon

The arrogance of the man! She knew she should accept what he offered without a qualm. Any woman in her position would do so. He was a wealthy earl; she was a struggling shopkeeper and a forger's daughter. But she had pride. She didn't want his charity, hated having to accept it. They'd managed their own affairs and survived just fine for five years without him.

Yet how could she refuse the doctor's services or the medicine for Chloe?

It was all troublesome. She hadn't been able to stop thinking about him since his kiss. Common sense told her he wanted something from her other than what she'd already agreed to.

But what more could he want? Dorian Reed wasn't expected back in town for four more days. Why couldn't Huntingdon just leave her alone until then?

Eliza paced around the racks of prints in the shop, clutching his letter in her hand, when the shop's bells chimed. She whirled to the door, hopeful that a customer had finally arrived. A short, lanky youth stepped inside with a gust of cold air. A dusting of snow covered his shoulders and battered hat.

"Mrs. Eliza Somerton?"

"Yes."

"I 'ave a delivery for ye," he said, thrusting a package in her arms.

Eliza glanced down at the bundle. The package was wrapped in plain brown paper and tied with string. "Who sent it?" she asked, even though she already knew the answer.

"I don't know, miss. I only get paid to make deliveries." He left the shop as quickly as he had come.

Eliza set the package on the counter and unwrapped the brown paper to find three beautiful shawls made from the softest wool she'd ever felt. Each was a different color—

green, blue, and rose—and she could picture a fine lady sitting in her parlor on a cold afternoon sipping oolong tea with one of the colorful shawls draped around her shoulders.

Heart thrumming, Eliza searched for a note, but didn't find one. It really wasn't necessary. She knew Grayson had sent them.

Footsteps sounded on the stairs as Amelia descended. "I heard the bells chime. Have we a customer—" she halted as she spotted the shawls spread across the counter, "Oh! How beautiful!"

An hour later, Chloe had joined Amelia, and together they giggled with glee as they admired the workmanship of the shawls and the fine wool. Chloe sat before the fireplace with the rose shawl draped around her shoulders, drinking tea. Her health had slightly improved since using the doctor's tonic. The lingering cough had lost some of its concerning force, and the fever was down.

"I told you he was courting you," Chloe said to Eliza.

"There'll be a price to pay, I'm telling you," Eliza muttered.

Chloe settled in the cushions of the settee. "Maybe he'll visit the shop after he finds the stolen painting. His reputation alone as a premier art critic will increase business tenfold."

Eliza didn't have the heart to contradict Chloe.

All men left. They were selfish and untrustworthy. She certainly couldn't rely upon them. Hadn't Father abandoned them to fend for themselves? Eliza had been left behind to care for her two younger sisters with little more than a shilling. She'd learned to trust herself. Lord Huntingdon was no different. He was worse, in fact. As soon as he had what he wanted—the stolen Rembrandt—then he would leave as well.

Eliza pulled Amelia behind the counter. "I'm going to see Huntingdon."

"What for?"

"He's after something. I want to know what it is." She'd demand an answer, and this time, the earl would give her one.

Chapter Nine

Eliza decided to wear the sable cloak Grayson had provided just so she could leave it with him. She wouldn't make her sisters give up theirs. They had few niceties in life and she wouldn't let her pride stop them from enjoying the gifts.

As she left the shop, a blast of frigid air struck her face. For a fleeting instant, she wanted to turn and rush back into the shop, where Grayson's coal burned brightly in her fireplace grate.

Strengthening her resolve, she plodded onward. She had difficulty hailing a hackney in the snow-packed lane and was forced to walk three blocks to Bond Street before finding a vacant cab. With shoes soaked through, her feet and hands numb, she was grudgingly grateful for the warmth of the cloak.

This time when she knocked on the front door of the earl's Mayfair mansion, the stern-faced butler recognized her.

"Mrs. Somerton to see Lord Huntingdon," she said.

The servant arched a knowing brow. "Is he expecting to conduct business with you again?"

"We already have an arrangement," she said.

The butler remained composed as he held the door open. Stepping inside, Eliza nearly sighed out loud as warm air surrounded her. A liveried footman came forward to take her cloak.

"No, thank you. I'd like to keep it until I see his lordship."

A flicker of surprise crossed the footman's face.

The butler appeared unmoved. "This way, Mrs. Somerton."

Passing the drawing room she'd been taken to on her previous visit, he led her further down the carpeted hallway. She passed a second drawing room, a music conservatory, and a spacious dining room with a table that could easily seat fifty guests. A dazzling chandelier holding dozens of candles hung from a ceiling frescoed with frolicking cherubs from the Baroque period. He opened a closed door and motioned for her to enter.

She swept inside. Huntingdon sat behind a massive mahogany desk of what could only be his study. Tall shelves lined with scores of books bound in supple leather occupied both sides of the room. Set in the opposite wall a large fireplace topped with a stone mantle held a crackling log. A gilt framed portrait of a jet-haired man wearing a neck ruff hung beside the mantle. Glancing at the figure's sinfully dark eyes, she knew it to be one of Huntingdon's ancestors.

"Ah, Mrs. Somerton. I've been expecting you," he drawled.

"Am I that predictable, my lord?"

He stood and walked around his desk. For such a tall man he moved with remarkable grace. His jacket of navy superfine stretched across broad shoulders, and a diamond pin glittered in his snowy cravat. He was strikingly handsome, every inch the aristocrat and exuded an air of command. She'd forgotten what a powerful opponent she had chosen. But here…now… among his wealth and splendor her own position struck her in stark contrast. The difference in their stations could not have been more pronounced.

He halted before her and raised her gloved hand to his lips. Her skin prickled pleasurably.

He smiled lazily and his gaze traveled her form, missing no detail—even to the damp hem of her gown and her sodden shoes. "I thought you would come, but I hoped you would wait until it had ceased snowing. By the look of your shoes, I'm concerned you walked here."

"I took a hackney, my lord."

"Did Stevens not offer to take your cloak?"

"You know very well that he did. I suspect you train your servants better than to omit such a detail."

His eyes crinkled at the corners, and a lock of his dark hair rested across his forehead. She had a ridiculous urge to reach out and smooth back his hair.

"Then I can only hope it's that you simply can't bear to part yourself from my gift," he said.

"To the contrary, I'm here to return it." She attempted to take off the beautiful cloak and hand it to him, but he stopped her with a hand on her shoulder.

Their eyes locked, and a strange tingling began in the pit of her stomach.

Her voice was shakier than she would have liked. "My family is not a charity project, my lord."

"I don't consider them to be one."

She swallowed hard. "I don't need your pity."

He dropped his hand from her shoulder. "Pity?" he chuckled. "You are not the type of woman to inspire pity. Other emotions, perhaps. But never pity." His eyes darkened a shade, and her traitorous heart skipped a beat.

"Then why?" she said.

"Pardon?"

"The coal. The shawls and cloaks. Why send them?"

"I thought I made my intentions quite clear. You are to accompany me to interrogate Dorian Reed, remember?"

She tilted her head to the side and shot him a disbelieving look. "You've already ensured my cooperation. If I fail to meet my end of the bargain, you will turn over the forged painting to the constable."

He frowned as if he wasn't pleased with the memory. "I need you in good health. It bothered me that your shop was so cold. There's no reason for it to be so."

The sincerity in his tone took her aback. "Is that all?"

"Yes."

"You expect nothing more?"

"No."

She bit her lower lip. "You must understand I've done just fine without your gifts. My sisters, however, are a different matter. I do not have the heart to deny them any comfort that may come their way, but I suspect you very well know that."

"Your sisters are charming ladies, and I'd rather they be warm this winter."

He was making her feel churlish. "I am truly grateful for the doctor you sent to see to Chloe. I will reimburse you for the man's services as soon as I'm able."

"That's not necessary."

"It is to me."

He tsked. "Stubborn."

She raised her chin a notch. "I prefer prideful."

He smiled easily, as if expecting her vehement protest. "Fine. I'm in need of your opinion. Consider it recompense for the doctor's services."

"My opinion?"

"Your professional opinion as the owner of a business."

She halted, looking up at him with surprise. No man had ever asked for her opinion.

"May I?" This time he was the one to reach for her cloak. She stood still as he whisked the fur off her shoulders and laid it across a chair. Her simple brown wool dress was crude in comparison to the rich luxury of the sable.

Taking her hand, he placed it on his sleeve and led her to the study door. Curiosity welled within her, and she followed docilely. With a simple proposition and charming smile, he had easily disarmed her.

As they ventured down the hall, side-by-side, she could not help but notice the muscles of his forearm beneath the fine fabric of his jacket and the pleasant scent of his shaving soap. His nearness kindled unwanted feelings and her pulse quickened. Fearful of meeting his gaze, she glanced down to discover that her sodden soggy shoes were leaving wet marks on the polished marble floor. His butler was sure to raise a brow.

Then every mundane thought fled as he opened a door and escorted her inside a sun-lit room.

Oh, my.

A multitude of brilliantly colored works of art lined the walls. Her eyes were drawn to portraits of his ancestors by Thomas Gainsborough, Francis Cotes, and George Knapton, sporting artists George Stubbs and John Wootton, and cloud-tossed landscapes by John Constable and George Lambert. The collection wasn't limited to English painters as splendid Dutch, Flemish, and Italian artists were also displayed.

His private gallery. And it was *stunning*.

"It's beautiful," she breathed.

"Yes, beautiful," his voice was husky.

She turned to find him watching her. The invisible web of attraction was building between them again. She glanced away nervously to study the art. It was much safer than studying *him*.

Eliza walked the perimeter of the room, taking in the hanging canvases like an aspiring artist gifted with her first set of brushes. Even though her father had been a talented painter, she'd never had an opportunity to visit museums or the Academy as a child. He'd been too busy working to take her.

She pointed to three vacant spots on the wall. "Are there missing paintings?"

"Those are on loan to the British Museum. I don't believe in keeping artwork hidden in a private collection. It's the duty of anyone blessed to own such work to share it with the public."

She stared at him in astonishment. "Not everyone would agree with you, my lord. Many of Father's clients never loaned their priceless artwork. They hoarded it, obviously believing it existed for their sole viewing pleasure."

A wry grimace thinned his lips. "I'm not surprised. Jonathan Miller's clientele were not the most moral."

She stiffened slightly, unsure whether he was passing judgment upon her, but the hardness and dislike that usually turned his eyes to glacial ice whenever he spoke of her father was absent in his gaze.

"Tell me, Eliza, what do *you* believe?" he asked.

She hesitated for a heartbeat, then sighed. "Masterpieces should be shared with the world."

He smiled in approval. "Good. Then as a lover of art, please tell me which ones I should loan next?"

"You're asking me?"

"Yes."

Again she was surprised by his willingness to seek her opinion. She turned back to the paintings, gazing at them in wonder. Which ones to choose? Each was breathtaking in its own way.

"These," she said, indicating two watercolors by Paul Sandby, a founding member of the Royal Academy.

"Excellent choices. Anything else?"

Walking slowly, she studied each piece and halted by an engraving. "This one," she said, pointing to *Icarus* by the

Dutch artist Hendrick Goltzius.

"It's from Goltzius's 1588 series, *The Four Disgracers*, and the only engraving in my collection. Why do you like it?" he asked.

She sighed with pleasure. "His talent with the burin is magnificent. His repeated patterns of swirling lines...his ability to reflect light and shadow on Icarus's rippling muscles and convey the fear on his face as he falls to his death is remarkable."

"Fascinating." She jumped at the sound of Grayson's voice close behind her and whirled to find him studying her.

"I felt the same way when I first saw the engraving, and I knew I had to possess it, no matter the cost."

She was reminded of the first time he'd spoken similar words to her when he sat beside her at the Tutton auction. But this time, she was strangely flattered by his interest. A tingling began in the pit of her stomach.

His gaze traveled over her face and searched her eyes. Keenly aware of his scrutiny, she felt exposed, emotionally naked in a way that alternately thrilled and frightened her.

"You lied to me," he said softly.

"Excuse me?"

"You lied about the Jan Wildens painting."

A prickle of unease ran along her spine. "Whatever do you—"

"You are not the forger of the painting."

Her heart thumped madly, and fear knotted inside her. "Of course I am."

"No. You are not an artist. Amelia is responsible."

"That's ridiculous!"

"Oh, I realize you have a love for art, but your father's talent did not fall to you."

Denial was her only option. "You're wrong," she said, shaking her head.

"No more deception." His voice, though soft, carried a silken thread of warning.

The tension between them increased frighteningly. For breathless seconds he held her panicked gaze. There was no lying to him, no escaping it. Impossible as it was, he knew.

"Please...please keep Amelia out of this," she pleaded.

He grasped her arms and the shock of his touch ran through her body. "I'm not interested in turning Amelia in to the authorities."

"Then what? What do you want?"

"This." He jerked her into his arms and his mouth swooped down to capture hers.

Unlike the first time, his lips were hard, demanding. He grasped her firmly about the waist, walked forward until she found herself pressed against the wall between two priceless paintings. He tilted his head, slanted his mouth more fully across hers and ravaged her senses.

She was trapped, her hands crushed against his hard chest. Gasping, her lips parted beneath his onslaught. He took the advantage, his tongue sweeping inside her mouth.

She tried to resist, but the combustible spark between them flared to life and stole her will. The wanton in her responded, to his scent, to his heat...to *him*. Her tongue grazed his and then sucked him into her mouth. He groaned and somehow her hands were free and grasping his shoulders and then tangling in his hair.

She loved the feel and texture of the dark locks and her nails raked his scalp. He kissed her, long and deep, causing desire to course hotly through her veins. His hand caressed her waist, then moved slowly up her side to cup the fullness of her breast. His thumb grazed her nipple through the worn material of her gown. She gasped as exquisite pleasure radiated from her breast and liquid heat pooled low between her legs, making her long for more...so much more.

Sensing her need, he deepened his kiss, his hands explored the soft lines of her back and hips, then lowered to grasp her buttocks and press her tightly against him until the hard, throbbing part of him thrust against her belly. Shocked, she gathered every last bit of her resistance and yanked viciously on his hair.

He grunted and lifted his head to look in her eyes. "Hellcat! I want the truth. Who are you, Eliza Somerton?"

For a heart-stopping moment, she feared he could read the truth behind the mask. That he could see her for who she really was.

Vulnerable. Lonely. Tired.

She had to end this. He couldn't be trusted.

No man could.

Her mind churned, groping for the most damaging thing she could say.

"I'm my father's daughter, Jonathan Miller's offspring. You'd best not forget it, my lord."

Chapter Ten

Grayson's arms tightened around Eliza. *Of all the bloody things to say.* "You admit it then?" he said tersely.

"Admit what? You know Miller is my father," Eliza said.

His pulse thrummed. His groin throbbed. The feel of her pressed tightly against him was intoxicating. "Not that, damn it. You admit to using Amelia's talents to forge paintings?"

"There was only one and we were desperate. It was soon after father left. We had no choice," she said.

"How desperate were you?" he demanded.

"Our circumstances were dire. Chloe was ill again. We needed food, shelter, and medicine."

His brow furrowed. He didn't like the image of Eliza and her sisters struggling to survive. "And what of your husband?"

Her green eyes widened. "I didn't marry until afterwards."

"Did he ever learn of your crime?"

"No. I never told him."

"You're willing to go to prison for Amelia's mistakes?" he said.

"I would," she said with conviction. "Amelia was never to

blame. I was the mastermind. I arranged for the painting to be sold to Viscount Tutton. I never considered his estate would hold an auction after his death."

"Would you do it again?"

"Yes." She lifted her chin. "Yes, I would!"

Her breasts heaved in the bodice of her worn gown and it took every ounce of his willpower not to lower his gaze, not to reach out and caress her flesh.

He'd forget his anger, lose his advantage.

He dropped his arms from around her. "I won't let you. Innocent people could be hurt."

She quickly stepped aside and met his hard gaze. "Only the rich, my lord. Father often said the wealthy can afford it. Forgery is a victimless crime."

Grayson recalled the humiliation he'd felt when it became known he'd raved about a forged painting. The newspapers had been quick to print his mistake. He hadn't shown his face at the Royal Academy for close to a year afterwards.

His thoughts turned bitter. *I was a laughingstock.*

Grayson hadn't been alone. Jonathan Miller had other victims as well, dozens who'd fallen for his scams. They weren't all wealthy and had taken considerable blows to their finances after learning that they had purchased worthless paintings and not valuable pieces of art from one of the masters.

In short, people *had* been hurt.

Anger and lust simmered in Grayson's veins, a volatile mix. "You and Amelia are fortunate. Viscount Tutton never learned the truth behind the Wildens forgery before he died. I have the painting now, and I won't allow you to do it again. I'm going to watch you, Eliza. Closely. Carefully."

Every curve of her body spoke defiance. "You do not *own* me, my lord. That was never part of our arrangement."

His eyes raked boldly over her. "It is now."

⋯

She had been foolish to incite him.

Eliza sat back in the earl's coach as it drove away from the mansion. She would have hailed a hackney if Grayson hadn't insisted his driver return her to her home.

She shifted restlessly against the luxurious squabs and pulled the sable cloak more tightly around her. She'd come with every intention of returning the cloak, but as she'd stood in the vestibule after their heated argument, preparing to leave, he'd wrapped it around her and she'd been afraid to protest.

She'd always believed Grayson was dangerous, but now that he knew the entire truth—that Amelia was the forger—she was even more convinced he could destroy them.

But so far he hadn't acted on the knowledge. Instead, he'd kissed her.

Bone-melting kisses in the seclusion of his stunning gallery. She'd been easily seduced. He was unlike any other man she knew. So different from the wealthy merchants who frequented her shop and made their illicit interest in her known. As a widow and shopkeeper without the protection of any male relations, she'd had her fair share of men who'd thought she should be freely available. She'd never been the slightest bit interested in any of them.

Until Grayson.

Each time they were alone, she found it difficult to recall he was her adversary. And when he swept her into his arms and kissed her…

Her stomach fluttered wildly. The touch of his lips was sensual and seductive, making her knees weaken. But more alarming than her physical response, his kiss revealed a hidden yearning buried deep within her.

Huntingdon was a complex man—kind one moment and

cold the next. He'd sent coal, shawls, and cloaks. He'd paid for a doctor to treat Chloe. He'd asked for her opinion on which of his valuable works he should loan to a museum. But just as quickly he'd revealed his knowledge of her family secret and warned that he'd watch her closely to ensure she'd not commit another crime.

It was all so confusing. There was only one thing she knew to be true. He was a powerful, dominant male who was used to getting what he desired, and she shouldn't—*couldn't*—allow further intimacy.

The risks were perilous.

What if he thought he could kiss her any time he wanted in exchange for keeping Amelia's secret? Or, heaven forbid, required more than that? A shiver of fear ran down her spine. If she were truthful to herself, she didn't fear Grayson, but the effect he had on her senses. Would she be able to resist him if he kissed her elsewhere…touched her elsewhere? Her pulse quickened at the thought.

Good God. What was she thinking?

He was an earl, and she was a shopkeeper and a criminal's daughter. They were as different as a colorful oil painting compared to a simple charcoal sketch. There could never be a future between them.

Her only thoughts should be of her sisters and how she could keep Amelia out of trouble. She needed to focus on what was most important and not allow Grayson to distract her. He could watch her as closely as he wished; she had no intention of selling another of Amelia's forgeries.

Once the stolen Rembrandt was found, Grayson would return to his prior existence—his realm of wealth and privilege—and she, without further worry of scandal, would return to her old life and the print shop.

Just as it should be.

...

As an earl and an important art critic, Grayson had certain obligations among polite society. Attending the annual ball hosted by Lord and Lady Ruskin—both generous patrons of the Royal Academy—was one of them.

Grayson stepped into the crowded Mayfair ballroom. Dozens of chandeliers holding hundreds of candles illuminated the room. He reached for a glass of champagne from a passing footman's tray and surveyed the guests.

The ballgowns were a rainbow-like display rivaling an artist's palette, from vibrant tones to pastels to the occasional white. The women's hairstyles were just as varied—dyed ostrich plumes swayed from towering turbans beside braided coronets and Roman style ringlets with hair bandeaux.

The men were not to be outdone. The dandies of the *ton* strutted about with brightly colored coats, striped and checked waistcoats, high, pointed shirtpoints, and intricately tied cravats. But the expensive silks and satins could not compare to the sparkle of diamonds, sapphires, and emeralds—the dazzling abundance of precious stones and gold.

He'd never given the opulence and wealth of the *beau monde* a second thought. He'd been raised as the heir to an earldom. But tonight, for the first time, he was seeing it through different eyes.

"You're looking particularly glum tonight," Brandon said.

Grayson sipped his champagne. "I didn't want to attend, but the host, Lord Ruskin, is a friend."

Glasses clinked and laughter floated. The elegant ballroom offered warmth, expensive champagne, and fine food. But his thoughts were of a small shop with novice artwork and colorful décor.

Brandon raised his glass of claret. "Why not? The mamas of the *ton* are nearly throwing their daughters at your feet.

Soon you'll have to choose one."

Grayson didn't care about the eligible debutantes and their eager mothers who reminded him of vultures circling their prey.

The orchestra began a lively country reel and dancers swirled on the parquet dance floor.

His mind kept turning to yesterday's confrontation with Eliza.

She'd intended to leave his home during a snowstorm wearing only her gown and wet shoes. Her wellbeing shouldn't matter to him, but it did. He didn't want her suffering frostbite or coming down with pneumonia, and his reasoning had nothing to do with their upcoming visit to Dorian Reed.

The mystery that was Eliza Somerton was slowly unraveling. She wasn't the calculating charlatan that she wanted him to believe. Her eyes had flashed emerald fire when she'd insisted that she would sell another of Amelia's forgeries. His temper had risen, but afterwards he'd had time to calm and think.

He didn't believe her.

She'd been desperate to reclaim the forged Wildens painting. If she intended to sell another of Amelia's forgeries, then why bother with the Wildens painting? Why not let it sell at auction? Chances were no one would suspect it was a forgery. Amelia's work was meticulous. He'd discovered it only because of Eliza's avid interest in the painting at the Tutton auction. Otherwise, he'd never have given it a second glance.

No, Eliza's bold retort had been an attempt to anger him. She'd only been half successful. He had been angry, but he'd been even more aroused. He'd swept her into his arms then pinned her against his gallery wall and claimed her lips. He had not imagined the fervor of their first kiss. It didn't matter that it had been swift; the undeniable magnetism was present.

She'd tried to resist, but her passionate nature had quickly taken over.

He relived the feeling of her hands slipping up his arms to caress the strong tendons in the back of his neck then tangle in his hair. Her body had arched toward his, and her moans had been a heady invitation. Her nipples had been taut beneath the thin fabric of her dowdy gown. In his hunger and desire, he'd wanted to peel off her clothing, and crush her breasts to his broad chest. He'd rouse her to the peak of excitement, then lay her down on the settee in his gallery and plunge inside her hot, welcoming body.

"I've been thinking about Miss Amelia," Brandon said.

"What?"

"Amelia. I've been thinking of her."

Grayson's brows drew downward. "I'm not surprised."

"I plan to visit the Peacock Print Shop. I want to offer her a commission to paint my portrait," Brandon said.

"Have you lost your wits?"

Brandon shrugged matter-of-factly. "You told Eliza that you know Amelia is the painter, correct?" Brandon didn't wait for Grayson's response. "Since it's no longer a secret, I've decided to seize the opportunity. My grandmother has been pestering me to have my portrait painted."

"So? Go to the Academy. There are dozens of qualified portrait painters."

Brandon shook his head. "There's something special about Miss Amelia. I can't stop thinking of her. It's a perfect solution. I need a portrait; she needs the money."

"Don't fake generosity on my behalf. You're like a randy schoolboy. You told me to find a mistress; maybe you should take your own advice."

"It's more than that," Brandon snapped. "She's different."

"What about the Duke of Townsend's daughter?"

"Don't even mention it. The duke and his family are

present tonight."

Grayson followed Brandon's gaze across the ballroom where Townsend and his family gathered. Brandon's grandmother had been pressing for a match with Townsend's daughter, Minerva.

A pale blond with an ample bosom, Minerva had an annoying tendency to speak incessantly. She was the type of woman Grayson couldn't tolerate—too much chatter, too little intellect. But Brandon didn't have a choice. He'd inherited his father's title along with his massive debt.

They were similar in that regard; but where Grayson had managed to pay off his debt and earn money in the Stock Exchange, Brandon was not as successful. He desperately needed Minerva's large dowry.

"What about you? You must marry soon. Sara's coming out will be here before you know it."

"I know it," Grayson said tersely. He needed to find a suitable wife, a titled heiress would be best. But he would have to be forced to the altar before he'd willingly bind himself to someone like Lady Minerva.

"The duchess and Lady Minerva have spotted me and are coming this way." Brandon swallowed. "I feel as if my cravat is cutting off my air supply. You'd best escape while you can, Grayson."

"I'll be on the terrace if you can extricate yourself," Grayson said.

He wove through the crowd, intending to exit through the French doors. The smell of hot candle wax and perspiring bodies was overwhelming.

"Grayson." A brisé fan tapped softly against his wrist. "I've been waiting to catch you alone."

"Leticia," he said, looking down at a blond woman.

"I didn't know you'd be in attendance tonight."

"I do get out and about."

She arched a well-plucked brow. "Other than gallery visits, you used to visit *me.*"

They'd had an affair months ago. Leticia, otherwise known as Lady Kinsdale, was a wealthy widow of a marquess. She was also a beautiful woman with sleek blond hair, blue eyes, and a willowy figure. She had been a good choice as a lover at the time, adventurous in bed, but had grown far too possessive. She made it known she'd wanted more than a pleasurable bed partner and sought to remarry.

Marrying Lady Kinsdale would be perfectly acceptable in the eyes of polite society. She was rich, titled, and an admired hostess. The perfect choice to help launch Sara into society.

But Grayson had stopped calling.

Leticia took a deep breath and his eyes were drawn to the large ruby resting in her cleavage. She licked her painted lips. "I've missed you Grayson."

"It's good to see you well, Leticia."

She ran her fan down his arm. "Do you not miss me?"

"I've been busy."

"You were never too busy for me in the past." She leaned close and grazed the buttons on his jacket with a gloved finger. "Come to my home tonight," she breathed.

An erotic invitation. Grayson should seize what she offered. But her well-practiced seduction left him disinterested. Her expensive French perfume, which he'd never minded before, was suddenly cloying. He felt the beginnings of a headache and eyed the open doors to the terrace.

"Tonight is not possible," he said.

"Another time, then?"

"Lord Huntingdon!"

Grayson turned to see his host, Lord Ruskin, waving.

"If you will excuse me." He bowed to Leticia, glad for a reason to end their conversation. She pouted, but thankfully, did not seek to detain him.

Grayson made his way to Lord Ruskin and shook his hand.

"Lord Huntingdon. I've been looking for you all evening," Ruskin said.

A ruddy-faced man with a booming voice, Ruskin was a collector of anything expensive and thought himself an art connoisseur. He was also an immensely wealthy marquess and an important patron of the Royal Academy.

"I've acquired a painting and I'd like your opinion. A Scottish artist by the name of Sir Henry Raeburn," the marquess said.

"I've heard of him, of course," Grayson said. "Quite talented."

"I knew it! My wife thought I was wasting money."

His wife was usually right. Grayson's headache began to increase in intensity, and he glanced at the French doors. "I'd be honored to see the painting. I'll visit next week."

Grayson made to move past the man and continue to the terrace when Ruskin placed his hand on Grayson's sleeve.

"One more favor, Huntingdon. My niece, Mary, would love a dance," Ruskin said, pointing to a female standing beside a group of older women by the refreshment table.

Grayson glanced at the lady who was pretty with brown hair and eyes and a slim figure. She was a young debutante, possibly in her second or third Season, the type of female Grayson was expected to marry to ensure the integrity of the title. Lord Ruskin waited patiently for his response. Grayson couldn't decline without insulting the marquess.

"I'd be delighted," Grayson said.

He walked to where Mary stood beside her mother and bowed to both women. "If your card is not full, Lady Mary, I'd be honored for the next dance."

Mary's face lit with excitement and she nodded. Her mother smiled in approval.

As Grayson led the lady to the dance floor, he spotted Brandon dancing with Minerva Townsend. Even from across the parquet floor he could see the lady speaking nonstop.

Brandon's unhappiness struck a chord with Grayson. If he found pleasure in having Amelia paint his portrait, then who was Grayson to protest? Brandon could enjoy Amelia's company while he posed by the fireplace mantle or in his study or wherever he chose.

Grayson was suddenly envious. What he wouldn't give for the excuse to spend an evening alone with Eliza without the mention of Dorian Reed, the stolen Rembrandt, or her father.

What would it be like to take her to an establishment for a cozy dinner? To share a meal with her and speak of other things?

Glancing down into Mary Ruskin's smiling face, Grayson's gut clenched. He was supposed to find a wife, do his duty by ensuring an heir to the earldom and a successful first season for Sara. As it stood, next in line was a distant second cousin who had a bad gambling habit. He would no doubt drain the Huntingdon coffers that Grayson's investments had enriched, and he could not be trusted to provide for Sara's future.

That would never do. It was time he found a suitable wife.

Mary Ruskin, like Lady Kinsdale, was also a good choice. Ruskin was a wealthy marquess and his family line impeccable. His niece was attractive enough, but Grayson felt nothing special in their connection, no force drawing him to her. He felt only an overwhelming need to flee the dance floor.

A mounting frustration grew within him. He wanted to see Eliza again. It was pointless to deny his attraction to her. His life had grown routine, he realized, social events and gallery visits, until he'd sat next to Eliza at the Tutton auction. Her beauty was a drug, clouding his brain, stealing his logic, threatening his well-laid plans for vengeance.

An image of Eliza in his private gallery gazing at the Hendrick Goltzius engraving arose in his mind. Her eyes had darkened to a smoky emerald. Her full lips had parted with pleasure. She'd been as entranced by the artist's talent as Grayson had been when he'd first seen the *Icarus* engraving. He'd experienced that excitement again through her eyes—through the rapid pulse at her neck and the hitch of her breath—and a jolt of lust, swift and violent, had him reeling like a man starved.

Sweet Jesus.

He cursed himself as he spun his partner into the intricate steps of the quadrille.

Why Eliza?

Why the stubborn widow and shopkeeper who wanted nothing to do with him? Why her? What good could possibly come out of desiring the daughter of his nemesis?

Chapter Ten

The note arrived for Eliza on the morning of the fifth day.

> *Eliza,*
> *Dorian Reed has returned to town. I'll arrive at the shop at noon for you.*
> *Grayson*

Eliza scanned the letter, noting he had used their Christian names. Their relationship had become more familiar, and she frowned at the thought.

She walked to the back room where Amelia was working. "Dorian Reed has returned to London," Eliza said simply.

Amelia set down her brush and stepped away from the landscape she had been painting. "When will Lord Huntingdon arrive?"

Eliza folded the note and slipped it into her skirt pocket. "I'm going to see Mr. Reed on my own."

Amelia looked at her in surprise. "But you agreed to go with the earl."

Eliza sighed. "Things have changed. Huntingdon knows

you're the artist and forger of the Wildens painting."

"So? How is that any different from when he believed you were the forger?"

Eliza looked at her sister in disbelief. "I'm not willing to stand by and watch you arrested!"

"You think he'd turn me in to the constable?"

She didn't think so, not really. But what if she was wrong?

"I'm not willing to take the chance," Eliza said.

Amelia placed her hands on her hips. "What does any of this have to do with you going to see Dorian Reed alone?"

"Nothing. Everything. I can't help but wonder: what if Huntingdon wants to find Father more than he cares to find the stolen Rembrandt?" Eliza said.

Amelia shrugged. "It should come as no surprise. Lord Huntingdon's reputation was damaged."

"But if there's a real possibility that Dorian Reed knows where Father is, then I want to find him first. I may not get the chance if Huntingdon gets to him before me," Eliza said.

"It's dangerous, Lizzie."

"No more than any of the other times I've spoken with Father's acquaintances."

Amelia removed her apron. "If you insist on doing this, I don't think you should go alone. I'll come, too."

Eliza raised a hand. "No. I need you to stay here with Chloe."

She turned and left the workroom, conscious of Amelia trailing behind. Careful not to look at her sister in case Amelia's worried expression should sway the course she'd chosen, Eliza donned her cloak and opened the shop's door.

Amelia grasped her sleeve. "Wait! What do I tell the earl when he comes looking for you?"

Eliza spared her a quick glance. "I'll be back before he arrives."

She hailed a hackney and gave him the address for the artist's district. It was in a run down part of town, not quite the rookeries, but far from the fine town homes and shops near Bond Street. The buildings were much closer together here with dark, narrow walkways between them.

The cab stopped in front of a two-story red brick building. The exterior was unkempt, and the brick was crumbling in places. The shutters had peeling paint, the front step was broken, and the hedgerows were overgrown.

From what she recalled, the dealers that had sold her father's forgeries had lived affluent lifestyles. Dorian Reed must have fallen on bad times.

Eliza retrieved her reticule, stepped down, and paid the driver.

"Should I wait for you, Miss?" the driver asked.

She glanced nervously at the neighborhood. "Yes, please," she said, making a quick decision. It would cost her, but she knew she had no choice. This was not the sort of street that teemed with hackney drivers looking for patrons.

Gathering her skirts, she headed for the front steps. The door opened before she had a chance to knock. A tall man with massive shoulders and a crooked nose that looked as if it had been broken numerous times eyed her ominously. He was a far cry from Grayson's proper butler.

"What do ye want?" he said tersely.

She handed him her card. "I'm here to see Mr. Dorian Reed."

He glanced at it and scowled, making her wonder if he even knew how to read.

"Who are ye?" he demanded.

She raised her chin and met his hostile glare. "My name is Eliza Somerton. I'm Jonathan Miller's daughter." It had been five years since she'd willingly revealed her true identity for fear of the consequences.

He blinked, and his lips curled at the corners. "Miller's daughter, ye say?" He opened the door wide, grasped her arm, and pulled her inside. "Ye should 'ave said so."

He released her arm abruptly. She had to make a conscious effort not to rub the spot where his beefy fingers had grasped her.

"Is Mr. Reed at home?" she asked.

He eyed her from head to toe. "Who would 'ave thought Miller 'ad a pretty daughter like ye. Aye, Reed's 'ere and he'll agree to see ye. Follow me, then."

Eliza followed him past the small vestibule down a dimly lit hall. Dust motes swirled in a faint ray of light from a dirty window. The faded wallpaper was peeling, the furniture dusty and old, and the carpet runner bare in spots.

She stopped short in what had been a dining room. After the dimness in the hall, the bright light made Eliza squint. Two large candelabra with a dozen wax candles burned upon the mantle, with additional candles on end tables in the room. A man stood before an easel. Dressed in trousers and a striped waistcoat, his shirtsleeves were rolled up and he was humming softly to himself. A quick glance at his canvas revealed a charcoal sketch of a sword and a double-barreled pistol. Both weapons were artfully positioned on a nearby sideboard.

Dorian Reed turned when she entered the room. Her first instinct was that he was younger than she'd imagined. Late thirties, early forties, with a full head of straw colored hair and a classically handsome face. She'd expected a man her father's age.

"There's a lady 'ere to see ye. She says her name's Mrs. Eliza Somerton. She claims to be Jonathan Miller's daughter," the butler said, handing Reed the print shop's card before leaving.

Reed lowered the charcoal in his hand. "Well, well. Miller's daughter, you say? What a pleasant surprise."

His English was impeccable, and she could easily imagine him fitting in seamlessly in any fine London gallery. Yet there was a steely glint in his blue eyes that made her uneasy.

"Thank you for receiving me, Mr. Reed."

He studied her face with a curiosity with which one would gaze at an object displayed in a curio. Her hands, hidden from sight, twisted nervously behind her.

"I would never turn away Jonathan's daughter," Reed said. "I can't help wondering, however, how much of your father's blood runs through your veins? He could never stay away for long. Do you have artwork you'd like me to sell?"

Thank heavens, no.

"That's not why I'm here," Eliza said.

"Oh? Do enlighten me."

"I was approached by a gentleman looking for a stolen painting. I agreed to help him, and we will be arriving together later today," she said.

"But you decided to visit me alone first, Mrs. Somerton?"

She'd expected him to question her and was prepared with her answer. "Suffice it to say, I'm not interested in the stolen painting, Mr. Reed. I seek information about my father's whereabouts."

"And this gentleman that you will be accompanying also wants to know about your father?" he asked.

"I have reason to believe so, yes."

"You were wise to come alone." His eyes pierced the distance between them. "Tell me, Mrs. Somerton, do you know precisely what I did for your father?"

"I didn't know anything of you until recently," she admitted. "I can only assume that as an art dealer you sold Father's paintings to interested clients."

"You mean his forgeries."

"Yes."

He laughed softly. "It's true. We would split the profits of the sale. Your father was very, very good. Half of London still has a Jonathan Miller forgery hanging on their walls. Not all the paintings were traced back to him."

"I see."

"I consider myself a shrewd businessman, but your father was the shrewdest. You see he didn't only fool the clients and art critics. He fleeced me as well before he disappeared."

Her unease ratcheted a notch. "I...I'm sorry."

She hadn't expected this turn of events.

But she should have.

Silly, Eliza! She thought to herself. *We're talking about Father. How often will you give him the benefit of the doubt only to be disappointed time and time again?*

Reed stepped away from the easel and approached, until she could see the ring of blue ice lining his irises. The hair on her nape stood on end.

"Your arrival is perfect timing, Mrs. Somerton, as I find myself in need of money. Forgers of your father's ability are scarce. He stole a particularly large commission."

Dare she ask? "How much?"

"A thousand pounds, to be exact."

A thousand pounds! She stared at him, her mouth agape.

"As his offspring, you owe your father's debts," Reed said.

"You cannot be serious!" she said incredulously. "I don't have that kind of money."

"But you are the owner of a business, correct?" He held up her card and read aloud, "The Peacock Print Shop."

Her heart raced as she stared at him.

"I shall have to be content to take your business."

Take her business! "But...but—"

He waved his hand. "Don't fret. I'm not interested in the day to day operations of a print shop, just a reasonable share of the profits. Let's say a little more than half should do."

"We barely survive! Surely there's another way."

He arched an eyebrow. "Do you have a thousand pounds?"

Apprehension swept through her. She had nothing to bargain with nor any money to pay him. "Of course not."

"Then I see no other way."

"And if I refuse?"

He advanced toward her like a stalking predator, and she felt a jolt of panic.

"I'm not a man you want to cross."

...

Grayson's pulse pounded on his way to collect Eliza. Dorian Reed was back in town and she could help him get answers.

In particular, the answer to who had purchased the stolen Rembrandt.

But more importantly, the answer to where Miller was hiding.

Soon, he thought. Soon he'd possess the information to finally be able to find the criminal.

He buried a nagging guilt regarding Eliza. He'd waited for justice for five long years. He must not allow anyone—even Eliza and her sisters—to dissuade him now. Not when he was so close.

His carriage pulled up before the wooden sign emblazoned with a gilt and blue peacock that swung gently in the breeze. Not waiting for his footman, he opened the door and hopped down. Three strides later, he was inside.

Amelia stood behind the counter framing a print.

"Good afternoon," Grayson said.

She stilled and stared at him. "Good day, my lord."

He was relieved to find the small shop warm and coal blazing in the grate. He scanned the room with its racks of prints and shelves crowded with small busts, ivory trinket boxes, and miniature oils.

There was no sign of Eliza.

Amelia's gaze darted to the mantle clock then out the bay window, then back to him.

Grayson grew alert. "Where's Eliza?"

Amelia twisted her hands on the counter.

"Amelia, where is your sister?" Grayson demanded.

"She's gone."

"Gone where?"

"She went to see Mr. Reed on her own," she blurted out.

"Christ!" he bellowed.

Amelia jumped. She eyed the stairs leading up to their private apartments and Grayson had the distinct impression she wanted to flee like a frightened rabbit.

She took a deep breath and bravely faced him instead. "The truth is I'm glad you're here, my lord. Eliza was to be back by now."

"How long has she been gone?"

Amelia worried her lip. "At least two hours. I fear something untoward has happened to her."

His unease turned to fear. He had no idea what type of man Dorian Reed was.

Immoral art broker? Violent criminal? Both?

As if reading his thoughts, Amelia paled. "I wanted to go with her, but she insisted on going alone. She can be quite stubborn."

He knew all too well.

Amelia hurried from around the counter and grasped his hand. "Please, will you help her?"

Some strange emotion stirred in his chest as he glanced down at her small hand clasping his. It was ironic, really. One of Miller's daughters asking him for help. He felt no satisfaction, or sense of redemption, only an urgency to find Eliza and ensure her safety.

Looking into Amelia's blue eyes, he squeezed her hand and lowered his voice in an attempt to ease her torment. "Don't worry. I'll find her and bring her back. Stay here and look after Chloe."

Chapter Twelve

Eliza faced Dorian Reed with her fists at her sides. "I won't give you a lion's share of my shop."

Reed ignored her and went to an end table and pulled out a piece of foolscap. A nearby pen and inkwell followed.

He approached with the paper in hand, and his cruel gaze crossed hers. "You *will* sign over your business to me. Start writing. 'I, Eliza Somerton, of sound mind and body, give sixty percent of all profits from the Peacock Print Shop to Dorian Reed effective immediately.'"

"I said I won't do it!"

His voice was cold and exact. "I said start writing."

"Go to the constable, if you dare. You will undoubtedly be arrested as Jonathan Miller's accomplice," she said.

Reed laughed harshly. "Who said anything about involving the constable?" His eyes narrowed. "It's quite simple, really. You repay your father's debt, or your family will come to harm."

She felt the blood drain from her face at the thought of Amelia and Chloe in danger. "How did you know…"

Just as the words were out of her mouth, she realized her mistake. He *hadn't* known of her siblings.

But he did now.

"I knew there were more of you," he said smugly. "Brothers? Sisters?" At Eliza's silence, he shrugged. "I can only assume there are sisters. It's highly unlikely that a brother would allow you to come to my doorstep unchaperoned."

Something inside of her snapped then, pushing her fear beneath the surface.

No one threatened her sisters. If there was one thing Eliza had learned from the years since her father's abandonment it was that a woman must never display weakness. Many men—customers and artists alike—had expressed lurid interest. She was a widow without any living male relatives, a woman who worked for a living, and therefore unprotected in society. She had managed by showing an unwavering confidence to the outside world.

But now Dorian Reed threatened everything she cared for.

Her sisters.

Her business.

Desperation mingled with hatred for the man who stood before her. The print shop was their livelihood, their key to survival. And even if she gave him more than half of her business, she knew deep in her bones Dorian Reed wouldn't be satisfied for long.

Men like him never were.

There was only one course of action left to her. Her eyes darted to the sideboard, where the sword and double-barreled pistol lay, subjects of Reed's charcoal sketch.

I must appear calm. Distract him with questions.

"What about my father? Do you know where he is?" she asked.

Reed halted. "I have information you want."

She made herself smile coyly. "Perhaps we can make an arrangement. I'll write anything you want, if you tell me what you know." She inched slowly toward the sideboard.

"I can be quite agreeable," he said.

Eliza nervously licked her bottom lip, and his gaze dropped to her mouth. The lustful look in his eyes was unmistakable.

"You're an attractive woman, Eliza Somerton," he drawled.

Bile rose up her throat, and she forced herself not to show her disgust. *Act the part, Eliza. It must be the performance of your life.*

She tilted her head and regarded him. "You're much younger than I expected, Mr. Reed."

"Call me Dorian." He followed her, slowly stalking.

Her back brushed the sideboard. She struggled to recall which weapon was on top, the sword or the pistol.

Which would be more deadly?

"Dorian," she said.

Reed stood close now. He was breathing heavily and his breath smelled of onions and tobacco. His eyes dropped to her mouth.

Her hand groped behind her, searching for the sword, but instead settled on the butt of the pistol. Panicked and out of time, she shoved him hard with her free hand and aimed the pistol at his chest.

"Move and I'll shoot," she said, cocking the first hammer.

A flicker of alarm crossed his face before his eyes narrowed to slits. "I see you inherited your father's cutthroat demeanor as well."

Her father cutthroat? She wanted to laugh at the statement. He may have been immoral and greedy, but as far as she knew, he had never physically threatened others.

"Tell me what you know," she demanded.

"How do you intend to leave here, my dear? One shout

and my man will come running. Do you intend to shoot us both?"

She cocked the second hammer. "There is a barrel for each of you."

A twisted smile crossed his face. "I'm duly impressed by your fierce tenacity, Mrs. Somerton. You'll make a fine business partner. There's only one problem with your current plan to escape."

Her composure was a fragile shell around her. Her hand trembled. "What might that be?"

Still smiling, his cold gaze passed over her. "You're assuming the pistol is loaded, then? You should have gone for the sword."

He lunged for the weapon.

She pulled the trigger.

A click sounded. No explosive crack.

For a heart-pounding instant, she stood holding the pistol and he smiled knowingly.

Instinctively, she threw the gun at his head just as his hand snaked out to grasp her with strong fingers.

Before she could make it past the sideboard she found herself pulled roughly and hurled toward a settee. Reed was upon her in a flash, holding her down with his body.

"You like a chase, then? I can accommodate you."

His mouth was on hers, wet and bruising. She pushed against his chest, but he had a wiry strength. She slapped at his ear with her open palm. "Get off!"

"You shouldn't have done that," Reed spat, "but if you like it rough, I'm more than happy to oblige." He grasped her hair and yanked her head back. His hard mouth smothered hers, crushing her lips against her teeth and bloodying her lower lip. His fingers dug into her shoulders through the thin cotton fabric of her gown.

Panic engulfed Eliza. She fought wildly, twisting beneath

him, and raised her leg to knee him hard in the groin. He grunted in pain, and she attempted to push him off her.

Suddenly Reed was seized from behind and tossed to the floor.

Grayson's face was a mask of fury as he towered over Reed.

Reed's eyes darted from Grayson's menacing presence to the door. "Sam!" he bellowed.

"Don't bother," Grayson growled. "Your guard was easily bribed."

Reed's face turned a mottled red. Scrambling to his feet, he lowered his head and charged at Grayson like an enraged bull.

The thud of Grayson's fist and the crack of Reed's nose echoed through the room. Bright blood spurted from Reed's nose and splattered across the floorboards. Reed stumbled back, tripped on the easel. He fell hard on his backside, toppling the easel, canvas, and scattering a box of charcoal across the hardwood floor.

Clearly dazed, Reed cupped his broken nose, howling in pain.

Grayson rounded on Eliza. His brows were drawn downward, his expression tense. "What the hell were you thinking by coming here alone?"

Her eyes were wide as she stared at the crimson flowing between Reed's fingers. "I…I—"

"Good God, Eliza. Are you hurt?" Grayson demanded.

"No," she said, and then gave a squeak of alarm as Reed struggled to rise.

Grayson whirled and grasped Reed's shirtfront and hauled him to his feet. "I assume the lady advised you of my impending visit."

Blood seeped through Reed's fingers as he nodded.

"I want to know if a stolen Rembrandt recently came

onto the market," Grayson said.

Reed wiped his nose on his sleeve, leaving a streak of red across his face. "Pickens bid on it."

"You mean *Viscount* Henry Pickens?" Grayson said.

Reed struggled against Grayson's hold, but to no avail. "Yes! It was the viscount."

Eliza couldn't believe how forthcoming Dorian Reed had become. A broken nose and the cad could not get the words out fast enough.

Grayson shook Reed once. "And the lady's father? Where is he?"

"The last time I saw Jonathan Miller was two years ago. He never said where he was headed and I didn't ask," Reed said.

"Two years ago! He's alive then?" Eliza said.

Dorian Reed looked at her. His eyes narrowed, but he appeared much less menacing bloodied and in Grayson's grasp. "Who knows? But I still want my money."

"What money?" Grayson demanded.

"Her father stole a thousand pounds from me before he disappeared. He's gone, but she's here," Reed said, pointing to Eliza. "I want my money."

"He wants our shop in exchange for Father's debt," Eliza said.

Grayson abruptly released Reed, who stumbled backwards. Reaching into his jacket, Grayson pulled out his purse and threw it at Reed's feet. It landed with a loud chink of coins. "Take that and don't ask for more."

Greed glittered in Reed's eyes as he bent to retrieve the pouch.

Eliza stared, heart pounding. Shock at Grayson's gesture caused words to wedge in her throat.

Grayson's dark eyes narrowed as he glared at Dorian Reed. "In exchange for my gold, you are never to go near the lady in the future. Understood?"

Grayson waited long enough for Reed to nod, then twisted Reed's shirt in his fist and threw him headlong into the settee.

Grayson's fingers clamped around Eliza's wrist. "Let's go."

He gave her no choice but to follow along. His hand was like a vice on her arm. They left the house and she dared a glimpse at his profile. A muscle jumped along his tight jaw.

He had a right to be furious, of course. She'd gone behind his back with every intention of obtaining information and keeping it secret. But what did he expect? He wanted her father imprisoned for his crimes. She couldn't let that happen. She had to find her father first, to finally understand why he'd abandoned his daughters, had never tried to reach out to them.

Grayson strode down the hall and she struggled to keep up with him. She felt light-headed at the sight of the large guard lying face down in the small entry. A garden brick lay close by.

"Lord! Is he dead?"

"No."

"I thought you bribed him."

He stepped in front of her, his broad shoulders blocking the body. "There was no time for any sort of negotiation. I knew you were inside."

He opened the front door, and she saw his fine, crested carriage where her hired hackney had previously stood.

The footman immediately came forward and opened the door. Grayson helped her to board and then sat in the bench across from her, his long legs brushing her skirts.

The carriage started forward with a jingle of harness. Silence hung between them like a heavy cloud. She dared glimpse at him, and the fierceness in his dark eyes gave a stark look to his handsome face. She shivered.

"I understand why you're angry with me," Eliza blurted out.

"Oh? Pray, enlighten me."

"You're angry because I attempted to learn my father's whereabouts on my own. That you will miss your opportunity for vengeance."

"Wrong. I'm furious that you put your life at risk."

"I'd hardly go so far as to say—"

Grayson leaned close, all solid muscle and menace. She pulled away from him. Her head back against the padded leather bench, she could go no further.

"What would you call it then? Had I not shown up when I did, who knows what that whoreson would have done?" he said.

Her stomach heaved. "You…you must understand. I searched for my father for a full year after his disappearance. If there is a chance…any chance that I can find him, then I must try. If he's arrested and sent to Newgate before then, I will miss any opportunity."

"You're more likely to miss any opportunity if you come to harm."

"I realize I took a risk."

"A foolish risk."

He startled her when he reached out to brush her lower lip with the pad of his thumb. He withdrew his hand, stared at the smear of blood there, and his mouth clenched tight.

"The bastard," Grayson hissed. He withdrew a kerchief from his waistcoat and gently dabbed at the bruised flesh.

Several long seconds passed while he tended to her.

Gathering her courage she finally spoke. "How did you know where I was?" she whispered.

"Amelia told me when I arrived at the shop. She is worried sick for you."

Guilt pierced Eliza's chest. The need to justify her actions arose again. "I didn't know Father owed Reed money. He threatened to harm Amelia and Chloe if I didn't sign over more than half of the shop's profits to him."

"I'm not surprised."

She fussed with her skirts. "Thank you for the money. We would have lost the print shop and would be destitute if we were forced to pay Reed. It will take me some time, but I promise to reimburse you every shilling." Her voice shook.

He ran his fingers through his dark hair and exhaled. "Eliza, when I arrived at the shop and learned that you had gone on your own, I was furious. But not in the way you believe. I was more angry that you put yourself in danger than because you tried to deceive me."

She froze, her muscles taut. She'd had all her defenses prepared, ready to fight, but this wasn't a battle. His revelation was as unexpected as it was thrilling. His eyes caught and held hers, and a lurch of excitement skittered through her nerve endings. His gaze hinted of perilous secrets and something else…something more.

Could he possibly care for her?

"Promise me you'll never do something so reckless again," he said, his voice tense.

Under his steady scrutiny, her thoughts were jumbled. "I…I don't know."

Grasping her shoulders, he gently shook her. "Promise."

"I shall do my best."

"Not good enough. I can see you will take some convincing."

He pulled her into his lap and kissed her. His lips were soft, and he was careful to avoid the tender spot where Dorian Reed had injured her. His mouth played with languid sensuality over hers. After her harrowing experience, Eliza needed to feel the strength of his arms around her. She arched forward against his broad chest. Boldly, she took his cheeks into her palms and pressed her lips to his.

He groaned low in his throat, but to her utter frustration he didn't deepen the kiss, didn't plunder her mouth. Instead, he pulled away.

His gaze darkened. "I want to thoroughly kiss you until you promise me what I've asked, but I don't want to cause you pain."

He shifted her in his arms and simply held her. She rested her face against his chest and felt the strong beat of his heart. The heat from his body seeped into her, warming and comforting. She had been shaken by Dorian Reed's attack, but now, in Grayson's arms, she felt safe.

She also felt utterly and totally grateful to him. He'd paid her father's debt, a man who had humiliated Grayson and evaded justice. The man whom Grayson had hunted unsuccessfully for years.

Shifting in his arms, she looked up at his strong profile. "Why did you give Dorian Reed the money?"

"You mean why pay off your father's debts?"

Her heartbeat quickened. "Yes."

"Because men like Reed will do anything for money, and I don't want him to ever trouble you or your sisters again."

Her heart was pounding so hard now she was amazed he couldn't hear it in the carriage.

"I will pay you back somehow. It may take me months… years, but I will manage to pay — "

"I don't expect it," he said.

Something shifted in her mind. She was starting to trust him. No, that wasn't entirely true. She *did* trust him. Perhaps it had been unfair to compare Grayson to her father. They were cut from a different cloth. Her father had neglected and abandoned his daughters whereas Grayson had helped her and her sisters survive.

She made a quick decision. Climbing off his lap, she sat across from him. "Then I'd like to fulfill my part of the bargain."

"Which bargain? The one where you agree never to go searching for Jonathan Miller?"

She grimaced. "I said I'd do my best. But that's not what I meant just now."

"Then what?"

"I want to help recover the stolen painting. Reed mentioned the name of a viscount who expressed interest in the Rembrandt."

Grayson nodded. "Viscount Pickens. His private collection exceeds mine. We have not always seen eye to eye."

"How can I help?"

He hesitated, his dark eyes contemplative. "The Royal Academy is hosting an exhibition next week. The viscount will undoubtedly attend."

"You mean to ask Pickens if he's recently purchased a stolen painting?"

Grayson chuckled. "Not directly."

"Then how?"

"Every year the viscount holds a ball for his wife's birthday. I mean to obtain an invitation," Grayson said.

"I'm surprised you are not already on the guest list."

"As I mentioned, our interactions haven't always been amicable."

She stifled a laugh. "Imagine that. Someone who doesn't get along with you."

He smiled at her teasing tone, but then his gaze lazily roved her figure. "What other dresses do you own?" he asked.

She was suddenly conscious of the plain blue cotton. Her clothing may not be of the sort required in his circles, but it was perfectly serviceable for a shopkeeper.

"Why?"

"I want you to accompany me to the Academy."

She hadn't anticipated such a request and her thoughts scampered with excitement. Oh! To see the Royal Academy and all the magnificently displayed artwork. An exhibition during the winter may not be the wildly popular Summer Exhibition, but she didn't care. She'd yearned to go to the place for years, but feared she might somehow be recognized as the daughter of the forger of the *ton*.

But if she arrived with Lord Huntingdon, who would suspect her? She'd accompany the highly regarded art critic her father had harmed.

No one would believe it.

"There is a dressmaker on Bond Street who I understand to be all the rage with the ladies of the *beau monde*. I'd like to take you shopping," he said.

"I cannot accept any more of your charity, my lord."

"It's not charity. If we are to attend the exhibition, it's necessary that you be dressed the part. Consider it a costume and the Academy a stage. Nothing more."

She'd be acting. As she had been doing for the past five years.

For some reason, disappointment welled within her. Grayson wasn't offering to take her as a fellow art connoisseur. He didn't simply wish to spend time with her, leisurely perusing the Academy's treasures, discussing new artists and studying the masters. She had a purpose: to help him engage Viscount Pickens and find the stolen artwork. He'd never otherwise have extended her an invitation to accompany him to the Academy.

Best she remember that and not allow any silly fantasies to take flight. She may trust him, but she wasn't foolish enough to lose her heart.

"Very well. I'll see the dressmaker, although I'm not as knowledgeable about ladies' fashions as I once was."

"I'll accompany you, remember?"

Lord Huntingdon to help her choose dresses? She pictured him in a ladies' dress shop. The dressmaker would undoubtedly fawn over the handsome, masculine lord as soon as he walked into her establishment. The experience would be entirely too intimate, like a man buying clothing for his lover.

His lover.

Her face grew hot. A warm shiver ran down her spine as her thoughts turned torrid. She imagined herself with Huntington, naked in bed together, their limbs entwined. Would he be a gentle lover? Or one consumed by passion?

The carriage came to a stop in front the Peacock Print Shop.

She reached for the door handle when Grayson placed a hand on her sleeve. Her skin tingled pleasurably.

"I'll send my carriage for you," he said.

Eliza didn't trust herself to meet his gaze. He was too intelligent and far too intuitive. He would surely know what she was thinking.

Nodding mutely, she fled into the shop.

Chapter Twelve

Grayson placed his empty glass on the table. "One more."

"It's unlike you to drink yourself into a stupor. I take it the lady is behind your demons?" Brandon said as he raised a crystal decanter.

Grayson sipped his drink. "Eliza nearly got herself killed. All because she wants to find her father before me."

"Do you blame her?" Brandon said.

Grayson swirled the amber colored alcohol in his glass as he contemplated the question. He was in a foul mood. After he'd escorted Eliza to her shop, he'd immediately sought out his friend at his home. Brandon had taken one look at Grayson and locked them in his study and handed him a glass.

"Miller abandoned her and her sisters. Eliza probably married old man Somerton just to survive," Grayson finally answered.

Brandon shrugged. "So? Miller's still her father. It makes sense she'd want to speak with him after all these years."

"After today, she better not act impulsively," Grayson said tersely.

When he'd learned she'd gone off to see Dorian Reed without him, he'd panicked. And when he'd found Reed straddling Eliza on the settee, fury almost choked him. Then the sickening fear that Eliza had been hurt, or worse, violated, panicked him into violent action. Both emotions were frighteningly unfamiliar.

What had come over him?

He was a man of self-restraint and control, highly respectable in his circles, and a deep thinking art critic. He experienced unleashed passion only when viewing a masterpiece hanging on a gallery wall. Yet he'd exhibited uncharacteristic violence twice now—first with the warehouse owner and now with Dorian Reed—all on Eliza's behalf.

Then there was their time in the carriage where *she* had cupped his face and kissed him. Her lips had been sweet and warm, and his response had been hot and urgent. He wanted to crush her to him and thoroughly kiss her, but at the first taste of blood from her bruised lip he'd immediately pulled back. He longed to seduce her, not hurt her. So he'd controlled the harsh uneven rhythm of his breathing and reined his lust.

Brandon lowered his glass and chuckled. "I was right the first time. Grayson Montgomery, the mighty Earl of Huntingdon, is in lust. I never thought I'd see the day."

Grayson scowled. He wanted Eliza Somerton. There was no sense denying it. She was unlike any woman he'd encountered, and she had enraptured him, enthralled him. At night, he was plagued by erotic dreams in which he kissed and licked every inch of her exquisite flesh until she cried out his name as she climaxed.

He was torn by conflicting emotions—lust, the need for revenge, and possessiveness. He didn't like it.

His thoughts turned again to the afternoon's events. She'd had enough good sense to acknowledge he'd come to her aid. Not only had he physically pried Dorian Reed off of her, but he'd paid her father's debts. Looking back, he should be furious he'd paid off Jonathan Miller's debts, but the odd thing was he wasn't. He'd acted impulsively when he'd thrown his purse at Reed's feet. He hadn't hesitated then, and he didn't regret it now.

Christ! Had he begun to separate the daughter from the father's sins?

The question hammered at him. At least one good thing had come of it. Eliza had agreed to help him find the Rembrandt. Oh, she'd grudgingly agreed before, but only because she believed she had no choice and he would turn her and her sisters in to the authorities for forgery. But after the fiasco with Dorian Reed, her gratitude had been clearly reflected in her jade eyes, and she now truly desired to help him.

But how much longer could they work together without him touching her, making love to her?

Brandon was right. Grayson was in lust.

In aching, painful lust.

"When will you see Mrs. Somerton again?" Brandon asked.

"I'm taking her shopping."

Brandon threw back his head and laughed. "Another first for you, my friend."

"It's not like that," Grayson snapped. "She's accompanying me to the Royal Academy to engage Viscount Pickens. I believe he purchased the stolen Rembrandt."

"Pickens? He's an arrogant ass."

"I'm aware," Grayson said dryly.

"The Viscount despises you. Aren't you two like oil and water?"

Grayson's lips thinned. "One can describe our relationship that way."

"Maybe Eliza can charm him. He has a fondness for

pretty brunettes, and I suspect he'll try to steal her away just to spite you," Brandon said.

"I'm counting on it."

It was all part of his plan. It wouldn't surprise Grayson if Pickens were drawn to Eliza. After all, what breathing male wouldn't notice her?

And Brandon was right. If Pickens believed Grayson was taken with Eliza, then he'd do anything to steal her away from him.

Grayson knew it could help his cause. Ease his efforts in finding the stolen Rembrandt. It's what he wanted, right?

Then why did the thought of another man with Eliza make his gut clench tight?

...

Grayson had sent word in advance of his arrival, and Eliza was waiting outside her print shop when his fancy, crested carriage arrived. The cold afternoon air stirred tendrils of her hair as she clutched the fur-lined cloak around her.

She fought the ridiculous urge to run to him as he stepped out of his carriage. Dressed in a navy jacket with damask waistcoat and buff trousers, his sensual lips curled in a smile when he spotted her.

Goodness. He nearly took her breath away.

"I like a lady who is prompt," he said, his tone teasing.

Her fingers tightened on her reticule. An angry earl she could handle; a handsome, charming man posed more of a challenge. She feared her defenses could easily crumble under this type of attack.

He was a rare type of male, one that possessed an irresistible combination of masculine confidence and a streak of dangerousness. The kind of man that women swooned over.

Eliza always considered herself a logical, practical

woman, a shopkeeper who survived using her intelligence. But something about the Earl of Huntingdon caused all rational thought to fly from her head.

Grayson waved aside the footman and held the door to assist her himself. She placed her gloved hand in his and alighted into the carriage.

She was aware of his strength and warmth of his body as she settled on the padded bench across from him. The footman shut the carriage door, and she immediately felt cocooned inside the warm, comfortable coach.

Yet she couldn't completely relax. Not with the good-looking man sitting across from her, the only man she reacted so strongly toward.

"Are your sisters aware of everything?" he asked.

"You mean do they know you are taking me shopping? Or do they know what happened yesterday with Dorian Reed?"

His lips twitched. "Both."

Eliza sighed. "I confide more in Amelia than Chloe. That being said, I decided not to worry them unnecessarily. I told them that Reed was not helpful at first and wanted a share of our print shop in order to pay off father's debt. I did confess you paid the thousand pounds on our behalf. Both are very grateful to you."

"As I've said before, they are lovely ladies and I wish them no harm."

"Oh, Chloe is in awe of you. And Amelia is now convinced you are good-hearted."

He laughed. "You don't agree?"

She wrinkled her nose. "You do not strike me as a man who needs flattery."

"True," he said. "As for your sisters, I agree with your decision not to tell them everything that occurred at Dorian Reed's town home. Amelia was very concerned for your safety."

She felt her face color. "I'm sorry I caused her worry. That's why I left the distasteful parts out. Omission is not lying, and I prefer to forget it myself."

His expression turned serious. "Nonetheless, there's a lesson to be learned from it."

She fidgeted in her seat. "I'm not a child in the schoolroom."

"No. You're not. But I do believe I've aged a year after yesterday's scare, and I would like to think you won't repeat any foolish visits on your own."

She blinked at the worry in his voice. Had he truly been that affected by it? She'd had nightmares last night in which she fled from the dark-cloaked figure of Dorian Reed. She ran and ran and yet he somehow had seemed to gain on her. She'd woken in a sweat, breathing heavily in her bed, and had tried desperately not to wake her sisters.

"It's in the past, Eliza. I won't let you come to harm," he said.

His softly spoken words eased her nerves. She swallowed hard and looked away. How could this man, someone who had every reason to hate her father, offer her his protection?

She twisted her fingers in her lap. "Tell me again what you need me to accomplish at the Academy."

"I want you to gain an invitation to Lady Pickens's birthday ball."

She looked up. "Me?"

"Yes. I'm certain you can charm Lord Pickens."

"May I point out that I do not get invited to society balls on a regular basis, my lord. Shopkeepers do not wear ball gowns and waltz with aristocrats in their free time."

"I'm perfectly aware of how society functions, but I'm not concerned. Viscount Pickens invites all his artistic friends, those that are influential art critics, collectors, and even Lord

Yarmouth, the Regent's own art collector."

"And precisely how do I fit in?"

"His guest list also includes artists—those who are on the cusp of recognition and those that are struggling. He surrounds himself with all types and proprietors of art shops have been on the guest list—even Rudolph Ackerman."

"Still, I—"

"I'm confident."

At her silence, he touched her chin with his forefinger and raised her eyes to his. She met his gaze and gasped.

He stared at her. Possessively. Protectively.

And lustfully.

And just like that it was there. The ever-present sizzling current between them. The air crackled with their desire.

The carriage came to a sudden stop. He was first to break their gaze and turn to the window. "We're here."

It took a moment for her to realize his meaning. Her mind floundered, and she recalled their destination.

The dress shop.

She took a deep breath and eased her grip on her reticule in her lap. Any more time in the confines of the carriage and she would have ended up in his arms, crushed against his chest, his kisses sending the pit of her stomach into a wild swirl.

The thought of stepping away should not leave her feeling bereft.

But it did.

Sweet lord, it did.

Chapter Fourteen

The step was lowered for Eliza and she hurried from the carriage. She needed fresh air to clear her head and space away from Grayson to calm her racing heart. Looking up, she glanced at the bay window of the Bond Street dress shop.

Eliza had walked by the shop many times, but she'd never been inside. There had never been a need. The dressmaker was currently the premier modiste for the *beau monde*, and Eliza no longer mingled with its members.

Tiny bells chimed as Grayson opened the door and it closed behind them, alerting the proprietor to their presence. A tall, thin-boned woman with a long face and upturned nose came forth to greet them.

"May I be of assistance sir…"

"Lord Huntingdon, and yes, I hope you will be of great assistance."

The dressmaker's eyes widened when she realized an earl was in her shop. She quickly curtsied and smiled. "Of course, my lord. I'm Mrs. Gardner, the owner of the shop."

Grayson motioned to Eliza. "May I present Mrs.

Somerton. The lady requires a gown that must be at the height of fashion."

If Mrs. Gardner thought it odd that an earl was accompanying a woman and giving fashion advice, it did not show on her face. *A consummate professional*, Eliza thought. The dressmaker could probably sniff out wealth from across the street.

Mrs. Gardner eyed Eliza from head to toe. "I have just the color in mind for the lady. Please follow me."

When Grayson's hand brushed Eliza's low back and ushered her farther into the shop, she suspected Mrs. Gardner's shrewd gaze didn't miss the detail.

Eliza stood straight and tried not to flush at his intimate touch. Heaven only knew what the dressmaker suspected of her relationship to the earl. Mrs. Gardner must assume she was the earl's mistress. And if so, she didn't seem perturbed by that notion. Which made Eliza wonder if men brought their mistresses shopping that often?

Eliza trailed behind the dressmaker. The shop was elegantly decorated for its distinctive and rich clientele with Egyptian inspired chairs with lion paw feet, silk drapes, and Oriental carpet.

"The lady requires the gown in a week's time," Grayson said. "She also needs walking dresses, evening dresses, and undergarments just as quickly."

Mrs. Gardner halted and whirled to Grayson. "A week! But I have other orders to fulfill, my lord. I would be forced to hire additional seamstresses."

"I'll pay double the cost if the clothing is ready in a week's time."

An avaricious gleam lit Mrs. Gardner's eyes, and she nodded. "I shall do my best. Right this way, if you please."

Eliza knew Huntington was wealthy, but the ease in which he offered to pay extra to have the clothing ready astonished her. She pictured her tiny print shop with its slightly faded curtains and settee in need of refurbishing.

The dressmaker motioned for them to follow her down the hall. Grayson glanced sideways at Eliza. "We'll have to go to the shoemaker's for the slippers and other shops for accessories."

Eliza looked at him in alarm. "Is all of this necessary?"

"It is if you are to accompany me to the Royal Academy."

"But the additional dresses and undergarments?" she whispered.

"I have no doubt the viscount will invite us to his wife's ball," he said dryly. "As for the other dresses, you may have to accompany me elsewhere."

"Elsewhere?" What was he talking about? She knew about the Royal Academy, and even a possible ball if things worked out and Viscount Pickens invited them to his wife's birthday celebration. But what else did he have in mind?

"You promised to help me find the painting, remember? It may require more outings," he said.

Grayson considered everything a costume, she reminded herself, similar to his liveried footmen. She felt a moment's dismay. But her thoughts fled when the modiste led them past racks of clothing and easels of sketches to the back of the shop where the bolts of cloth were stored.

Oh my! Shelves stacked with colorful bolts of silks, satins, cashmere, crepe, brocades, merino, velvets, taffeta, and twill made her gasp in delight.

Eliza immediately thought of her sisters. Amelia would be drawn to the colors and textures like an artist to a varying color palette; Chloe would be ecstatic. Eliza suddenly wished they were here to experience the dress shop firsthand.

Mrs. Gardner reached for a bolt of sapphire silk and unrolled a yard to show Eliza. The material was so fine it felt like a waterfall between her fingers. She couldn't imagine the cost to make a gown of such luxurious material.

"It's lovely," Eliza breathed.

"You will wear it well," Grayson said.

A satisfied smile crossed the dressmaker's face. "I have sketches you must see and pick the design of your gown. Whatever you decide upon, this silk will be ravishing."

"Mrs. Somerton also requires an evening dress for the day after tomorrow. Something suitable for a visit to the Royal Academy," Grayson asked.

The dressmaker halted. "All my clothing is made to order; however, I do have something a customer never picked up."

Mrs. Garner motioned to a forest green dress on display in a corner. With a high waist and rounded bodice adorned with crystal beading, Eliza's breath caught. She longed to feel the satin against her skin. Years ago, when Chloe was a child and her father was knighted and selling his own original paintings, they had worn fine, fashionable dresses.

"This is the one," the dressmaker said. "Simple but elegant, and with a few adjustments it can be ready quickly." Removing the garment, she held the fabric to Eliza's cheek. "See how the color brings out her emerald eyes. Exquisite!"

"Exquisite, indeed," Grayson said softly.

His attention was riveted on Eliza's face, not the dress. A shiver of excitement ran down her spine at the intensity in his eyes.

"If you would follow me to the fitting room, you can try on the dress and I shall make adjustments," Mrs. Gardner instructed.

They followed the dressmaker to the back of the store into a chamber with four closed-off spaces with curtains. A round pedestal was in the center of the room before a cheval glass mirror.

Mrs. Gardner pulled back a drape, hung the dress inside, and motioned for Eliza to enter the space. "I shall help you with your stays." Turning to Grayson, she said, "My lord, you will be comfortable sitting in the showroom."

"No, I want to see it," Grayson said, choosing a chair in the corner.

Eliza's gaze flew to Grayson, then Mrs. Gardner. Surely the dressmaker would protest?

But Mrs. Gardner didn't blink. "Of course, my lord."

...

Grayson didn't know what he was doing sitting inside the dressing room. He felt like a fool. Waiting for the curtain to open like a child at a magician's show, he sat on a dainty, rosewood chair that was far too small for his frame. Only he was no child and a magician was not hidden behind the curtain.

He could come up with all manner of arguments to explain his behavior. He needed Eliza to accompany him to the Royal Academy. He needed her to engage Viscount Pickens and obtain an invitation to his upcoming ball.

But none of those arguments could explain why he sat and waited.

He wanted to see her in a beautiful dress. He wanted to see her out of the dress.

He wanted to see *her*.

The curtain opened and Eliza emerged, followed by Mrs. Gardner.

He sucked in a breath as Eliza stepped up onto the pedestal.

The dressmaker clapped her hands in excitement. "Just as I thought! The color is lovely and the seams can easily be taken in."

Grayson's mouth went dry at the sight. The dressmaker had pinned the dress so that it fit Eliza like a second skin.

The low beaded neckline accentuated her magnificent breasts and the high waist revealed the feminine curve of her hips and made her legs look endlessly long. He imagined those long legs wrapped around him as he slid inside her body. He became instantly aroused, and his tailored trousers grew tight.

Eliza's face was flushed with happiness. She spun around on the pedestal, revealing a glimpse of slender ankles.

Grayson shifted restlessly in his seat and looked away.

A scrap of sheer, black silk hanging from a sewing basket caught his eye. He envisioned Eliza wearing undergarments made from the silk, and his heart pounded.

Why the hell was he torturing himself?

The dressmaker retrieved her pincushion and hovered around Eliza like an overzealous mother hen. "Stand straight for the hem."

Eliza ran her hands down the skirt lovingly. "It's such a beautiful fabric. It's been years since—" She stopped midsentence and a flush crossed her face.

A true professional, Mrs. Gardner did not comment on Eliza's slip.

Grayson wondered when was the last time Eliza had purchased a dress or any new item for herself. He experienced satisfaction in seeing her happiness. She was so unlike the spoiled ladies he normally associated with at society functions. His prior mistresses would never protest if he spent money on their wardrobe. To the contrary, they had demanded it.

But Eliza demanded nothing.

He was amazed by her integrity. She was a struggling shopkeeper, a young woman who was thrust into the role of providing for her younger sisters. Desire for a beautiful woman like Eliza was understandable, expected even. But admiration and respect were entirely different emotions—uncomfortable emotions that complicated his already perplexing feelings toward her.

"A pin has come loose. Raise your arms and I'll refasten the bodice," the dressmaker said.

Eliza complied, and the already snug bodice stretched across her ample breasts. Grayson thought he would burst with need. He realized he wanted to buy her pretty things, and experienced a sudden desire to lavish her with silks, satins and jewels. He pictured her as his mistress, dressing for his pleasure.

His mistress.

Why hadn't he thought of it before?

It was a simple solution. He would buy a town house where they could spend long, lustful afternoons and sizzling evenings—far way from her business, her sisters, and his tedious estate ledgers and the bevy of hounding aspiring artists who sought his constant attention.

He couldn't marry her. He must consider Sara's reputation and future as well as his title. But he needn't offer her a ring. Men of his status wouldn't blink an eye at the notion of him claiming Eliza Somerton as his mistress.

"That should suffice," the dressmaker said, interrupting Grayson's erotic thoughts. "For the other garments, you must choose from sketches and fabrics. Excuse me a moment while I fetch the sketches." Mrs. Gardner rushed off.

Eliza stood perched on the pedestal. With the dress pinned, she was forced to wait until the seamstress returned. She bit her bottom lip, obviously uneasy alone in his presence. She was such an enigma to him. She acted the part of an experienced, worldly widow, but there was such sexual innocence in her eyes. He couldn't remember a time he wanted a woman so badly.

A sudden need to learn more about her compelled him to sit forward in the dainty chair.

"Was it a love match?" he asked.

Her delicate brows furrowed. "Pardon?"

"Your marriage. Did you love him?"

She hesitated and glanced at the tips of her stockinged feet. He thought she wouldn't answer, but then she raised her eyes. "As I explained, Mr. Somerton was much older."

He stood. "Ah, I understand."

Even perched on the pedestal, she had to look up to meet his eyes. Her hair was pinned at her nape revealing her cat-like green eyes and elegant neck. "What do you mean by that?"

"There was no passion between you."

Her eyes sparked. "There was passion!"

"I'm not speaking of mere consummation of the marriage vows."

"Then what?"

He took a step forward. "Lust. Desire."

She stiffened, and for some reason her nervousness aroused him further.

"You speak out of place, my lord," she said.

"It's Grayson. Call me Grayson," he demanded.

Her stubborn little chin jutted forward. "Fine. You speak out of place, *Grayson.*"

"I don't think so, Eliza," he said softly. He stepped closer, until he could see the pulse beating rapidly at her nape. He wanted to make her heart beat faster, and an image of her gasping for breath as she climaxed beneath him flashed through his mind. "I'd like to teach you about passion."

Her full lips parted. "It's wrong," she whispered.

"An attraction this strong cannot be wrong."

She was poised before him like a piece of ripe fruit. He was starving, he just needed to reach out and touch her.

He cupped her cheek. "You feel it. Don't you?"

Her green eyes widened. "No." Her voice broke.

"You remind me of rare art. Beautiful and exotic at once. Meant to be viewed for pleasure and handled with utmost care."

Her breasts rose and fell in her bodice. "Stop."

"I'd like that privilege," he said huskily. "I'd treat you well. Teach you about the pleasures of the flesh, teach you everything you haven't experienced and always yearned to learn."

Her eyes were like liquid pools at his erotic words. Her pink lips parted.

Nothing could stop him from kissing her at that moment. A flash of eager anticipation mirrored in her eyes when she realized his intent, and he felt a thrill of male satisfaction. He'd kiss her and convince her of his plans to make her his mistress.

It was brilliant. It was perfect.

He pushed aside a nagging guilt about his intent to bring her father to justice. At that moment his heated blood was focused on *her*.

He dipped his head, his lips inches from hers…

She inhaled deeply, then suddenly winced and grasped the edge of her bodice. "Ouch!"

Startled, he swiftly pulled back.

She raised her arm to reveal a protruding pin. A trickle of blood oozed from a scratch on the tender skin of her underarm. "The blasted pin!"

"Hold still," he commanded.

He studied the fabric and realized the head of the pin was inside the bodice. Reaching inside the dress, his fingers touched the soft, warm flesh of the side of her breast. His nostrils flared as the delicate scent of lilacs filled his senses. Careful not to cause her more pain, he slid the pin from the fabric. The satin gaped slightly and revealed a glimpse of rosy nipple above her chemise.

His blood ran hot and heavy through his body. His eyes rose to hers, and a ripple of excitement passed between them. His thumb grazed the wound where the pin had injured her.

She didn't move. Didn't breathe.

He slowly bent his head to kiss the side of her breast.

She sucked in a breath, but didn't push him away. Emboldened, he licked her skin, and she made a strangled sound.

She was sweet and warm and exotic at once. "Don't deny you feel the attraction between us. We must explore it further," he murmured against her skin.

"No," her voice was weak.

He straightened and looked in her eyes. "Yes. It's rare and special."

"We cannot," she breathed.

He was desperate. He just needed to kiss her once. No pins or distractions. He lowered his head to her lips.

Just then footsteps sounded in the hall. Eliza jerked back, clutched the green fabric to her breast, and leaped off the pedestal to flee into the fitting room. She pulled the curtain closed just as Mrs. Gardner rushed into the room with a stack of sketches in her arms.

"Perhaps you can help with the selection, my lord." She dumped the pile of sketches into his arms. The shop's bell chimed in the distance alerting her to another customer in her shop. "Pardon me for a moment as I see who has arrived." She turned and once again hurried down the hall into the showroom.

Frustration roiled inside Grayson at the shopkeeper's untimely interruption. He glanced down at the sketches in his arms. He couldn't care less about them. His mind was consumed with what was happening behind the curtain. He pictured Eliza taking off the dress, the material sliding down her long legs, her upthrust breasts swelling above her corset. The curtain was only feet away. He could easily part the fabric, help her with her hooks and stays. Plant the seeds of seduction once again. Hint toward his plans of making her his lover.

He dumped the sketches on the chair. He stepped forward, his hand outstretched to reach for the curtain.

"Is that the Earl of Huntingdon's carriage in front of the shop?" The frighteningly familiar voice pierced his sexual haze, and his hand dropped to his side.

He'd know that feminine voice in his sleep. In fact he *had* heard it in his sleep.

Leticia. His former mistress was here.

Damn.

Chapter Fifteen

Eliza breathed heavily in the tiny fitting room and rested her head against the wall. The plaster was cool, unlike her overheated skin. There was no point in denying her attraction. Grayson exuded a potent masculinity that effortlessly stole her senses. She was drawn to him and her rioting emotions were impossible to control when he was near. She relived the moment his lips grazed her exposed skin and then he'd licked her...

Sweet Heaven! Her knees still felt weak.

She shook her head. Such an attraction was dangerous. What good could come from her growing desire for him? A future was out of the question.

She had to regain some semblance of control. She had to protect her sisters, her business, and her way of life. Huntington already knew too much, and his shrewd intelligence had led him to suspect even more. He talked of the lack of passion in her marriage only to speak of exploring the ever-present desire between them. She agreed to help him, she even trusted him with Amelia's secret, but that did not give him free license to delve into *all* of her past.

No one must know the full truth.

Taking a deep breath, she tried to calm her racing heart. She was ensconced behind a curtain. Yet she felt anything but safe. Grayson was just beyond and waiting. One step, maybe two, and he could fling open the curtain and pull her back into his arms.

The question was: would she be able to resist him?

She made a renewed effort to reach for the back of the dress, but the pinned fabric made it too difficult. Where in heaven's name was the dressmaker?

She was just about to peek between the curtains, when she heard the rustle of skirts and a feminine gasp.

"Grayson! What an unexpected surprise." A woman's voice — definitely not Mrs. Gardner's.

"Good afternoon, Leticia," Grayson said.

Eliza listened with bewilderment. The woman must be on very familiar terms with him to call him by his Christian name. Eliza froze as a memory surfaced in her mind. Then Eliza recalled what his sister, Sara, had said when she'd climbed into her carriage. Hadn't Sara mentioned a woman by that name who'd frequently visited Grayson in the evenings? Wasn't Leticia's formal title Lady Kinsdale?

"I haven't seen you since the Ruskin ball, darling. I never knew you had an interest in ladies' fashions," the woman said.

"Leticia—"

The lady's tone turned husky. "You must come calling again soon, Grayson. You can review the state of my wardrobe."

Eliza gasped at the outrageous comment. Parting the curtain an inch, she peeked out to see a stunning blond woman. With fashionably styled silvery hair, fair skin, and blue eyes, she looked like a porcelain doll. She was in complete contrast to Eliza's dark looks. She was also a lady. Her gown of fine silk appeared costly and was the height of fashion. And her jewels! Her gold necklace had a large ruby the size of a walnut that glittered between her breasts.

Leticia placed a slender hand on Grayson's sleeve and leaned close to whisper something in his ear. The intimate gesture was even more telling than her words.

Eliza's stomach sank and her fingers fisted in her skirts. She'd nearly succumbed to Grayson's skillful seduction moments ago. His words reverberated through her mind: *Don't deny you feel the attraction between us. We must explore it further. It's rare and special.*

What had she been thinking?

He wanted to bed her when he was still having an affair with that woman? Leticia's arrival, no matter how distasteful, reminded Eliza of her place.

They were from different worlds. She was a shopkeeper and he was an earl with ladies like Leticia at his whim. They had nothing in common.

What a fool she'd been!

Ignoring the potentially treacherous pins, Eliza pushed the curtain aside and swept into the room.

"Has the dressmaker returned, my lord?" Eliza said.

The blond woman's eyes widened in surprise, and Eliza experienced a flash of triumph. But just as quickly, Leticia's shock was replaced with a facade of indifference.

"Have I interrupted something?" Leticia's painted lips curled in a sly smile.

Grayson's expression had changed from when Eliza had stood on the pedestal before him. The heated look in his dark eyes was replaced with a cool detachment.

He turned to the blond woman. "If you would be kind enough and summon the dressmaker. That would be most helpful."

The woman stiffened slightly at the obvious dismissal,

then recovered with a sultry smile. "Of course. Don't forget my offer." Leticia departed with a swirl of silk skirts.

Several heartbeats passed as Eliza and Grayson stared at each other. Eliza finally came to her senses. If he wasn't going to leave, then she would. She intended to find the dressmaker as quickly as possible and get out of the pin-riddled dress.

Head raised high, Eliza tried to move past him, but Grayson grasped her arm. "It's not what you think."

She blinked. "Don't be silly. Your affairs are none of my concern."

"Damn it, Eliza. It's over between us. I haven't been with Leticia in months."

She shot him a haughty stare. "Who you cavort with means nothing to me."

"Oh? That's not what it looked like to me."

She refused to allow him to see how much he'd wounded her. "Then you are mistaken, my lord."

His fingers tightened a fraction on her arm. "It's Grayson, remember?"

"Don't worry, my lord. I gave my word."

His brows drew downward. "What does that mean?"

She pulled her arm back and he released his grip. "I still intend to accompany you to the Royal Academy and help you find the stolen Rembrandt. But do not think you can take liberties. I may work for my living, but I'm not a whore."

...

Things couldn't have worked out worse. Grayson couldn't believe Eliza's change in demeanor. Just moments ago she had responded to his caresses and her body had instinctively arched toward him.

Everything had been going well. He was sure of his seduction. Certain she longed for his touch as much as he craved to touch her.

Leticia's unexpected arrival had changed it all.

Grayson stared at Eliza's stiff back as she marched down Bond Street. She'd been polite and cool and had barely spoken to him after the dressmaker had assisted her out of the green dress and back into her drab shopkeeper's garb.

He'd had plans for them. He wanted to take her to a dining establishment and share a hot meal and a glass of fine wine. He wanted to hear about her upbringing, her marriage, her past. Not because he wanted to coerce information from her about her father, but because he wanted to learn more about her.

It was all impossible now. She'd uttered one-word syllables to him since leaving the dressmaker's shop. They ventured into a shoe establishment and ballroom slippers were ordered to match the gowns they had ordered. At another shop, fans and accessories followed.

This time Eliza didn't protest at the cost.

Neither did she speak to him.

But she did freely converse with the shopkeepers. She smiled gaily and enjoyed the items they brought forth for her inspection. Grayson was forced to watch helplessly as the male shopkeepers were entranced by her smile, her easy laughter, and her quick praise of their shops.

His participation was limited to standing in the back, nodding in approval at her selections, and paying the bill. If Brandon were present, his friend would laugh and say he had turned into a brooding and jealous man.

Both foreign emotions for him. Since when was he jealous over a woman?

At last they returned to his carriage. She settled on the bench across from him as beautiful and as untouchable as an ice queen.

"Do I have everything I need?" she asked.

It was the first full sentence she'd spoken to him other than "yes" and "no."

"Everything for the Royal Academy. We'll have to return for the fittings."

"Are you certain Viscount Pickens will invite us to his upcoming ball?"

He was. But he didn't share the full truth. "I believe he will find you delightful and charming," he spoke with light bitterness.

She must have misunderstood his tone for she shook her head. "I agreed to help you and I shall."

"I never doubted you."

"But this," she said waving her hand at what he could only assume was the tangible bond between them, "must cease between us. We cannot keep kissing."

"I disagree."

"That woman—"

"Is in my past."

"That wasn't what I was going to say. She is a lady, a woman in your circles. I don't belong in your world."

He didn't expect the argument. Leticia may be a titled widow of a marquess, but she didn't consume his thoughts. His logical mind understood Eliza's argument, but it didn't matter when two people were so strongly drawn to each other.

"We can't fight it."

"I have to. Don't you see? You have nothing to lose. You're the Earl of Huntingdon. Wealthy. Powerful. Society wouldn't blink an eye to learn you had an affair with a lowly shopkeeper, while my reputation would suffer. Do you mean to harm me?"

Her question took him off guard. She was right, her reputation as a shopkeeper would be damaged if it were discovered she was his lover. Many men would think she was freely available and make their lurid intentions known.

But no one would know, he told himself. He had no intention of shouting the news of their liaison off the rooftops.

"What happens between us will remain secret. I mean you no harm," he told her.

But could he honestly make that promise? When he finally found her father and sought his arrest, he couldn't promise that the full truth wouldn't be revealed. If it were discovered she was Jonathan Miller's daughter, she'd be destroyed along with her sisters. No one would frequent the Peacock Print Shop if they knew the infamous forger's daughters owned the establishment.

She shook her head. "Go back to your lady friend."

He was stopped from arguing when the carriage halted and his footman jumped down to open the door. Grayson waved the footman aside and helped her alight himself. "I shall see you soon, Eliza."

He waited until she was out of sight and in her shop.

Grayson climbed back in the carriage and leaned against well-padded squabs. Her words turned over in his mind. *Go back to your lady friend.* No doubt Leticia would welcome him with open arms.

The problem was he didn't want Leticia. He wanted Eliza.

His desire for Eliza Somerton was maddening. He was angry and frustrated with his lack of control whenever she was near. He should respect her wishes and keep his distance. But how much could a man take? How much longer could he work closely with her, have erotic fantasies about her, and not entice her into his bed?

The need for justice still burned in his gut. He was more determined than ever to find Jonathan Miller and see him tried for his crimes. And he still wanted to find the Rembrandt, keep it out of Viscount Pickens's private collection so that it could be loaned to the museum and shared with the masses.

But he also wanted Eliza, and if she were discovered to be

Miller's daughter, then her reputation, her way of life would be torn apart. Once again, she'd be left alone to see to her sisters' survival.

He now wanted much more than vengeance by capturing the criminal who'd damaged his name, humiliated him among his peers, and harmed others with his criminal forgeries.

The simple had now become complex. His goals were changing—to seduce her for sure yet protect her from ruin after her father was arrested and tried for his crimes.

Chapter Sixteen

The following days were difficult for Eliza as business had slowed to a trickle. Eliza poured over the accounts in the evenings, truly concerned at their expenses and lack of income. At least they didn't have to worry about heat. Grayson's supply of coal would easily see them through the remaining winter months.

On a particularly slow day, the jade dress was delivered from Mrs. Gardner's shop. Her sisters fussed over the beautiful satin dress with its long sleeves and hemline trimmed with delicate rosettes. Chloe wondered over the fine batiste material of the undergarments, and Amelia tried on the matching satin slippers that also arrived from the shoemaker's.

The afternoon of their visit to the Royal Academy arrived a day later. Excitement hummed in Eliza's veins as she sat across from Grayson as his carriage pulled up before the Academy on the Strand in front of New Somerset House. She smoothed her hands over the green satin.

"You look lovely this evening, Eliza. The gown does

indeed enhance your beauty."

Dressed in black and white attire, he looked stunning. A powerful man. She could easily drown in his eyes.

Don't act the besotted fool!

She swallowed. "Are you certain Viscount Pickens will be present tonight?" she asked. "From what I understand the exhibition during the winter is not nearly as well attended as the annual summer exhibition."

The summer exhibition was a popular event of the Season, and a favorite of many members of the *ton*. Unlike the endless soirees, garden parties, musicales, and balls, the Royal Academy displayed stunning artwork and was a refreshing change of scenery.

"It's no matter," Grayson said. "Pickens wouldn't miss this. Not all the aristocracy travels to the country in the winter."

The footman opened the door. Grayson didn't wait, but helped her alight. His hand held hers a fraction longer than necessary. She looked up at him questioningly.

"Thank you for attending with me," he said.

Oh, he was charming when it suited him. She needed to remind herself of why he wanted her. With women like Leticia waiting in the wings, he needed her only to help find the Rembrandt and, heaven forbid, her father.

She placed her gloved hand on his sleeve and they entered the Academy's vestibule. A nervous unease gripped Eliza. Her father had never taken her along with him on his ventures to sell his forged artwork. Yet years before, when he had been a legitimate painter, she had accompanied him to several functions. As the eldest daughter she had assisted him and carried his wooden art box containing his oils and brushes.

It may have been years since Jonathan Miller mingled with these people, but anxiety coursed through Eliza. Would someone recognize her?

Grayson must have sensed her unease. He squeezed her hand. "It was years ago; no one will recognize you. And you are accompanying me, remember? They would never suspect that I'd bring you along."

He meant as Jonathan Miller's daughter. She didn't know whether to laugh at the irony of it or not. She glanced at him through lowered lashes. She didn't find a mocking glint in his eyes as she'd expected, but a surprising sincerity.

Then all thoughts fled as he escorted her into the main gallery. Paintings hung from floor to ceiling. Exquisite pieces of work ranging from revered masters to new talent—a kaleidoscope of brilliant colors—a feast for any art lover's eyes. She recognized paintings from several of the Academy's Founders—Thomas Gainsborough, John Baker, and Sir Joshua Reynolds. A painting by Sir William Chambers, the Academy's first treasurer and the man who'd designed New Somerset House, was prominently displayed.

The paintings weren't grouped by subject. Portraits hung beside landscapes and charcoal sketches. Colors and talent whirled together to create a fantastic display. She could spend hours here.

A throng of well-dressed people milled through the room, viewing the artwork. The exhibition was indeed well attended, and many of the guests knew Grayson. He nodded in greeting and stopped to shake hands with several distinguished-looking men. A gentleman with white hair, bushy eyebrows, and a pronounced limp approached them.

"Lord Huntingdon! It is a pleasure to have you in attendance. I wondered if you would be in Huntingdon House in Lincolnshire at this time of year."

"The country can wait, Henry. I wouldn't miss an exhibition."

Grayson turned to Eliza. "May I introduce Mrs. Somerton. This is Mr. Piper, the Academy's Exhibitions Secretary."

The Exhibitions Secretary! Her father had never been important enough to be enthusiastically greeted by such a man.

Eliza curtsied. "It's a pleasure."

Mr. Piper smiled kindly. "The pleasure is all mine." He motioned to the room. "Please continue. I'm anxious to learn the earl's opinion on several of the pieces."

They strolled forward, her gaze riveted on the walls. "It's stunning. A dream come true to finally attend."

"Your father never brought you here?"

"No. He never saw a need."

Something flared in his dark eyes. "He was a fool."

She stiffened. "I'm not surprised by your opinion."

"No, you misunderstand. He was a fool not to have recognized your love for art and to have taken you to every London museum."

She looked up at him. She'd expected criticism of her father, but only because of his criminal acts, not because he'd wronged *her*. The intensity in Grayson's gaze was back, and the excitement between them was present again. He gently squeezed her gloved fingers. Her pulse quickened.

"Ah, there you are, my lord."

Eliza whirled to see a tall, thin man rush over. Dressed in a plain brown jacket and waistcoat, he held a notepad and pencil in his hand. "Lord Huntingdon, there is a painting by a new artist, the *Times* seeks your opinion."

Eliza blinked at the newspaperman. His attention was focused entirely on Huntingdon.

Grayson offered his arm. "Shall we, Eliza?"

He led her to where the painting hung. It was slightly above Grayson's eye level, but many others hung much higher, closer to the ceiling, and she realized one would need a tall ladder to hang them.

"Positioning of the paintings is a constant battle with the

artists," he whispered.

Grayson tilted his head and clasped his hands behind his back as he stared at the painting. A group had gathered around to watch, and she was struck by just how influential his opinion was. His words could make or break a new artist's career.

Eliza stood entranced as she watched him. Candlelight reflected off his dark hair, and his profile looked almost fierce as he studied the work.

Her heart skipped a beat. Must his every movement remind her of his sexual attractiveness?

Eliza forced her gaze away. The artist stood by, a young man close to Eliza's age, and he shifted nervously from foot to foot as Grayson studied his work. Eliza thought the painting was a beautiful portrayal of the battle of Trafalgar. The artist clearly had talent, and with more tutelage, could become a great painter.

"What do you think, Mrs. Somerton?" Grayson asked, catching her by surprise.

She blinked. Was he truly asking her opinion before all these people?

The crowd around them seemed just as surprised.

She met Grayson's gaze to see if he was mocking her, but he looked at her in earnest.

She cleared her throat. "I find the painting very dramatic and inspiring. The fighting is portrayed in vivid detail and takes me back in time to the battle."

"Excellent description," he said firmly. "I concur with the lady's opinion."

She was aware of the newspaper reporter furiously scribbling in his notepad.

"Mrs. Somerton owns the Peacock Print Shop near Bruton Street. I find it a charming respite," Grayson said offhandedly.

The reporter glanced at her, then continued to write in

his pad.

Eliza was shocked. She understood the importance of what had just transpired. One word from Grayson and her shop could become noticed overnight.

Grayson turned to the young artist. "I would be interested in attending your future exhibitions. If I like the rest of your work, we could discuss my being your patron."

The artist's mouth opened and closed. "It is an honor, my lord. A true honor."

Grayson tucked Eliza's arm beneath his and led her away.

"Why did you do that?" she said.

"The artist has talent; I was under the impression you liked his work as well."

"Not that. You mentioned my shop to the reporter. Why?"

He shrugged offhandedly. "I think it's a charming place."

She eyed him warily. "Why else?"

"You need the customers."

She did. The shop was suffering from the endless winter. Still, she couldn't believe he thought to ask her opinion and praise the Peacock Print Shop in front of the reporter. "But you needn't have—"

"Ah, there he is," Grayson said, cutting her off.

Confused by his abrupt change in topic, Eliza followed his gaze. "Who?"

"Viscount Pickens. He approaches."

A heavy-set man with brown hair and eyes who appeared close in age to Grayson walked a direct path to them. His eyes narrowed as he met Grayson's gaze.

Viscount Pickens stopped before them. "Huntingdon. I understand you just viewed a new artist's work. Why am I not surprised you found it inspiring? I've seen stains on a chamber pot that showed more artistic talent."

Eliza gasped.

Grayson arched a dark eyebrow. "Perhaps your quizzing

glass is in need of an adjustment, Pickens."

"Ha!" Pickens bellowed. "Your arrogance will be your downfall."

"I'm not opposed to fisticuffs, but I'd prefer to compose myself in front of the lady," Grayson said dryly.

The viscount's gaze settled on Eliza. "You're right. I don't need my glass to see the loveliness of the lady accompanying you."

Grayson made the introductions. "Mrs. Somerton. This is Viscount Pickens."

As Pickens bowed gallantly over Eliza's hand, she curtsied and gifted him with her most charming smile. "I've heard so much about you, my lord. As a lover of art, I understand you have the best private collection in all of London."

His chest puffed with self-importance, threatening to pop the buttons on his waistcoat. "It is my life-long ambition to claim all things beautiful," he said, his beady eyes raking her form.

She glanced sideways at Grayson. A muscle twitched at his jaw.

Could he be jealous? Ridiculous. He wanted her to engage the viscount, didn't he?

"Pickens never misses an Academy exhibition. He believes himself an art connoisseur," Grayson said.

The viscount's brow furrowed. "Don't listen to a word he utters, Mrs. Somerton. Huntingdon and I seem to be in constant disagreement. If you're searching for a truly knowledgeable art collector, you need not look further. As for Huntingdon," the viscount's eyes darted to Grayson, "he's not as reputable as he undoubtedly led you to believe."

She felt Grayson stiffen beside her.

"But Lord Huntingdon is very well respected," Eliza pointed out.

Pickens snorted. "He was fooled in the past." His lips

curled mockingly, and he turned to Grayson. "Why don't you tell her, Huntingdon? That you raved about an oil painting, believing it to be Raphael's work, only for it to be discovered a forgery. A forgery!" he guffawed.

"I never denied it." Grayson's voice was tense.

Pickens looked to Eliza. "He was fooled by the infamous forger of the *ton* himself. I would have never made such a mistake," he boasted.

Grayson stood stock still. Eliza's gaze darted from him to Pickens and back to Grayson. Coldness settled in her chest. She'd never truly thought about the consequences of her father's crimes. Grayson carried himself with such confidence that she'd come to believe him impregnable to harm.

Forgery, her father had said many times, *is a victimless crime when sold to the rich.*

Her father had repeated the mantra so often that she'd begun to believe it from an early age.

For the first time, she saw how it had harmed Grayson. How it harmed him still.

How many others had ridiculed him for his mistake?

She had a strong need to defend him. Not her father.

But Grayson.

"That must have been years ago," she said.

"Not so far back that others don't remember. He didn't show his face at the Academy for a full year. Isn't that right, Huntingdon?"

Grayson stood silently. Did he truly not care to defend himself against the arrogant viscount? Pickens's comments were slanderous and insulting. Huntingdon had a right to call him out. Instead he remained still, his expression unflinching.

Why on earth didn't he say something?

"I recall the forger," Eliza said. "I believe his name was Jonathan Miller."

"Yes," Pickens said.

"He fooled many people. Connoisseurs, collectors, and critics, like yourself. There's no shame in what happened. If I were you, I'd double check the authenticity of the paintings hanging in your own private collection, my lord," she said.

Pickens's smile wavered, and Eliza suppressed her own self-satisfied smile. She was not ignorant of men like Pickens. Men who had an overinflated sense of themselves. Her father had made a living swindling such fools.

Careful, she thought. *Putting the viscount in his place is not why we're here today.*

She laughed lightly and touched the viscount's arm.

Pickens's tight expression eased. "You're teasing me, Mrs. Somerton."

"Perhaps."

"The lady is your defender, Huntingdon," Pickens said.

"I don't need a defender," Grayson said at last. "But I must admit that her efforts are quite attractive, and I find her fascinating."

Grayson's eyes bathed her in admiration, and her pulse hammered. How much of his statement was true and how much was for the viscount's behalf?

"Lord Huntingdon! A few more questions, if you please."

Eliza turned to see the newspaperman swiftly approach Grayson.

"It appears Lord Huntingdon is busy," Pickens said. "May I escort you about the exhibition, Mrs. Somerton?"

She hesitated and looked at him beneath lowered lashes. Here was her opportunity, her chance to charm the viscount. She gifted him with a coy smile and placed her gloved hand on his sleeve. "That would be lovely, my lord."

Chapter Seventeen

Grayson watched as Viscount Pickens led Eliza across the room. Her fingers rested on his sleeve, her green eyes focused on his face, and a sensual smile curled her full lips. Pickens responded as any red-blooded male would to the rapt attention of a beautiful woman—his chest inflated by several inches and he strode with an arrogant sense of self-importance.

Grayson's gut clenched. Just as he expected, as soon as he'd introduced Eliza, Pickens had taken an interest her. But when she'd ardently defended him in front of the viscount, she had truly captured Pickens's interest.

The viscount wanted to hurt Grayson any way he could. What better way than to use Eliza? If flinging insults at Grayson in front of the lady failed, he'd attempt the next best thing—seduce the lady away from him.

Grayson had felt a cold fury, a dangerous anger, when Pickens had brought up his past. He remained silent, fearing if he spoke or moved it would be to wrap his hands around the viscount's thick neck. Instead he stared at Pickens with barely concealed hatred, thinking how ironic it was that he had no idea the forger's daughter stood before him.

Five years may have passed, but the humiliation of being fooled by Jonathan Miller was still fresh in Grayson's mind. His reputation had suffered—still suffered. Pickens may be the only one to insult him to his face, but he knew others still whispered behind his back.

At one point Grayson imagined his mistake would be etched on his tombstone: *Here lies Lord Huntingdon, earl of the realm and mostly successful art critic, save for being fooled by the infamous forger of the* ton.

Yet just as his temper threatened his control, Eliza had surprised him by defending him. She wasn't playing a part when she'd spoken. Her beautiful face had paled, and she'd flashed Pickens a look of disdain. Her words had been earnest and her set down of Pickens satisfyingly true.

He still struggled to comprehend how she—the daughter of Jonathan Miller—had defended him. It was unbelievable, incredible.

He'd never forget it as long as he lived.

"Lord Huntingdon. Are there any other notable paintings you'd like to point out?"

Grayson turned to the newspaperman. He had already peppered him with questions about the new artist, and Grayson's patience was quickly expiring. He was having a deuced difficult time concentrating on his answers. He glanced back to where Eliza and Pickens stood in the corner of the room.

Eliza stood inches away from Pickens. She threw back her head and laughed at something the idiot said.

Grayson's fingers clenched into fists at his side.

She was playing her part all too well, and he didn't like it. The viscount's wife was noticeably absent, and Pickens had free rein to gaze upon Eliza like a besotted fool.

Free rein to try to seduce her.

Eliza turned and the candlelight radiated off her skin and her green skirts shimmered. Any man would picture her naked body beneath the hugging silk, her long limbs wrapped around him. Surely Pickens was imagining the same erotic scene, and the viscount believed her to be Grayson's lover.

And that's what he wanted her to be, dammit.

He was accustomed to having beautiful women vie for his attention, whether it was Leticia or other widows seeking a lover. His wealth and title ensured success, never rejection, but with Eliza Somerton everything was unnerving...

He should feel satisfaction that Pickens' interest was captured. It was part of his plan to gain an invitation to the ball and access to his mansion. But the problem was he felt anything but satisfaction.

Pickens touched Eliza's low back with his hand under pretense of gaining her attention. He pointed to a watercolor hanging at the level of her breasts. She looked at the painting; Pickens looked down her bodice.

Jealousy, fierce and dark, surged inside Grayson.

Enough was enough.

"Excuse me," Grayson said to the newspaperman, then stalked over to where the couple stood.

"Lord Huntingdon." Eliza smiled as he approached. "Viscount Pickens has just told me of a ball he is hosting in a fortnight and has extended me an invitation. He assures me yours will be delivered straightway."

"Mrs. Somerton is a jewel of an art lover. Wherever did you find her, Huntingdon?" Pickens asked.

The pompous bastard was standing too close to Eliza. Grayson wanted to pull her away. "You must be speaking of your wife's birthday ball. Is she well?" Grayson asked.

Pickens's face darkened. "Of course, she is. But I find it odd that you of all people should inquire about her welfare."

"I will be sure to personally extend her my congratulations when I attend your ball." He made a curt motion to Eliza. "Come, Mrs. Somerton. I am finished with the reporter." Grayson took Eliza's arm and tugged her along beside him. He efficiently wove through the crowd, evading further conversation, and led her into the vestibule.

They made it to his crested carriage. As soon as the footman shut the door, Eliza whirled on Grayson. "What was that about?"

"What?"

"The way you asked about the viscount's wife. The animosity between you and Pickens was palpable. Something obviously occurred to cause such dislike. Something other than artistic rivalry."

Grayson's jaw tightened. "He believes I had an affair with the viscountess."

"Did you?"

"No. I've never been with a married woman, even an unhappy one."

"Then why does Pickens think so?"

"Harriet has solicited me on several occasions."

Her lips pursed. "I see. No wonder you have never been invited to her birthday ball. A woman scorned is not a woman to be taken lightly."

"There is truth to that statement," Grayson scoffed. "Pickens and I never liked each other to begin with, but needless to say, Harriet told him that I had solicited her, and *she* had rejected *me*."

"It makes perfect sense now. No wonder he wants to have an illicit liaison," Eliza said.

"He said that?"

"Of course not," she snapped. "A man doesn't need to speak the precise words for a woman to understand his intent."

Grayson frowned. She spoke like he was a simpleton who didn't understand a man's motives or desires. He understood all too well, and the idea of Pickens attempting to seduce Eliza made his blood boil.

He was even angrier at himself for his lack of control when he was near her. He wanted to be the one to seduce her, no one else. Every moment they spent together made it more difficult to focus on the reason he'd enlisted her aid in the first place. It didn't help that every time he'd kissed her, she'd responded with fire to his touch.

The carriage sped across the street and she glanced outside. A tense silence enveloped the carriage.

They turned a corner and she finally caught his gaze. "Why didn't you say something?"

He knew exactly what she was referring to. She was too persistent not to demand the truth. "You mean why didn't I defend myself against Pickens' attack on my character?"

"Yes."

"Would it have mattered? It's true I was fooled by your father's work. His forgery was meticulously crafted."

"You must have been devastated. Devastated and furious."

"Men like Pickens will always attack. You didn't need to speak on my behalf."

"I believe I did," she said softly.

"It wasn't your forgery that fooled me, remember?"

"Yes, but—"

"Leave it, dammit," He said in a tense, clipped voice that forbade further argument.

Once again silence stretched between them. She twisted her hands in her lap and bit her bottom lip. He felt uncomfortable for venting his anger and causing her distress. He wanted to reach out and smooth her fingers. To ease her torment the way she'd tried to ease his under the viscount's attack.

"I never fully understood the consequences of selling forgeries back then," she said. "I thought it was just taking money from those that had more than enough. But there is more, so much more harm done by the deed."

He sighed and ran his fingers though his hair. "Don't think of it. You did well today, Eliza. You ensured invitations for both of us to the Pickens' ball."

She leaned forward and touched his sleeve. "Thank you for taking me to the Academy. For as long as I live, I'll never forget it."

His heart hammered at her touch. "You speak as if you will never attend again."

"I may not get the chance."

"As I said earlier, your father should have taken you and Amelia. He should have seen how much you all enjoy art; should have recognized Amelia's budding talent."

Her lips parted. Her emerald eyes were liquid pools. No deception reflected in their depths, only an honest need.

"Our wants weren't important to father. He thought only of survival."

"Why? What drove him?"

Eliza sighed. "He was a successful and legitimate portrait painter for years. He was even knighted by the Crown. Then our mother died from a lingering cough that affected her lungs. She was a good mother and their marriage was a true love match. He changed after her death, and he became withdrawn and aloof. At the same time new painters came upon the scene, younger ones, and competition for work became fierce. He adapted," she explained.

"By becoming a forger?"

"It was simple for him, you see. He was already painting. Why not copy other works? He should have ceased early on. But greed took hold of him," she said, a note of sadness in her voice.

"He stopped thinking of his daughters."

"Yes, he did. But to his credit, he somehow inspired the love of art in all of us."

Grayson nodded. "It's why you opened a print shop, not a dress shop or some other business."

A hint of sadness crossed her features and her eyes were downcast. "I suppose so."

He reached for her hand and began to stroke the inside of her palm. Slow circular strokes, meant to relax her clenched fingers. "We are similar creatures in that regard, Eliza. We experience an inexplicable joy when we are immersed in the artistic world."

She sucked in a breath at his touch. He felt the familiar pull between them as strongly as an artist feels the first brushstroke on a blank canvas—compelling and sure, with a heighted sense of awareness of the pleasure to come.

"Another business would have been safer," he pointed out. "But you could never stay away, even at risk of society learning your true identity. You need to be surrounded by artistic beauty; you crave it and feel whole only when you are immersed in it."

She glanced up, her green eyes alight with awareness and something else.

Excitement. Desire. For him.

"Yes, I believe it's true," she whispered.

His heart pounded as lust ran rampant through his blood. "Imagine if we can capture that together," he said hoarsely.

"It's not safe."

"That's what makes it so exciting." Reaching out, he pulled her to him.

She didn't protest. She appeared as caught up in the moment as he was.

His mouth covered hers hungrily. She was all soft,

feminine curves. She kissed him back, wrapped her arms around his neck, and buried her fingers in his hair. Their tongues met, tentative at first, then more urgently. His lips left hers to nibble at her earlobe, licking the delicate shell, and she shivered. He continued on, trailing kisses down her nape and above her embroidered bodice. His breath heated the curve of her breast through the silk and she trembled in his arms.

Compelled by a strong urge to touch and taste more of her, he unbuttoned the top buttons on the back of her gown, slid the silk and her chemise down her shoulders to reveal her lush breasts. Her rosy nipples hardened like diamonds in the cool air, and he nearly groaned out loud at the sight of her flesh.

Cupping the globes in his hand, he licked one nipple then sucked it full into his mouth. She gasped and arched forward, offering herself in splendid abandon. She grasped fistfuls of his hair, urging him on. He turned his attention to the other breast, licking and laving until his cock throbbed and strained against the fabric of his breeches. She squirmed against him, rubbing against his hardness, and his heart pounded in his chest as if he had sprinted ten miles.

"Jesus," he moaned. "I have to have you, Eliza."

His hand moved under her skirts, trailed his fingers up the silk stockings encasing her long legs until the fabric of her drawers made him want to tear the cotton to get to her skin. He longed for a bed, not the cramped confines of the carriage.

The carriage hit a rut in the road and she nearly toppled from his lap onto the floor.

"Oh!" She scrambled back to her bench, struggled to right her dress, and covered her breasts from his gaze.

He mourned the loss, nearly groaned out loud. His breath was ragged. He'd never been so painfully aroused in his entire life.

"Eliza, we have to—"

"This can't keep happening!" she cried out. "I seem to lose my senses around you. It's wrong, all wrong."

"It didn't feel wrong to me."

She ignored him, and continued to struggle with her dress. The buttons were in back; she'd never reach them.

"Let me." He spun her around and set upon the tiny pearl buttons with a vengeance. He tried not to think about the softness of her skin as he closed the gap of silk.

"Thank you," she murmured.

He frowned. He didn't want her thanks; he wanted her naked and writhing beneath him.

She began to fuss with her hair. Ebony locks had come loose from her coiffure; one curled deliciously around her right breast. His fingers itched to reach out, trace it.

He was so lost in his erotic thoughts that he was slow to realize that the carriage had stopped until he heard the squeak of the footman's perch as the man jumped down. Moving the drawn tasseled shade aside, Grayson saw they had arrived outside of her shop.

"Thank you for taking me to the Academy today, but we must keep distance between us. A working relationship. No more kisses. I insist."

"Splendid." Had he much choice?

"I'll see you at the Pickens's ball in a fortnight."

Two weeks. There was no way he'd wait two weeks to try and seduce her again. A thought occurred to him. "Your fittings, remember?"

A panicked expression crossed her face before it was replaced with a polite smile. "You needn't trouble yourself, my lord. I'm sure you have much more important duties than to attend a fitting."

He did. Surely he did. But he couldn't think of a single one at the moment.

Chapter Eighteen

"I don't believe it! More customers are coming," Chloe said, as she hurried to clear the counter of invoices.

Amelia thrust a copy of the *Times* at Eliza. "This newspaper article is wonderful," she said, before rushing off to help another customer who just walked into the shop.

Eliza couldn't help herself. She unfolded the paper and read the article for the third time that morning.

> THERE WAS QUITE A STIR AT THE ROYAL ACADEMY THIS WEEKEND. THE INFLUENTIAL ART CRITIC, LORD HUNTINGDON, ASKED AN ANONYMOUS WOMAN FOR HER OPINION ON A NEW ARTIST'S WORK. SURPRISING TO EVERYONE, HE AGREED WITH HER FLATTERING DESCRIPTION OF THE PAINTING, AND HUNTINGDON EVEN OFFERED THE LUCKY ARTIST A PATRONAGE. TURNS OUT THE MYSTERY WOMAN IS MRS. SOMERTON, OWNER OF THE PEACOCK PRINT SHOP ON BRUTON STREET. ONE CAN ONLY ASSUME LORD HUNTINGDON IS A LOYAL CUSTOMER OF THE ESTABLISHMENT.

Eliza glanced up and pasted a smile on her face as the

shop bells chimed once again.

"We told you he would help us," Chloe whispered before she too walked off to assist their new patrons.

Her sisters were right. Business was thriving and at no better time. The winter had been harsh and Eliza was exhausted from spending evenings reviewing the books and worrying if they would make it to spring. The *Times* article, accompanied by a break in the snowfall, had led to a surge in customers. Prints and paintings were selling as were bric-a-brac décor. Eliza had no doubt the sales were a result of Grayson's comments to the newspaperman.

She owed him in more ways than she could admit.

Amelia stifled a yawn as she assisted a customer choosing a print. Eliza stopped short in dismay. Her sister also seemed tired this morning. Could it be because the shop had been so busy or was she coming down with Chloe's illness?

Or was there something else?

Amelia turned and caught Eliza's gaze, then quickly looked away. Eliza waited until the customer paid for his purchase and departed before pulling Amelia aside. "I know I've been preoccupied lately, but is there something wrong?" Eliza asked.

Amelia shrugged. "I was up late painting. The truth is I was considering selling one of my forgeries to help with the rent."

Eliza's mind floundered. "You know I'm against it."

"I'm aware how you feel."

"Then why?"

"For you. For us. For the household. Because you worry all the time."

Eliza blinked. Was it true? Did they perceive her as worrying all the time?

"You must understand why I want to help," Amelia said, reaching out to clutch Eliza's hand. "You're always the solid, responsible one."

"I am the eldest. It's my duty," Eliza pointed out.

Amelia shook her head. "That's nonsense. I'm a full-grown woman. You always shoulder our burdens and are the logical sister who exhibits control of her impulses."

In control of her impulses? Had they any idea how close she had come to giving herself to Grayson on the way home from the Royal Academy? He had been right about her. Viewing great works of art unleashed her passionate nature—a passion he alone understood and shared. She had been caught up in the excitement of her surroundings and with the handsome man who'd accompanied her. She had easily forgotten about her worries, thinking only of her base desires.

She had never been in *less* control.

"I don't fault you for wanting to help the household, but I also don't want you to go to such extremes as to sell forged artwork without my knowledge. My attempts to gain the false Jan Wildens painting are what got us into trouble with Lord Huntingdon in the first place."

"Involving the earl has helped us more than harmed us," Amelia argued.

"Perhaps, but promise me you won't do anything rash."

Amelia hesitated, then hugged her. "All right. Business has picked up, and there doesn't seem a need for me to step in now. But please understand that I want to help. You shouldn't be the only one to worry. You used to smile, be light-hearted… laugh."

Eliza frowned. When was the last time she laughed with her sisters? Had it been that long? Eliza's arms tightened around Amelia. "I shall, I promise. Now I need to leave for my fitting at the dressmaker's shop. Will you and Chloe be able to handle the shop?"

"Of course. Please go. You must take advantage of

the luxury no matter how it came about. You should seize happiness when it crosses your path."

...

Eliza returned to the dress shop with mixed feelings of excitement and trepidation. She couldn't wait to see how the dressmaker had turned the luxurious sapphire silk into a ball gown. But at the same time, she was fearful of running into Lady Kinsdale. She couldn't say what upset her more—the idea that the lady had been Grayson's lover or that the thought made Eliza maddeningly jealous.

Mrs. Gardner ushered her into the back room of the dress shop, swept aside a curtain of one of the partitions, and hung the gown on a wall hook. "Is it to your liking?"

Eliza's heart skipped with joy as she gazed at the shimmering sapphire gown. It was stunning with a beaded bodice, full sleeves, and hem trimmed with silver ribbon. Her long-buried female vanity surfaced as she touched the soft fabric. "It's absolutely lovely."

The dressmaker eyed Eliza from head to toe. "It will look exquisite on you. Please wait while I fetch my measuring tape and pin cushion," she said before departing from the room.

As soon as Mrs. Gardner left the fitting room, Eliza peeked beneath the curtained partitions and was relieved to find the adjoining room vacant. But her relief was short-lived when she heard footsteps and female voices in the hall.

"It's a riding gown, not a ball gown. I'm tired of all the frilly pink dresses in my wardrobe. I prefer something violet or burgundy. Something a grown lady would wear," a young female voice said.

"His lordship likes pink," remarked an older woman's disapproving voice.

"I doubt my brother would even notice," added the young

voice.

"I have just the color and material in mind. If the young lady would please wait in the back room," said Mrs. Gardner.

Eliza whirled to the doorway just as Mrs. Gardner entered, followed by a young girl with curly, dark hair. Eliza recognized her as Grayson's sister, Sara.

"I shall return shortly with sketches and fabric samples," the dressmaker said on her way out a second time.

The girl's brown eyes widened when she spotted Eliza. "Mrs. Somerton! What a wonderful surprise."

"Hello, Lady Sara. Are you alone?"

Sara shook her head. "My maid accompanied me." A sudden mischievous glint lit her eyes. "If you're inquiring about my brother, he is not present. Huntingdon wouldn't set foot in a lady's dress shop," Sara said, giggling.

Eliza smiled. She wouldn't contradict the girl and ruin her opinion of her brother.

Sara skipped over to clasp Eliza's hand. "I've been thinking of you."

"Oh?"

"I'd hoped you would visit again. My maid is dozens and dozens of years older, and it can be lonesome in a big house."

Eliza's eyebrow arched at Sara's description of someone so much older than her thirteen years. "You are a charming young lady. You must have many friends," she said.

"I suppose. But I'm anxiously waiting to turn eighteen for my coming out so I can attend all the exciting balls and parties."

"Ah, I see. You want to dance with the gentlemen," Eliza said.

Sara shook her head, causing her curls to bounce. "Only one interests me."

"You have a favorite? Lord Huntingdon will want to meet the fellow," Eliza pointed out.

Sara dropped Eliza's hand and began to pick imaginary lint from her skirt. "My brother would never approve of him."

"How do you know? You must give your brother a chance."

"You don't understand. Mr. Samuel Neal is the most handsome gentleman I have ever seen, and his family is quite well off."

"Then—"

"They are not aristocracy, but in trade. Samuel's father owns a shipping fleet, and Samuel is being groomed to take over the family business. My brother wants me to marry a duke's son," Sara said.

Poor Samuel is just like me. Eliza was no longer the daughter of a baron, but the offspring of a criminal. A woman in trade.

"I take it you don't like the duke's son?" Eliza asked.

Sara's eyes narrowed a fraction. "He's pompous, arrogant, and talks only of himself. He has no interest in my opinions. I could never be happy with him."

"You must explain your concerns to your brother."

Sara let forth an unladylike snort. "An impossible task. All that concerns him is the title and family line. Grayson used to be fun. We used to talk. Ever since mamma and papa died, I've become his responsibility rather than his sister."

Eliza froze. Hadn't Amelia said something similar about her? Could she have much more in common with Grayson than she'd thought? Both had lost their parents and had accepted responsibility for their younger siblings. Granted, her father wasn't dead, but he'd been long gone and of no help to Eliza when it came to her sisters. Amelia had said she should enjoy life and seize moments of happiness.

When had she stopped?

"That's why I was hoping you'd visit," Sara said. "My brother has been uptight and short-tempered lately. He's quite unpleasant to live with. A visit from you would undoubtedly help."

Eliza wasn't sure about that. "What about his lady friend?" she found herself asking.

Sara's brow furrowed. "Who?"

"The one you mentioned when you climbed into my carriage. Lady Kinsdale."

Sara wrinkled her nose. "Leticia hasn't visited in months, thank goodness. My brother has much more sense than to keep her company."

He told the truth. Eliza's heart sang. Grayson had said he'd ended the liaison months ago. She'd been unsure whether to believe him. She shouldn't care, but she did.

Was there harm in their flirtation? She'd been so worried about their survival for so long that she'd become a creature of habit. She already agreed to help Grayson, so why not enjoy herself at the same time? Why not seize the moment?

The Royal Academy had been a lifelong dream. Attending the viscountess's birthday ball would also be a once in a lifetime experience. She'd get to dress like a wealthy woman, mingle with the *beau monde,* and dance with Grayson. She eyed the waiting silk dress, hanging in the curtained partition. Sunlight from a nearby window made the sapphire silk shimmer. It would look like a rippling waterfall on her body.

She turned back to Sara and found the girl studying her. A sudden impulse struck Eliza and she smiled.

"Sara," Eliza said. "Have you been to Gunter's for ices?"

Sara's eyes lit. "Grayson used to take me. He never has time anymore."

"I shall take you."

"When?"

"How about today?"

"Truly?"

When Eliza nodded, Sara threw herself into her arms. "I

knew I was right about you."

Mrs. Gardner returned, and Eliza's gown was efficiently measured, pinned, and fitted. Sara picked fabric for a riding outfit, and selected a style from several sketches the dressmaker offered.

Sara's maid trailed behind as they emerged from the dress shop. Out of the corner of her eye, Eliza spotted a fine carriage with the Huntingdon crest waiting for Sara. A footman hopped down to open the door.

Sara tugged on Eliza's sleeve. "You must promise not to repeat anything I've told you in confidence about Mr. Samuel Neal to my brother," she whispered, drawing her attention away from the coach.

Eliza's brow furrowed. "You will have to tell your brother your feelings for Mr. Neal and your dislike of the duke's son. You must trust him."

"Not yet. Will you keep my secret?" Sara whispered more urgently this time.

Eliza patted Sara's arm. "No need to get upset. I'll agree for now."

"Agree to what?"

Eliza started at the sound of an all-too familiar masculine voice. She whirled to see Grayson leaning against the side of the coach, and her hand flew to her chest. "Goodness! You startled me."

"Pardon. I came to fetch my sister and I'm pleasantly surprised to find you with her." Dressed in a striped waistcoat and navy jacket, his shoulders appeared a mile wide.

Her heart beat rapidly. She hadn't seen him since their passionate embrace in the carriage. She'd thought of him often enough, and counted the days with anticipation and trepidation until the Pickens's ball.

One week left.

His lips curved in a lazy smile. "My carriage is parked

openly by the curb. I wasn't hiding."

"Mrs. Somerton has invited me to Gunter's for ices," Sara told Grayson.

Grayson's dark eyes looked at Eliza inquiringly. "May I accompany you?"

Sara looked at him questioningly. "I thought you were busy today. A curator—lord something or other—to visit."

Grayson waved a dismissive hand. "He can wait. What could be more important than accompanying two beautiful ladies to a confectioner's shop on this lovely afternoon?"

Sara's face beamed as she turned to Eliza. "I told you that you would put him in a good mood."

Eliza kept quiet. The girl was quite innocent and she didn't want to ruin her perception. What would she think if she knew the true reason that had brought her together with her brother?

A short carriage ride later, they arrived at 7 Berkley Square in the West End of London. A charming storefront with a sign with a pineapple read *Gunter's*. Grayson held the door as they entered the confectioner's shop.

Sara gasped in delight at the array of treats on display in the open cases—Italian wet and dry sweetmeats, chocolates, creams, sugar plums, pastries, ices and numerous ice cream flavors including orange, lemon, pistachio, jasmine, even burnt filbert and Parmesan.

Sara and Eliza both ordered lemon ices and Grayson the pistachio ice cream. They sat in the corner of the shop on dainty chairs at a table with clawed feet. Eliza tasted a spoonful of the ice, and the sugary sourness of the lemon melted on her tongue in a burst of flavor.

It had been quite a while since Eliza had indulged herself at Gunter's. The confectioner's clientele consisted of finely dressed ladies and gentlemen. Gunter's was one of the only establishments that a gentleman could be seen with a lady and not harm a woman's reputation. During the summer months it was customary for patrons to eat the treats outside, and waiters would run through traffic to deliver frozen ice cream or ices before they could melt. But it was still winter and people sat at tables and chairs enjoying the treats inside the shop.

Sara shifted in her seat and craned her neck to see a family seated across the shop. "I see Miss Abigail Evers, my school friend. May I go speak with her?"

"Of course," Grayson said.

Sara stood and kissed his cheek. "I'm so glad you decided to come with us," she said, then rushed off with her lemon ice in hand to speak and enjoy her treat with her friend.

Grayson turned his gaze on Eliza. "The weather has given us a reprieve. People have seized the opportunity to leave their homes. I take it the Peacock Print Shop has seen some business?"

Eliza bit her bottom lip to prevent a smile. He'd delivered the question offhandedly, but she knew his true purpose behind the question. "Yes. But the weather is not the only reason the shop is busy and you know it."

"Oh?"

"Have you read the article in the *Times?*"

"I haven't read the newspaper this morning," he said.

Eliza opened her reticule, pulled out a folded newspaper sheet, and held it out to him. "You should. You are portrayed quite favorably in the article." He glanced at the newspaper in her hand, but made no move to take it from her.

"Are you surprised by the article?" he asked.

"No. What does surprise me is the number of new customers who have asked for my opinion on what painting they should buy," she said.

Humor lit his eyes. "I've never doubted your good taste, Eliza."

She laughed. "You're outrageous."

Grayson set down his empty ice cream bowl and spoon and looked at her. "Thank you for inviting Sara."

"She's a delightful young lady. You should spend more time with her. She misses you."

"She told you that?" he asked.

"In so many words."

"I've been busy."

"You feel responsible."

"I do. I will do right by her when the time comes for her first Season."

Eliza hesitated, unsure exactly how to phrase her thoughts. "Be sure to do what's right for her and not what you think is best."

His brow furrowed. "What does that mean?"

Eliza gazed down at her lemon ice before looking up at him. "I never realized before today, but we have something in common when it comes to our younger siblings. I've been looking after my sisters since our parents have gone."

"Your father isn't dead."

"True, but he's not in our lives either."

They'd never have closure wondering what happened to him. She wasn't the only one disturbed by it. Amelia might say she didn't care, but Eliza suspected she dabbled with forgeries as a way to be close to her father. Chloe was overly fond of the male species, and Eliza believed she kept looking for a father figure.

Eliza lowered her spoon. "What I mean to say is that I understand how you feel. Amelia is impulsive. Chloe naive about men. I've always felt that I must do right by them, but perhaps I've been going about it all wrong. They must choose their future paths for themselves."

"You're making no sense. What does any of this have to do with Sara?" Grayson asked.

Eliza hesitated. She'd promised to keep Sara's secret about Mr. Samuel Neal. But she'd never said she wouldn't mention the duke's son. She could still help a little, couldn't she?

"Sara talked about a certain duke's son. Someone you prefer for her," Eliza prodded.

"Yes, the Duke of Trent's son is an excellent choice."

"Perhaps. But you must make sure your choice is hers."

He stayed silent for so long she feared she'd gone too far to interfere with the raising of his sister. But then he held her gaze. "Sara's getting attached to you, isn't she? It's easy to do."

What did that mean? "I don't mean to meddle, my lord."

He leaned forward and touched her hand. His expression stilled and grew serious as he studied her face unhurriedly, feature by feature. "What if I tell you I don't mind? I like it."

Her pulse quickened at his admission. She tried to quench the dizzying current racing through her at his intense perusal. Not sure how to answer, she pulled her hand away and picked up her spoon.

"How were your fittings?" he asked.

She glanced up. Thankfully this was a topic she felt comfortable discussing. "They went well. The gown will be ready for the Pickens ball."

"I was willing to attend with you," he said.

"Why?"

"I've a confession. I wanted to see you again and I didn't want to wait until the ball."

The intense look in his eyes combined with his words left her momentarily speechless. She lowered her gaze and swirled the melting lemon ice with her spoon.

"You must not say such things. We agreed to a working relationship." She swallowed the last remaining spoonful of ice. The sugar now seemed overly sweet on her tongue.

He lowered his voice. "I tried not to think of you, but to

no avail. I want to kiss you."

She choked on her ice. Gunter's may be the only place they could be seen together without fear of damaging her reputation, but not if he kissed her. The sparks were flying as it was, and Eliza feared anyone who glanced at them was certain to see the attraction between them.

Her gaze dropped to his perfect lips. How could she look at him without imaging his kiss? If they were alone, she wouldn't be able to resist him.

"We shouldn't associate with each other until the viscount's ball." Her mind floundered with something that would distract her from his hot stare. "Perhaps we should discuss our strategy for that night."

"Not here," he said.

"When?"

"I'd like to take you to dinner."

"Attending Gunter's with your sister is one thing. But it's unwise for us to continue to be seen publicly together," she said.

"There's a quiet establishment where we could dine. I know the proprietor and the fare is excellent. I will arrange for us to have a private room."

She thought of Amelia's advice to enjoy what life offered. But she wasn't an artist who could fling worries aside and live and paint with abandon. She wasn't Chloe, who lost her head when she first gazed upon a handsome face. She was Mrs. Somerton, a respectable shopkeeper on Bruton Street.

The truth was she was thankful for all Grayson had done, but she was also scared. She couldn't afford to fall in love with him, and she knew that she risked the emotion if she continued to spend more time with him. What would that gain her but a broken heart?

Grayson was an earl, the type of man who married a wealthy, titled heiress, but certainly not the daughter of his enemy.

At the same time, logic told her they needed to discuss what would happen at the ball. She was unsure of her role and how Grayson planned to find the stolen Rembrandt in the viscount's large mansion.

"When?" she found herself asking.

"Tonight. Expect my carriage at seven."

Chapter Nineteen

Grayson and Eliza were greeted warmly at the Foxwood Arms. The proprietor, Nicholas Foxwood, had been expecting Grayson and shook his hand as soon as they entered the establishment. Grayson had helped Foxwood's brother when he'd been a fledging artist. The brother was now painting portraits of wealthy merchants and Foxwood had been grateful to Grayson ever since.

They were led to a cozy private room. A fire burned brightly in the grate and a waiter opened a bottle of the inn's finest wine and filled their glasses. Eliza sipped the wine and watched Grayson from across the rim of her glass. Sharp cheekbones slanted across his face, and as he leaned slightly forward in his chair, his jacket stretched taut across his broad shoulders. His body was lean and hard, and she vividly recalled being pressed against his chest in the carriage ride home from the Royal Academy.

"You must try the turtle soup. It's a specialty here," he said.

A flutter of nerves swam low in her belly as she sat across

from him. She doubted she could eat much tonight. She'd known Grayson for little more than a month and she'd never dreamed she would be seated in a private parlor sharing an intimate meal with him. They'd started off as enemies and now they were…

What exactly were they?

Allies to retrieve a stolen Rembrandt? Or on opposite sides when it came to finding her father?

It was all so confusing. Her attraction for the man heightened those feelings and put her in a precarious situation.

She drank more, and he attentively refilled her glass. She knew she shouldn't imbibe too much, but the fine wine went down smoothly and warmed her blood and eased her nerves.

The waiter delivered the first course, a steaming turtle soup. He served it from a silver tureen and quietly withdrew. Eliza picked up her spoon, dipped it in her bowl, and tasted it. The perfect blend of spices made the warm soup mouthwatering.

"Umm," she said, her eyelids fluttering closed. "It's absolutely delicious."

She opened her eyes and found Grayson's gaze intently focused on her face. A familiar shiver of awareness ran through her.

"Watching you savor the food gives me pleasure," he said, his voice low and smooth.

Eliza caught her breath. "You shouldn't say such things."

"Why not? I forgot how good the food is until watching you enjoy it."

"It sounds like I simply amuse you."

"It's not simple amusement, Eliza. The truth is I find everything refreshingly new when I'm with you. Most shockingly, even artwork."

Oh, my. She'd never expected him to make such an admission. She reached for her glass and swallowed. "You shouldn't examine it too closely, my lord. There's a simple explanation. You are accustomed to the finer things in life. As a shopkeeper, I am not. You are merely observant and notice my reactions."

His eyes filled with amusement as he shook his head. "I believe there's more to it than that."

The door opened and the waiter brought the second course. The aroma of roast lamb made her mouth water. The waiter set a plate of lamb with cauliflower and asparagus before her.

Eliza dutifully picked up her fork and took a small bite. Everything was cooked perfectly and well-seasoned. Grayson never seemed to take his eyes from her as they dined.

She shifted in her seat. "Perhaps we should talk about the Pickens' ball."

"What's there to discuss?"

"Now that we have both received invitations, what do you hope to accomplish?"

"I plan to find the stolen Rembrandt." He spoke as if it was a simple task.

She blinked in surprise. Did he truly believe she'd be satisfied with such a vague answer? "Even if Pickens did purchase the painting, he wouldn't be foolish enough to keep it in his home at the same time he's hosting a ball. Only an idiot would openly display it on his ballroom wall."

He grinned as he leaned back in his chair. "No, but a man of his arrogance would hang it in his private gallery."

"You intend to just waltz inside his private gallery?"

He chuckled. "I doubt he'd invite me."

A thought clicked in her mind. "You think he'll escort me?"

His smile wavered, and his eyes narrowed a fraction. "I considered it, but I don't want you alone and unprotected with the man."

Not for the first time, his tone was possessive. She should take offense. Instead her pulse quickened.

"Then what are you planning?" she said.

"I'm going to conduct an illicit search while Pickens is occupied with his guests," he said as if the answer was obvious.

"You can't be serious! What if you're caught?"

"I won't be."

She couldn't help herself from laughing at his display of arrogance. "And to think when I met you I thought you were just another pompous aristocrat."

A dark eyebrow shot upward. "Pompous?"

"And boring," she added.

"Now I take offense to *that*. Haven't you experienced excitement and adventure since we've been working together?"

She eyed him. "You know I loved attending the Royal Academy."

The waiter delivered dessert—strawberries and Devonshire cream. Grayson ordered another bottle of wine. She watched as he topped off her glass.

She picked up a strawberry and bit into the ripe fruit. A sweet burst of flavor tickled her tongue. She couldn't remember the last time she'd eaten a strawberry. The fruit was a luxury they could never afford.

"You must eat it with the cream," he said as he plucked a red berry out of her hand and dipped it into the thick cream. Leaning forward, he raised it to her lips. "Taste."

Whether because of the wine, or the man, a thrill of excitement skittered down her spine. Looking into his eyes, she leaned close and parted her lips. He fed her and she bit the tip of the strawberry. The combination of the fruit and the rich cream was heavenly. She chewed slowly, aware of his eyes darkening as he watched her.

"You're right. It's delicious together," she said.

"There's a touch of cream on your lip."

She reached for her napkin.

"No." He rested his hand on her wrist. "Let me."

Instead of raising his napkin, his gaze dropped to her lips and he leaned even closer until she could feel his breath on her cheek. She froze, her heart thundering in her chest, as his head lowered inch by inch. He didn't restrain her in any way and she was free to sit back, to pull away.

She didn't move. Didn't breathe.

His tongue idly licked a trace of cream from her lower lip. It felt like the lightest swirl of lush wetness. She sensed the tension and power coiled in his muscles. But there was nothing rough about his kiss as his mouth gently brushed hers once…twice…teasing her senses.

She sighed and parted her lips in anticipation of his deepening the kiss. Her heart leapt as his lips fully covered hers, and her mouth parted beneath the domination of his lips. When his tongue idly brushed against hers, an unbidden shiver of wanting coursed through her.

He kissed her slowly and thoroughly, skillfully unlocking her inhibitions and rousing her passion. The spicy scent of his shaving soap coiled about her as he sipped at her mouth like it was fine wine. Her excitement grew along with her desire. All her pent up emotions surged forth and swept away her misgivings. The differences between them melted away. She wanted this, craved the contact. The harsh uneven rhythm of her breathing echoed in her ears.

"Oh, Grayson," she heard herself whisper.

Her fingers grazed his sleeves across the table until she clutched his muscular forearms. She wanted to touch his shoulders, run her fingers through his hair. His lips promised secret delights and tenderness that touched upon a loneliness she'd long denied. Feelings she'd buried in these years since her father had left them and survival had been an all-consuming concern suddenly erupted.

It wasn't only emotional yearning she craved, but physical as well. Liquid heat gathered between her legs as they kissed. She was all too aware of the width of the table between them. She wanted to press herself against him. Feel the strength of his arms about her, his heat, the hardness of his body. Surely he could sense her need. He would know how to ease it. She moaned into the kiss, a demand and request at once.

He cupped her cheek and pulled back an inch. She made a mewling sound in frustration.

"Eliza," he whispered against her lips.

"Hmmm."

He withdrew a fraction more. She raised her eyelids in confusion and met his gaze. He'd been kissing her...why on earth did he stop?

His voice was a deep rasp. "There was never a Mr. Somerton, was there?"

Her mind fuddled. She was slow to come to her senses and clear her head of the haze of passion that threatened to consume her. His eyes were clear and she could only imagine how she appeared to him—green eyes glassy from too much wine and too much passion.

"Must you know everything?" she said, her voice shaky.

She should be frightened that he knew the truth. In the short time since she'd known him, he'd stripped her of all her secrets. From the beginning, he'd quickly discerned that she was Jonathan Miller's daughter. He'd learned Amelia was the forger, not her. And now, he knew she'd concocted tales of a false husband.

She searched his face, but there was no trace of anger at her deception. Rather a strange curiosity and some other emotion flickered in the depths of his eyes. Fascination? Admiration?

"I want to know," he insisted.

She shook her head slightly.

"Please. I *need* to know."

She wasn't expecting a plea, and the tone of his voice tugged at her heart. He wanted to know the truth, and not because he would use it against her. Deep down she knew he wouldn't reveal her secret to ruin the business she'd worked tirelessly to build.

"It's true. Mr. Somerton never existed," she whispered.

"Why pretend all this time?"

She realized she still grasped his forearms. She tried to pull away, but he clutched her hands. More surprised than frightened, she looked up. She stared wordlessly across at him, her heart pounding.

"Why else? A widow is much more acceptable as the proprietor of a business than three young, unmarried ladies," she said. "I could never have obtained a lease for the print shop without my alias. And even with my fictitious background, I was still at the mercy of unscrupulous merchants and customers. The warehouse owner Mr. Cain is merely one example."

Grayson's jaw tightened at the mention of Cain's name. "You haven't gone back to that blackguard, have you?"

"No. There hasn't been a need." Not since she had received Grayson's list of suppliers who willingly did business with her.

"How long have you known about my past?" she asked.

"I've suspected for a while."

"How?" If he knew perhaps others would as well.

"Your kisses."

"My kisses?" What on earth did he mean? She thought he'd looked into her past, wandered into the nearest cemetery in search of a gravestone with the Somerton name, or even searched the records for a death certificate.

"Your kisses are passionate, but inexperienced," he said simply.

Eliza bristled. Again she knew she should react with anger, but instead his explanation wounded her vanity. She pursed her lips, leaned on her elbow, and looked him in the eye. "Don't you like kissing me?"

...

Grayson knew Eliza was emboldened by the wine. She also looked hurt. It was a ridiculous response on her part since he'd never been more aroused. It had taken all his self-control not to strip the table of the tablecloth, spread it before the fireplace, and ravage Eliza right then and there. He envisioned undressing her and taking the pot of cream and spooning it on her breasts, her soft thighs, her woman's center and slowly and leisurely licking cream off every luscious part of her body.

He also knew there was only one way to ease her concerns. He had to show her.

Desire made his voice hoarse. "We should leave."

He stood and helped her to her feet. Thankfully, she didn't argue. She swayed slightly as he led her from the inn and helped her into the carriage. She sat beside him.

Grayson banged on the roof, and the carriage lurched forward.

"You never answered my question," she said.

"What question?"

"About kissing me. Don't you like it?"

He was beginning to sweat. "I like it very much. I also think you drank too much wine."

"I should be upset with you."

"Why? Because I don't like being lied to?"

She shrugged. "I didn't do it *to* you, remember? The story started long, long ago."

He'd suspected her secret for a while, but he hadn't been sure. He needed to know the truth and now he had it. She had never been married, which meant there was a good likelihood she was untouched. And damn if that thought didn't make his cock swell even harder.

What the hell was the matter with him? He had never bedded an innocent before. He avoided them like the plague. Virgins came with emotional complications. Why then did he want her more than ever?

She was a fighter, a survivor, and he respected her more than many men who were his peers. He also desired to possess her with a fierceness that was frightening.

She looked up at him. Her eyes were large green orbs in the carriage lamplight. "Now, back to kissing. What am I doing wrong?"

"Nothing," he said hoarsely. "And I never said I don't like kissing you."

She cupped his cheek and scooted close. "Show me."

He didn't need further encouraging. He swept her into his arms and kissed her soundly this time. She clutched fistfuls of his jacket, then wound her hands around his neck. Her nails scratched his scalp, sending a jolt of raw lust through him. She would drive him mad, completely mad.

He pulled back an inch. "That's why I needed to know the truth. Your first time should be in a bed," he said, his voice hoarse.

She trembled. "You've never minded kissing me in your carriage before."

"This is more than just kisses."

"It is?"

The carriage came to a halt as they arrived at Bruton Street. Grayson jumped down to help her. "I'll see you inside."

She fumbled for the key in her reticule. As soon as she had it out, Grayson took it from her, opened the door, and followed her inside the print shop. A single lantern was left to burn on a side table.

"Where are your sisters?" he asked.

"Shh," she said. "It's almost midnight. They are asleep upstairs."

He took a deep breath and ran a hand through his hair. He couldn't ravage her. Not when her inhibitions were loosened by wine and her sisters were asleep upstairs. "I enjoyed our dinner together."

She tilted her head to the side and studied him. "Our evening isn't over. Come." Picking up the lantern, she took his hand and led him into the back workroom.

He was powerless to resist and followed her. The faint smell of oil paint and turpentine filled the small space. Two fresh paintings rested against the wall to dry. He'd seen similar ones in the shop before and suspected they were Amelia's favorites that sold well—a painting of a bowl of fruit and a country landscape. The worn worktable was cleared of paints, but a jar of brushes rested in the corner.

Eliza closed the curtain partition, ensconcing them in a private art haven, and turned to face him. "I want you to kiss me again so that I may learn."

"You drank too much wine."

"So? Kiss me." She shrugged and sauntered over to him. Her fingers grazed his cheek, then lowered to rest against his chest. His heart raced beneath her hand.

She didn't wait for him, but stood on tiptoe and pressed her lips to his. His whole body stiffened. He stared down at her, his body tense and controlled.

She made a little mewl of frustration, and tried slanting her mouth against his. Her delicate pink tongue flicked across his lips, then she pressed closer, and sucked his full bottom lip into her mouth.

Grayson's control snapped as desire scorched through his entire body. He pulled her to him and pressed her against the worktable. His mouth opened, and his lips parted hers to make the first sweeping stroke of his tongue.

She didn't resist, but clutched his shoulders and arched against him in surrender. Her heated response fueled his desire. His hands slid up her waist to cup her breasts. Even through her gown, he felt her nipples tighten at his touch. Her full breasts were magnificent and he needed to see them again…to feel them again.

He worked the fastenings on the back, and pushed aside the gaping fabric of her gown and chemise to free her breast and it filled his palm perfectly. He kissed her as his thumb grazed the rosy tip of her nipple.

His other hand raised her skirts and skimmed her silk stocking all the way up to the bare skin past her garter. He parted her drawers and touched her enticing heat.

She was wet. *For him.* His growl of approval was met with her own gasp of pleasure. His fingers teased her. He slipped a finger inside then withdrew to trace a slow circle over her sensitive bud. She moaned and arched toward his hand. He imagined what it would be like to be inside her. All that silken heat encasing him. He took deep breaths, desperate to keep control. Her first time should be all pleasure, no pain. He wanted to feel her tremble, to watch her experience her first climax. He wanted her to remember him when she had erotic dreams.

"Let yourself go. I won't let you fall," he whispered huskily against her lips.

His fingers stroked expertly. He watched her as she writhed in his arms. Pure, primal possession took hold, and she was exquisite in her passion. Her body convulsed in his grip and mewling sounds of pure pleasure escaped from her lips as she climaxed.

He lowered his lips to her ear. "I want you."

Her eyelids fluttered open. "Where?"

Christ. Would she let him make love to her?

She struggled to sit on the table, and her hand swept out to steady herself. She hit a jar of brushes, sending it rolling off the table and shattering on the wood floor.

She gasped and her eyes widened in horror.

Seconds later a feminine voice called out from the print shop. "Eliza? Are you home?"

Eliza jumped to her feet and smoothed her gown. "It's Amelia."

Grayson needed no further explanation. He spun her around and helped her with her buttons. Her hair had suffered, but there was nothing he could do about it.

"Please stay here." She parted the curtain to the workroom and left. Moments later, Grayson heard the two sisters begin to talk.

"Yes, it's only me," Eliza said.

"Are you all right? I heard a noise," Amelia said.

"I apologize for waking you. I clumsily knocked over a jar in the back workroom. No need to worry. Go back to bed and I shall clean it up."

"Are you certain? I can help."

"No. I'm certain. Please go back to bed. I don't want to wake Chloe as well," Eliza said.

"Wait. How was your evening with Huntingdon? Was it romantic?" Amelia asked.

"Go back to bed, and I promise to tell you all about it tomorrow morning," Eliza said.

Seconds later, the curtain to the workroom parted and Eliza returned. "I'm sorry, but—"

"I heard." He raised her hand to his lips. "I had an enjoyable evening."

"I did too."

He wanted to pick her up, fling her across his shoulder, and carry her away like a pirate with his booty. "So do you believe me now when I say I enjoyed kissing you?"

• • •

Eliza tossed and turned that night. She kept reliving their passionate encounter in the workroom. He'd made her body come alive, and her own driving need had shocked her. Never had she thought such intense pleasure was possible.

If Amelia hadn't unwittingly interrupted, what would have happened? Would she have allowed Grayson to make love to her?

She could only blame so much on the wine. She'd known of the strong passion within her whenever they were together. But tonight was an awakening experience that had left her reeling. If Grayson could make her body unravel from just his touch, what would it feel like to be with such a virile man in an even more intimate way?

She wanted him. But could she give herself to him, and not fall in love? A future was out of the question. The differences in their stations could never be overlooked.

But the most frightening question of all was: had she lost a bit of her heart already?

Chapter Twenty

The night of the Pickens ball arrived two days later. They had decided that Eliza would arrive separately from Grayson. He'd sent an unmarked carriage for her and it was currently stuck in a long line of traffic leading up to the house. At last her conveyance stopped by the front door of the massive Mayfair mansion and a liveried footman opened the door and lowered the step.

Eliza alighted and immediately composed her features into one of calm as she observed the continuous flow of well-dressed guests up the front steps. Strains from the orchestra could be heard outside, and numerous lanterns by the front doors illuminated the scene.

Although she'd never previously attended a London ball, she had a role to play. No one must suspect she felt unease.

Especially not Viscount Pickens.

Out of the corner of her eye, she spotted Grayson approach. He must have blended with the crush of guests and waited for her outside the mansion. She glanced at his presence and tried not to stare. She assumed he would wear black and white, but he looked striking in a long-tailed coat of blue superfine, white waistcoat, and dark knee-breeches.

He stepped in line behind her as they made their way up the stairs to enter. "Stay close for now, Eliza. The crowd will disperse once we enter the ballroom. We will be introduced separately by the majordomo. No one should assume we have arrived together."

She surveyed her surroundings as they reached the ballroom. The light of hundreds of beeswax candles from crystal chandeliers reflected off the marble columns and black and white floor tiles. The scent of expensive perfumes and colognes and the vivid colors of the guests' gowns overwhelmed her senses. And the jewels…the diamonds, rubies and emeralds in the ladies' earbobs and around their necks were spectacular. The men were not to be outdone either, with gold pins in almost every cravat.

She spotted two gentlemen who had been at the Royal Academy. The rest were a nameless, faceless mass comprising the members of the *beau monde* who were in town either for the Pickens's ball or because they found the country boring. Either way, Eliza was uncomfortable with the pomp and the wealth. For a fleeting instant, she understood how her father had sold these people forgeries without conscience. The openly displayed wealth was beyond her wildest imaginings.

It is a victimless crime, Jonathan Miller had said. *They certainly can afford it.*

But money was only a piece of her father's crime. She had begun to realize there was much more to it than wealth. Father had hurt people in other ways. She recalled the viscount's humiliating barbs at Grayson for falling victim to her father's schemes.

Grayson eyed her. "Are you certain you're up to greeting our host?"

"Only if you are prepared to greet the viscountess."

He winked at her and she was caught off guard by how handsome he appeared in his evening attire tonight. As the receiving line moved along, Eliza was aware of women eyeing Grayson and of whispers behind fluttering fans. He had captured more than one feminine eye.

Eliza spotted Viscount Pickens ahead. Dressed in a robin's-egg blue jacket and checkered waistcoat, he looked like an overweight peacock. The viscountess, who was at least a decade younger than the viscount, was a tall, rail-thin woman whose taste for the flamboyant rivaled her husband's. Her pink dress was the exact shade of the papered walls and was trimmed with an abundance of silk flowers and ruffles. Her blond hair was swept upward with an ornamental headdress, which added to her already imposing height.

"Mrs. Somerton, it is a delight to see you again," the viscount said, his gaze lingering on Eliza's face before turning to Grayson. A flash of dislike crossed his features. "Huntingdon, I daresay I wasn't certain you'd attend."

"I wouldn't miss it," Grayson said.

The viscountess smiled at Grayson. "Lord Huntingdon, it's been years."

"Happy birthday, my lady."

She smiled coyly at Grayson. Eliza disliked the viscountess instantly.

Don't be ridiculous, she chided herself. The viscountess was a married woman and Grayson claimed never to have had an affair with her. *Besides, I have no claim over the man.*

She followed Grayson farther into the ballroom. The orchestra was in the middle of a lively country reel, and Eliza watched the dancers whirl by on the parquet floor. A dark-haired gentleman dancing with an attractive blond woman caught her eye. She shifted to the side and noticed the handsome man was Lord Vale. Upon closer scrutiny it appeared as if his female partner was continuously talking to him through the vigorous steps of the dance.

Goodness! How did she manage? She never missed a step.

"Who is the lady with Lord Vale?" Eliza asked.

"Lady Minerva, the Duke of Townsend's daughter. Vale's family seeks a match between them."

She shouldn't be surprised. Vale was an earl; it was expected that he dance with the daughters of dukes and make a good match. Yet she couldn't help but feel dismay. She'd seen the way Vale had looked at Amelia, and she certainly suspected Amelia's feelings toward the handsome man.

How would Amelia react to the sight of Vale dancing with a lady?

She'd be devastated.

But unlike the fanciful Chloe, Amelia was a realist and a survivor. She knew a future between them was impossible. Eliza had stressed all along that she wanted a good match for her sisters—wealthy merchants who would never question their pasts. Amelia had balked at Eliza's thinking, but Amelia would do what was expedient.

Grayson and Brandon shared similar titles. There was little difference between them when it came to the *ton*. They'd both be expected to marry to ensure the integrity of their titles. She couldn't allow herself to forget that. Her growing feelings for Grayson were troublesome. She must not allow him to occupy her thoughts more than necessary. The sooner they found the Rembrandt, the sooner she'd have her old life back without the temptation of Lord Huntingdon.

• • •

Grayson sipped a flute of champagne and watched as men made fools of themselves vying for Eliza's attention. He couldn't blame them. She looked exquisite tonight in the enticing sapphire gown that hugged her curves and displayed the lush mounds of her breasts. Another gentleman wandered over, increasing the number to four men who surrounded her. Every protective instinct made him want to stake his claim, but he couldn't act as Eliza's escort. They must appear to have been invited separately. He said her reputation mattered to him, and it did.

Still, he was perturbed, and he experienced an animalistic possessiveness. A young buck reached for her rapidly filling dance card and scribbled his name.

The orchestra struck up a waltz, and Grayson acted on impulse. He strode forward and elbowed his way past the men until he reached Eliza's side.

"The lady's first waltz is already taken." Grayson took her arm and whisked her away from her admirers and to the parquet dance floor.

He rested his hand on her slim waist and caught the music. She followed his lead and it occurred to him that she had no reason to know the waltz, but she was proficient in the steps.

"Where did you learn how to dance?" he asked.

She arched a brow. "You mean how could a shopkeeper know how to waltz?"

"I didn't mean to insult—"

She smiled up at him, and his pulse increased. "I'm teasing, my lord. I've been practicing these past two weeks with Amelia."

He whirled her around the dance floor, their bodies inches apart. Her delicate lavender perfume teased him, and he could scarcely think about his steps due to the tumult of desire he felt for her. He was tempted to spin her straight out to the terrace and find a secluded spot in the gardens. To claim those red lips and peel the magnificent gown down her slim shoulders.

"What are you thinking?" she asked.

Other than making love to you?

"The gallery, remember?" he said. "I'll slip away during the champagne toast celebrating the viscountess's birthday."

"Where should I meet you?"

"I don't want you to meet me. I want you to stay at the ball," he said firmly.

She raised her chin and boldly met his gaze. "No."

The music began to fade as the waltz ended and the orchestra prepared for its next ensemble. Grayson grasped her hand, fully intending to whisk her behind a potted palm where he could argue with her when, out of the corner of his eye, he spotted the young buck who had last written on Eliza's dance card eagerly waiting for her at the edge of the parquet floor. Grayson pivoted, steering her toward the open French doors leading to the terrace.

Cool night air engulfed him. Torches burned bright, illuminating the slate tiles of the terrace and the well-sculpted gardens below. A pair of gentleman smoking cheroots lounged in the corner. Grayson led Eliza to the opposite corner and leaned against the balustrade.

"I insist you stay here. I have to pick the lock. It may not be safe," he said.

Her magnificent green eyes shone defiantly in the torchlight. "I did not come all this way to be set aside. I'm coming with you."

Infuriating woman. He didn't know whether he wanted to vehemently argue with her or kiss her senseless.

"Fine. The viscount's private gallery is at the top of the stairs. We'll have to go up through the servants' staircase. If we're caught, we are lovers looking for a secluded room for a rendezvous, understand?"

"I'm an exceptional actress, remember?"

How could he forget?

"It's too risky to leave together. Wait five minutes after I leave to follow me."

They returned to the ballroom separately just as the footmen were making their rounds with trays of champagne. Guests gathered around Pickens and the viscountess with their glasses raised in celebration.

"A toast to my lovely, wife!" Pickens called out.

The guests cheered and the orchestra immediately began playing a lively tune.

"Well, well. If it isn't Mrs. Somerton," a feminine voice said at her side.

Eliza turned to see Lady Kinsdale approach. The widow looked stunning in a gown of silver tissue with a shockingly low bodice. Her golden hair was artfully arranged with wisps of curls accentuating her blue eyes and heart-shaped face.

"You learned my name, then?" Eliza said.

"It wasn't hard to discover. I aided Lady Pickens with last minute additions to the guest list. I was surprised to learn you are acquainted with Lord Pickens as well. I know he takes a fancy to anyone in the art world, even proprietors of small, inconsequential print shops."

Eliza's smile was strained as she turned her attention toward the dance floor. She refused to give the woman any satisfaction by responding.

"Are you looking for Lord Huntingdon?" Lady Kinsdale asked.

"No."

Lady Kinsdale shrugged a dainty shoulder. "No sense lying to me. You fancy yourself in love with Huntingdon, don't you?"

"Pardon?" Eliza turned.

"There's no need to be coy. You're in love with him." The statement was delivered with haughty rebuke and an arch of well-plucked brows.

"I don't see how that is—"

"I would not have thought you such a fool. He'll never offer you marriage. Don't you know that you are just a bit of bed sport to him?"

Eliza's lips thinned. "We are not lovers."

She laughed, a brittle, harsh sound. "I'm not a fool. Regardless, you are a commoner, *a merchant*," she said the word as if it offended her. "You are completely out of his realm despite your presence here tonight and the fine gown you are wearing that he undoubtedly purchased for you."

Eliza started as the guests clapped suddenly and cheered for Lady Pickens. The noise seemed to reverberate in her head. A heavy feeling settled in her stomach. The lady may be cruel, but her words rang true.

Eliza had known it all along, hadn't she? She was just playing a part, a temporary role for the time being.

She struggled to remain impassive, to not respond to the hurtful barbs.

Five minutes.

She only had five minutes and then Grayson would search the art gallery without her.

Pasting a smile on her face, she turned to Lady Kinsdale. "I may be a temporary diversion for Lord Huntingdon, but from what I've seen you are no longer a diversion to him of any kind."

Lady Kinsdale's mouth gaped slightly, and her eyes narrowed. "How dare you," she hissed.

"I dare, my lady. Now pardon me." Eliza turned and strode away.

• • •

Grayson was waiting for her at the bottom of the servants' staircase leading to the mansion's second floor. Her delicate features appeared pale save for two bright spots on her cheeks.

"You're late. Are you all right?" he asked.

"Yes."

He wondered if she were nervous to conduct a clandestine search of the viscount's home. "Give me your hand."

She slipped her hand into his grasp. "We have to be quick," he said as he hurried up the stairs with her beside him.

She rushed to keep pace with him. "How do you know where you're going?"

"I was here before, years ago."

"I thought you never had liaisons with married women?"

He shot her a sideways glance. "I don't. But Lady Pickens lured me upstairs under pretense of viewing a painting."

"Was it worth it?"

He grinned. "The painting, yes. The lady's wrath, no."

They reached the top of the stairs and stepped into a long hallway. Grayson counted the closed doors as they crept past. The servants were busy attending to the guests below stairs and no one was in sight. *Four, five, six...* He stopped at the next door. Reaching for the handle, he wasn't surprised to find it locked.

Eliza's eyes widened as he withdrew lock picks from his coat pocket. "And to think I called you a boring aristocrat."

"Are you retracting the statement?"

"It depends on whether you are successful in opening the door, my lord."

He grinned as he inserted two steel rods into the lock and began to manipulate the mechanism.

Footsteps sounded down the hall.

"Someone's coming," she whispered urgently.

"I almost have it."

"Hurry!"

Sweat beaded on his brow. She shouldn't be here; he should have insisted she stay at the ball. The lock released and the handle turned. Grasping her by the hand, he pulled her inside and shut the door.

They held their breath until the scrape of booted feet passed by the door and continued onward.

Grayson cracked the door and glanced outside. "It was just a passing servant."

"Thank heavens," she said.

They turned back to the room. It was dim, but he could make out the shapes of paintings hanging on the walls. Marble pedestals displaying ceramic plates, ivory and gold carvings, and bronze statues occupied the center of the room.

What he'd told Eliza was true. He'd been here years before when the viscountess had invited him under pretense of viewing one of the paintings. She had made her amorous intentions clear that evening. But that had been a while back, and he was curious as to how vast Pickens's collection had grown since then.

"See if you can find—"

Eliza cut off his next words with a gasp. "Look at that painting!" She pointed over his shoulder and caught his gaze, causing his heart to pound. "Do you see that landscape?" she asked in wide-eyed wonder.

He followed where she was pointing. She looked as if she'd just seen a Michelangelo.

"Yes. Why?" he asked.

"It's one of Father's."

"How can you tell?"

"I was with him when he painted it."

Grayson couldn't stop himself from laughing. "For the first time, I don't find fault with your father. I only wish I could point out that Pickens purchased a forgery himself."

"An eye for an eye?"

"In a way, yes," he said. "All those years of putting up with his taunting and Pickens was fooled himself."

Eliza glanced at him with regret. "You'll never be able to

tell him."

"No," he said bitterly. Pickens couldn't learn that they'd broken into his gallery. Grayson's thoughts turned as he glanced at the walls. "We haven't much time. Look for the Rembrandt."

They searched quickly, glancing at every painting on each of the walls around the room.

"It isn't here," Eliza said. "Maybe Dorian Reed was wrong and someone else purchased it."

Frustration roiled inside him. "No, dammit it. Pickens must have it stowed elsewhere."

"We have to return before we're discovered missing," Eliza said.

He didn't want to abandon their search, but she was right. There was always the possibility that Pickens would escort a guest upstairs to view his collection.

Grayson was careful to crack the door open and glance both ways before leaving the gallery. Making their way back down the stairs, they blended with the crowd in the overheated ballroom.

Chapter Twenty-One

Eliza sensed Grayson's disappointment as they returned to the ballroom. He had been so certain that the Rembrandt was in the viscount's private gallery. She wanted to find it just as badly as he did, but for different reasons.

She wanted Amelia's forgery returned. She no longer believed Grayson would turn it over to the constable. But at the same time, only when the forgery was in her possession could she rest easy knowing the crime could not be traced back to her sister.

If Grayson was convinced Pickens had purchased the stolen Rembrandt, then Eliza was as well. And she was going to do everything in her power to find it. She scanned the ballroom until she spotted the viscount.

He was by the punch bowl, a crystal glass in hand, surrounded by friends. He laughed at something one of them said and paid little attention when the amber colored liquor in his glass splashed on his lace cuff.

He was clearly deep in his cups. It was no secret he'd expressed his lascivious intentions toward her.

A perfect combination.

She thought of her father. Jonathan Miller often took every advantage.

So would she.

Grayson was occupied, his back to her as he talked with a distinguished looking gentleman. She headed for the refreshment table, a direct path to the viscount.

His watery eyes lit as she purposely brushed his shoulder. He motioned to a footman and she was immediately offered a tray full of flutes of bubbling champagne.

"You look ravishing, Mrs. Somerton. Are you having a good time?" the viscount said.

"Your home is magnificent, my lord. I must admit I was most excited when I met you at the Academy. I am a true lover of art."

His breath was hot on her cheek. "As am I."

She leaned close, placed a hand on his sleeve. "I've heard your private gallery is wondrous."

He leered at the swell of her breasts above her bodice. "Wondrous, yes. Would you like to see it?"

She licked her lips. "My blood sings at the thought. I'd find it most exciting."

Lust shone in his eyes. "Come. I'd be a bad host if I didn't oblige such a lovely guest."

The orchestra played a lively tune and the music reached a crescendo. She'd lost sight of Grayson as she followed the viscount out of the ballroom. This time she did not sneak up the servants' staircase, but ascended the winding front stairs.

Pickens weaved slightly and the strong odor of brandy wafted from him. He withdrew a key ring from his waistcoat pocket and that's when she saw it.

A second gold key on the ring.

What room was it for?

He fumbled with the key; dropped the key ring twice

before he successfully opened the door to the gallery.

She stepped inside for the second time that night. She roamed the room, pretending to see the pieces for the first time. "The works of art are exquisite." She halted before her father's forgery and a deviousness rose within her. "This is especially lovely."

His chest puffed with self-importance. "It was quite costly. I outbid many others for it," he said arrogantly.

A thoughtful smile curved her mouth. "Tell me, do you have other pieces squirreled away?"

"Perhaps."

She came close and ran her fingers up his arm. "You must know that expensive artwork makes me breathless…excited."

His eyes bulged in his ruddy face. "You are striking. A passionate woman. I knew the first time I saw you with Huntingdon."

"He means nothing to me. Whereas you and I share a special connection, my lord," she breathed.

She wrapped her arms around his neck. He needed no further invitation to kiss her. She turned her face at the last second and his lips met her cheek. His kiss was wet and sloppy on her face. She forced down her revulsion and her nimble fingers plucked the key ring from his waistcoat and hid it behind her back. She pushed against his chest with her other hand.

"I hear your wife's voice!" she cried out.

Pickens lifted his head, alarm battling his drunken haze. "My wife?"

He turned toward the door. Eliza hid the keys in her skirts and went to the door. "We best return to the ball before we are missed. Your wife must be searching for you."

"My wife. Yes, we have to go back," he said. "She'll make my life unbearable if she catches me here with you the night of her ball."

"Then let's not give her a reason."

Pickens face reddened and he opened the door for her to pass. "I'll return a few minutes after you," Eliza said. "If anyone asks, I'll say I was looking for the ladies' retiring room."

"Yes. Yes," he said, then hurried off down the stairs.

As soon as the viscount was out of sight, Eliza turned back around and withdrew the keys from her skirt pocket. She ran to the door adjacent to the gallery and fumbled to get one of the keys into the lock. Just as she thought she found the right key, a strong hand grasped her arm and swung her around.

Her scream was stifled beneath Grayson's hand. Her heart pounded like a drum until recognition calmed her and he nodded.

Grayson released her, but didn't step back. His eyes flashed dangerously and a muscle flicked angrily at his jaw. "What the hell are you doing?"

She held up the key ring. "Finding the Rembrandt."

"Is picking pockets another skill you learned from your father?"

"It wasn't difficult. Pickens is quite drunk."

"You could have been hurt or worse—"

"We haven't much time," she said, cutting him off. "Pickens admitted to owning more artwork, and I suspect this key opens one of these doors." She motioned down the hall.

He grabbed the key ring and began trying to open the door she had been working on. None of the keys worked. They went to the second, but had no success.

The third one opened.

Grayson cracked the door. Confident it wasn't occupied, they entered what was obviously the viscount's master bedchamber. Elegantly appointed with mahogany furniture and a canopied four-poster, it had an adjoining door that

Eliza suspected led to his wife's chambers. A portrait of Pickens with his horse and hunting dog hung above a stone fireplace. At first glance, it looked like any other aristocrat's bedchamber. But then she noticed a large package wrapped in brown paper and tied with butcher's string visible from behind a tall chest of drawers.

"Over there," Eliza pointed.

Grayson pulled the package out from behind the furniture and carefully unwrapped a corner of the brown paper. "This is it," he said.

Eliza's breath caught. The Rembrandt was magnificent, and she ached to remove all the paper and view it in its entirety. A mastery of brush strokes showed a self-portrait of a young Rembrandt in his studio painting.

"We can't take it with us. I'll send a note to Thomas Begley tonight," Grayson said.

She reached for the key ring in Grayson's hand. "I have to return this."

Grayson grasped her arm, his expression fierce. "That's the second time you outright defied me, Eliza. You could have been hurt or violated."

She knew what he referred to. The first time she'd defied him she'd visited Dorian Reed on her own. That had turned out to be a nightmare. But this time was different. They had only one chance to find the stolen painting.

"You cannot be upset with me," she argued. "We found the Rembrandt. Now let me return the keys before Pickens discovers them missing."

"How?"

"Leave it to me," she said.

His eyes narrowed and she feared he wouldn't release his grip on her arm, but he reluctantly let her go. "I'll be watching you downstairs."

They returned to the ball separately. She found Pickens

by the dance floor with a drink in hand. He bowed when he spotted her and lowered his voice. "The viscountess suspects nothing."

She feigned a smile of relief. "Thank goodness."

He offered his arm. "I would be a rude host if I didn't ask you to dance."

She accepted and he led her onto the dance floor. She smiled as she slipped her hand beneath his jacket and returned the key ring. "Thank you for the tour, my lord. I'll never forget such an enlightening artistic experience."

Chapter Twenty-Two

The following morning Eliza woke past noon with a terrible headache. The ball had seemed endless and she didn't return home until four in the morning. As a hardworking shopkeeper, she never slept past six, and she marveled at the frivolity of the upper crust.

Memories of last night returned. They'd found the Rembrandt. Her part of their arrangement had been fulfilled. After Huntington returned Amelia's forgery, there was no need ever to see him again.

The thought should have offered her comfort, but instead she felt an acute sense of loss, jagged and painful. She was being foolish. Huntingdon was no different from Lord Vale in that both would eventually marry rich, titled ladies. She was a mere shopkeeper, the daughter of the man who had fleeced him.

Still, when his note arrived later that afternoon she was filled with excitement.

Chloe handed her the missive. "This arrived for you this morning. I wanted to wake you, but Amelia said to let you rest and that you didn't come home until the wee hours of the morning."

Grayson's distinctive bold script was written on the front of the foolscap.

"You must tell me what the ball was like!" Chloe prodded. "What were the ladies wearing? And the gentlemen? Did you dance with the earl?"

Amelia's headache slid to the base of her skull. Her younger sister's incessant questions pounded against her. "The ball was decadent, Chloe. I'll explain it all later."

Eliza hurried into the back workroom and broke the seal.

> *Eliza,*
> *I would be honored if you would join me for dinner tonight at my home. As you have upheld your end of our arrangement, I shall uphold mine. My driver will arrive at seven.*
> *Grayson.*

Her heart thumped erratically at the thought of sharing another intimate meal with him, but this time in his home. She had no doubt what he meant; he was a man of his word and he would return the Jan Wildens forgery. But there was more there. He needn't invite her to his home. He could have the painting delivered by one of his many footmen.

So what more did he want?

And why was she questioning his invitation?

She wanted to see him one last time. Somehow she'd grown accustomed to him, to spending time with him, discussing their mutual love of art. He was intelligent, good at what he did as an art critic, and compassionate toward her sisters. And if she were honest with herself, she was highly attracted to him.

Then there was the issue of the Rembrandt. She had

questions of her own. Did the duke reclaim the stolen painting? And if so, how did he accomplish that feat? One didn't simply knock on a viscount's door, accuse him of theft, and search his house.

Amelia found her pacing the back room. "Did last night go as expected?"

Eliza whirled at the sound of Amelia's voice. "We found the Rembrandt. Pickens did indeed purchase it."

"That's good news, isn't it? Huntingdon will return my painting."

"He's asked to meet me tonight."

"You've grown attached to him, haven't you? And the thought of never seeing him again must be distressing."

Her sister looked so young and expectant standing beside a stack of canvases. Eliza thought of Lord Vale and the duke's daughter dancing together at the ball. Even though she knew Amelia hadn't seen Vale since his visit to the shop, her heart ached for her sister.

They were in the same predicament, weren't they?

A part of her wanted to tell Amelia, but she bit her tongue. Why ruin her fantasy? She would tell her later so that Amelia would have a chance to protect her heart, whereas Eliza feared her own was already lost.

. . .

Eliza wore one of her new dresses that evening. A simple, but elegant gown of pale green crepe embroidered with silver rosettes. Unlike the prior two occasions she had visited Grayson's Mayfair mansion, the butler, Hutchins, greeted her warmly.

"His lordship is waiting for you," Hutchins said.

She followed him through winding hallways and was surprised when they passed the formal dining room with its polished table and Chippendale chairs. They turned a corner, and she recognized the direction they were headed. Grayson's study was several doors down, and she wondered if they were to dine there, but when the butler passed the study and halted outside another closed door, her pulse quickened.

She knew this room as well...

Hutchins opened the door and she swept inside Grayson's private gallery. He was standing at the tall window, looking at the gardens below. He turned at her entrance and smiled. He looked magnificent in a navy jacket, snowy cravat, buff colored trousers, and polished Hessians. Candles glowed from the chandelier and candelabras on end tables around the room. In the corner was a table for two with snowy white linen and fine china.

Grayson held out his hand. "I've been looking forward to our dinner, Eliza."

She came forward and placed her gloved hand in his. "So have I."

He led her to the table and held out her chair. "I thought it would be fitting for us to dine here." Candlelight flickered off the priceless paintings.

His fingers lingered on her shoulders as she sat. She shivered in awareness and inhaled the distinctive scent of his shaving soap. He took the seat across from her and she was struck with a sudden nervousness.

The door opened and two footmen entered carrying silver covered trays. A plate of venison and fresh vegetables was placed before them, and her crystal goblet was filled with expensive wine. The food was delicious, but she ate without tasting. Her senses were attuned to the man before her.

He raised his wine glass. "A toast to our success."

She raised her glass. "To finding the Rembrandt."

She sipped the wine and then lowered it to find him staring at her lips. "You never told me what happened after the night of the ball. Was the painting in fact recovered and returned to its rightful owner, the Duke of Desford?"

"Yes. Thomas Begley, the duke's man of affairs, is a shrewd man. He knew he couldn't just accuse a viscount of knowingly purchasing a stolen painting, so he approached Pickens and told him that an art dealer who was arrested claims he sold the stolen Rembrandt to him. Pickens immediately panicked and claimed he did not know the painting was stolen. The Rembrandt has been returned to the duke."

"That's brilliant."

Dessert arrived, a sweet tart with a light coating of powered sugar. Grayson's dark eyes missed no detail as she ate the delicious confection and licked her lips.

He stood and held out his hand. "Come."

She rose and took his hand. He motioned to a velvet settee before the window and she thought he wanted her sit, but he shook his head and pointed behind the settee. She saw it then.

The Jan Wilden forgery.

"As promised. The painting is yours. I'll have it wrapped and will personally deliver it to you tomorrow morning."

She never doubted he would keep his promise. Yet a feeling of intense gratitude welled within her.

"What will you do with it?" he asked.

"Burn it."

He arched a dark eyebrow. "I hate to see art destroyed, even a forgery."

"It shall never end up in another collector's gallery again," she vowed.

He nodded, and she knew he understood how strongly she felt about the painting. "You're one of the most admirable women I have ever known," he said.

She looked up at him in surprise. "Admirable? Need I remind you of my family's history?"

"Those are your father's sins, not yours," he said firmly. "I told you I was wrong to blame you for his past deeds. You are a hard working shopkeeper, a woman of worth who has shouldered the burdens of caring for your sisters."

His words sent a thrill through her. Could it be true? Could he see her for who she truly was and not as the daughter of his nemesis?

"There's something else," Grayson said. He looked eager now and she was caught up in his excitement. He pointed to the *Icarus* engraving that she had originally admired the first time she'd walked into his private galley. "This is yours."

"Pardon?"

"This is my gift to you. I want you to have it."

Her mouth gaped. The engraving was worth a small fortune, but it was the gift of art that truly captured her senses.

"Why?" she asked.

"Ever since you first admired the work, it has reminded me of you."

Her heart pounded an erratic rhythm. She understood the vast differences between them. Socially, economically… morally, if one considered her family history. But now, none of it seemed to matter. Her eyes were open. Wide open. And she wanted this man.

Longed for him.

Their time together was limited—had come to an end. Was she willing to spend the rest of her life wondering what if?

The answer was a resounding no.

She was filled with a strange inner excitement as she studied the sensuality of his features. Just once, she wanted something for herself. One night that would last her a lifetime of memories. "I want more, my lord."

His brows drew downward. "Another painting?"

She stepped close and licked her lips. "No. More of what

I experienced in your arms," she whispered.

His dark eyes reflected glimmers of candlelight as he held her gaze. "Eliza, be sure of what you ask. I won't be able to stop this time."

"I'm sure," she breathed. "I want you."

He cradled the side of her face and his gaze dropped to her mouth. Her pulse quickened. She'd waited so long for his kiss tonight. Her lips parted in invitation and she rose on tiptoe to meet his lips with her own. He kissed her slowly and leisurely, his movements igniting a flame of desire. She wrapped her arms around his neck and arched forward in sweet invitation.

His kiss changed and he pulled her tightly against him from chest to thigh. All her senses heightened, and she moaned in approval. He gave her a passionate, openmouthed kiss, then his strong hands grasped her around the waist and he took two steps forward.

She found herself pressed against the wall between two paintings, just like an instance long ago. But this time she welcomed him, welcomed the thrust of his tongue, the pressure of his muscular chest against her sensitive breasts. She clung to him, her fingers grasping his broad shoulders. He flicked his tongue across the seam of her full lower lip, then reclaimed her mouth as if he was a dying man and she was his salvation.

He turned her to face the wall and swept her hair aside to place a hot kiss on her nape. She shivered at the touch of his lips on her neck, and desire pulsed through her in a dizzying rush. The heat from his body wrapped around her back as she pressed her palms against the cool plaster. Her breath caught as she felt his fingers undo the fastenings of her gown. She longed to feel her naked flesh pressed to his. The tiny row of buttons loosened, and her beautiful new gown slid down her body to pool at her feet. Her shift and corset followed, leaving her clad in only her silk stockings and frilly garters.

She was naked and he was fully clothed. She should be ashamed, but she didn't care, her need was so great. She wasn't a lady and she had eagerly made the choice to be with him. Then all thought fled as he kissed her back, licked each of her vertebrae down, down, down, until he reached her bottom and placed a hot kiss on her derriere.

She sucked in a breath. He was on his knees, cupping her breasts in his large palms and she'd never felt so vulnerable and hot at the same time. Her body cried out for his touch, for something she knew he alone possessed to give her.

He turned her around, sucked her breast into his mouth and flicked his tongue across her nipple. Searing sensations radiated from her breast to the aching heat between her thighs. She closed her eyes to savor the pleasure. He moved to her other breast and she felt she would go mad with need. He kissed a path down to her stomach, twirled his tongue in her navel, and blew on the patch of hair between her legs. Then he licked her hot, aching core.

Sweet heaven! Grasping fistfuls of his dark hair, she thought to pull him away, but at the first stroke of his hot tongue against her sensitive bud at the crest of her sex, her knees buckled.

His strong hands held her around her waist as he looked up. "I have you. I won't let you fall."

He lowered his head and continued his onslaught. He licked and laved her until she was quivering with need and her inhibitions fled. Her entire being centered on what his skilled mouth was doing to her. Her body tightened like a bow, and she was poised on a precipice of pleasure. With a last flick of his tongue, she hurtled into oblivion from an explosive climax. Gasping for breath, she sagged against him.

He stood and held her tight as her breathing slowed. At last she opened her eyes. His gaze was dark with passion and his body taut with need.

"I've wanted to do that to you since the first time I sat beside you at the Tutton auction," he said, his voice hoarse.

"Truly? I had no idea."

He brushed her forehead with his lips. "I know. I've had erotic dreams of you in my bed, and having you beside me without touching you has driven me to near madness."

She boldly met his eyes. "Show me more, Grayson."

"God, yes." Picking her up in his arms, he carried her to the settee beneath the window. The velvet fabric was soft and inviting against her naked skin.

Beyond half-closed eyed she saw the moon and stars through the window. She was aware of a rustle of clothing and watched as he tugged his cravat from his shirt points and unbuttoned his shirt. His chest was beautifully muscled with swirls of hair and a trail that ran down his flat abdomen to disappear beneath the waistband of his trousers. He pushed his trousers down his hips, and her gaze lowered.

His manhood jutted out long and hard. She felt a moment of unease at his size. She wasn't completely ignorant about what transpired between a man and a woman. She just didn't think he would be so *big* or that her body could accommodate him.

"Your body was made for me, for this," he said.

His dark gaze was so hungry and full of raw need that her heart lurched in her chest and her apprehension dissipated. She lowered her gaze once again, now fascinated by the size and length of him. She reached out to touch him. He was hardness encased in velvet. She slid her palm up the thick column and her thumb traced the head of his erection. He gave a strangled groan.

Placing a knee on the settee he lowered himself atop her. The feel of skin against skin set her aflame. Then she felt the tip of his rock-hard shaft slide over her aching flesh. She instinctively arched her hips.

"Easy," he murmured. "I want to go slow. Make this good for you."

Slow? She was too far gone and desperate for what he could give her. He entered her slowly, inch by inch, until she was wild with need. Her nails dug into his buttocks, urging him on until he groaned in pure male satisfaction and thrust deep. She cried out against his neck.

He immediately stilled, hot and throbbing inside her. His body invaded hers as his gaze seemed to penetrate her private thoughts.

"Are you all right?"

"Yes," she breathed.

He eased himself slowly out of her body. She thought he meant to leave her, but then he slid back inside at a deliciously slow pace. The possessive fullness was still there, but so was the pleasure. He increased his tempo and her hips rose of their own accord to meet his. She gripped his shoulders, watched his beautiful face through half-closed eyes.

Then he reached down between their bodies to stroke her sensitive bud and she shivered. Her body took over and she lost all thought but that of pleasure. Her climax built to a crest as he kept up his steady, powerful rhythm. Passion rose in her like the hottest fire, setting her body ablaze. Her breath came in ragged gasps as she rode the wave until she cried out as she was roused to the peak of desire, then hurled beyond into ecstasy.

His head fell forward, his breathing labored. Once, twice more he thrust within her, and then he stiffened and withdrew from her body as his seed spurted across her belly.

Eliza held him to her, their breathing labored. His breath warmed her cheek and she stroked his back. Love coursed through her and she knew what had transpired between them was an earth-shattering experience and she'd never feel the same for another man.

Chapter Twenty-Three

Grayson rolled to the side of the settee, careful not to crush Eliza beneath his weight. As his body recovered from an explosive climax, he struggled to get his equally ravaging thoughts under control.

Never had he experienced such great sexual satisfaction. Not with Leticia or his prior liaisons.

Only with Eliza Somerton.

And she had been a virgin.

"You're beautiful in your passion," he said gruffly.

She blushed and he found it arousing. His eyes were drawn to her magnificent breasts. The strawberry tips made his mouth water to taste her. His fascination was far from over.

He'd just taken her virginity. And damn if he didn't want her again.

He propped himself up on an elbow and watched her. Her lids fluttered and her breathing was slow and easy. He drew his fingers down the smooth skin of her arm, unable to keep from touching her.

"Stay the night with me," he said.

"I cannot. My sisters will worry."

"Next time, then—"

A rap on the door stopped him short. Grayson scowled. He'd left strict instructions that they not be disturbed after dessert was served.

He quickly donned his trousers and cracked the door to see Hutchins. The butler was clearly nervous and shifted from side to side.

"What is it?" Grayson asked.

"Lady Sara is asking for you, my lord."

"Sara? My sister is supposed to be spending the night at a friend's home."

"She has returned early and is in the kitchen eating scones with Cook," Hutchins said.

Grayson let out a frustrated breath and ran his fingers through his hair. "Tell her I'll be right there."

Damn. He had arranged it so that Sara would not be home. Did she have a spat with her friend?

His attention returned to Eliza. "I'm sorry. Sara was excited to spend time with her former school friend, Miss Abigail Evers, the girl she saw when we all went to Gunter's."

"I remember." Eliza rose and retrieved her dress. She bent over as she slid the garment up her legs, giving him a delectable view of her derriere. Desire pumped through his veins.

"Thank you for an unforgettable evening," she said over her shoulder.

That was it? She was dismissing him?

If she thought it was over between them she was mistaken. "Eliza—"

She smiled at him. "Please go see to Sara. She mustn't know of my presence. Meanwhile, I'll wait here."

• • •

Eliza paced the gallery for a full five minutes after Grayson departed. His lovemaking had been fiercely passionate and had touched her soul. More amazingly, he'd admitted that he no longer judged her for her father's criminal past. He saw her for who she strived to be—not the eldest daughter who inherited Jonathan Miller's morals and legacy.

She wished they had met under different circumstances. If her father had never turned into a criminal and remained a legitimate painter, perhaps she would have met Grayson at a Royal Academy exhibition. Or an art gallery. Or even a ball. What if they had a chance at a future?

Cease daydreaming, she chided herself. She should be grateful she'd experienced him for one night, however brief.

A sickening feeling of despair struck her. After Amelia's painting was returned, there was no need to see him again.

She breathed heavily. Tears welled in her eyes, and she wiped them away with the backs of her hands. Sara's interruption may have been for the best. Common sense dictated that Eliza should leave before they shared more intimacy that put her heart at perilous risk. Taking deep gulps of air, she garnered the strength to search for her reticule.

Footsteps sounded outside the room, and Grayson opened the door and slipped inside. "Sara's fine. Her friend has a cold, and Sara left so that she may recover. I apologize for the interruption to our evening."

"I'm glad nothing is amiss with your sister," Eliza said.

Grayson's eyes raked her and lowered to the reticule clenched in her fist.

"You're leaving," he said simply.

"I must."

"Stay with me. I can offer you so much." His voice was low, husky.

A knot rose in her throat. What was he saying? How could she stay with him? "I would never leave my sisters."

"That's not what I mean. We can still be together."

Her heart pounded so loud she was certain he could hear it. "You mean as lovers."

"Yes."

His eyes held hers, earnest and hot. She shivered at the scorching heat.

Could she do it? Could she become his mistress? Could she stay with him while duty required he marry a proper lady of his station?

A woman like Lady Kinsdale.

Eliza thought of Lady Kinsdale's cruel, but truthful words: *He'll never offer you marriage. You must know you are just a bit of bed sport to him.*

She already feared losing her heart to Grayson. Could she be his lover and further explore her sensual side without risk?

The answer was a resounding no.

Then there was the issue of her parent. Grayson may desire her as his mistress, but what about his vows for justice? Did he still want her father's neck in a noose? Did Grayson care enough about her to let the past go?

"What about my father?"

He stiffened. "What about him?"

"Let there be honesty between us. Do you still want to find Jonathan Miller and see him tried for his crimes?"

"What does that have to do with us?" he said tersely.

"Everything. I have come to suspect that finding my father was your utmost concern all along. But I also believed that you truly wanted to find the Rembrandt and that you do not wish me harm."

"I don't wish you harm," he insisted.

"But my father?"

Dark eyes stared down at her, probing her soul. "It's true I've hunted Jonathan Miller for years and have a burning need for justice. But you must understand that others came to me for aid as well. They lost fortunes and I tried to help them, promised them justice, but Miller slipped through my fingers time and time again."

At the simmering anger in his tone, a sudden disturbing thought came to her. "Did your plans for vengeance against Jonathan Miller include seducing his daughter?"

His expression was grim. "No. That's not what tonight was about. What happened here had nothing to do with anyone but us. Only us." At her dubious look, he shook his head and stepped forward. "How else can I convince you?"

She jumped back, knowing if he touched her, she'd be lost. "Convince me? You ask me to become your mistress, then admit that you will continue to hunt my father and send him to the gallows? How can you be so selfish?"

"Don't tell me that you have feelings for the man who abandoned you and your sisters to struggle to survive?" he said, a cold edge to his voice.

She listened with rising dismay. "Despite everything, he is still my father. You must also know there is a chance he may identify us as his daughters if he is arrested. And I must think of Amelia and Chloe. Amelia fears becoming like him and if he's captured and tried, it will cause her horrible inner turmoil. Chloe misses him terribly and only has fond memories of him. It's not as simple as you believe, and I can no longer be certain of your intentions. But the truth is that it no longer matters." Despite her resolve she glanced at the settee where they'd lain in each other's arms moments ago. "What happened tonight was a one time affair."

She clutched her reticule tight to her side and made to step by him.

He moved so abruptly to block her path that she squealed in surprise. Gripping her upper arms, his fingers caressed her skin. His gaze traveled over her face and searched her eyes. "This isn't over between us."

Her spine stiffened at his words and she tried to ignore the soft, rhythmic stroke of his fingers. Her heart seemed to rush to where he touched her, and a hot ache grew in her throat. "You had what you wanted. I trust you to deliver Amelia's painting. As for your 'gift,'" she said, motioning to the engraving on the wall, "you can keep it. Good evening, my lord." She attempted to pull away and sweep past him a second time.

His fingers stopped caressing her skin, but he did not release his grip on her arms. He refused to move. "Eliza—"

"Please let go."

He ignored her. "I'm not satisfied. I want you again."

Her heart tripped clumsily behind her lungs at the primitive need in his deep voice. Her fingers ached to reach out and touch him. "There can be no second time."

"I loved touching you. Making you come apart in my arms. You enjoyed it, too, Eliza," he said huskily.

Her face grew warm at his erotic words and her traitorous body responded. She must not allow him speak to her that way, not after he vowed to continue on his path for vengeance.

She twisted out of his grasp and lifted her chin. "Stop. It's over."

Grayson's eyes gleamed in a way that alarmed her. "I won't allow it."

"Arrogance does not suit you, my lord," she said.

"It's not arrogance when you were screaming out your pleasure, begging for more not long ago."

Her hand cracked across his face. He froze, his eyes narrowing. For a heartbeat she feared she had pushed him too far, but then he wordlessly stepped aside.

She halted by the door. "There's no need for you to personally deliver my sister's painting. A messenger will suffice. It's best if we don't see each other again," she said, then closed the door behind her.

Chapter Twenty-Four

The next morning, Eliza rose early and went downstairs to open the shop. She made a pretense of studying the ledgers, but her mind was far away in deep thought.

She was a fool. She'd trusted Grayson when he said Father's sins were not hers. He'd called her hard working.

Admirable.

Pain squeezed her heart. Grayson may desire her, but he wanted vengeance more.

She'd offered herself to him completely and freely…with all the pent up passion and desire she'd felt for him. Her mind burned with the memory of what he did to her body, how he made her feel. Allowing him to make love to her had taught her more about pleasure between a man and woman than she'd ever dared imagine. For as long as she'd live, she'd never forget the tantalizing caresses or the blazing passion.

She knew he could never offer marriage, but she'd foolishly thought that if they could share one rapturous night, then it would be enough to last her a lifetime. The opposite had occurred. She longed for him more fiercely than before.

There was no denying the truth. She'd fallen in love with him.

Leave it to her to want the unattainable.

She truly was a fool.

Eliza was vaguely aware of Chloe flitting about the shop, straightening a row of prints as she assisted a customer. Meanwhile, Eliza hunched on a stool behind the counter with a quill in hand scribbling in the ledger. Despite her best efforts, she couldn't concentrate, and the tiny numbers blurred before her strained eyes.

The shop's bell chimed and a man entered carrying a large package wrapped in brown paper.

"A delivery for Mrs. Eliza Somerton," the deliveryman announced.

Chloe glanced at Eliza over her shoulder. "What is it?"

Eliza's heart pounded. She knew, of course.

Eliza untied the string and peeled the paper aside to reveal Amelia's forgery of the Jan Wildens painting.

"Huntingdon returned it!" Chloe cried out. "I told you he was a man of his word. You must thank him for us."

Eliza wrung her hands and turned away.

Chloe frowned. "What's wrong, Liza?"

Eliza glanced at her sister. "Nothing. I'm pleased it's finally back in our possession."

Chloe was still staring at her. She tilted her head to one side and regarded Eliza thoughtfully. "You fancy him, don't you?"

Fancy was too frivolous a word. She'd fallen hopelessly in love with him.

"It matters naught, Chloe. I fulfilled my end of the bargain, he fulfilled his. We will both move on."

"But why does it have to end? You could marry."

Sweet Chloe. Her fascination with males was something that had always concerned Eliza. She still believed Father had no other choice than to run and that he would return as soon as he was able.

"He's an earl, Chloe. And I am just a shopkeeper."

"Rubbish. True love will always find a way."

"Members of the *ton* marry for wealth or title, and preferably both. I have neither."

"He's a powerful man, Liza. He doesn't need money and he already has a title. He can do as he wishes."

Innocent Chloe. There was no sense arguing with her.

"Where's Amelia?" Eliza asked. "She'll want to know that her painting has been returned."

"She's gone to the market and will be back shortly."

Eliza covered the forgery and stowed it behind the counter. She wanted to burn it. She knew it was childish, but the painting had caused her so much trouble.

Not entirely true. She never would have met Grayson if not for the forgery. Her thoughts twisted and turned. But if he'd never entered her life, she would not be feeling this much pain.

She ran her fingers down the gilt frame. She'd wait until Amelia was present to decide the fate of her work. It only seemed right.

"Tell me when Amelia returns," Eliza said.

"Why? Where are you going?" Chloe said.

"Out."

She needed to leave to clear her head. The shop's walls seemed to close in on her making it difficult to breathe. She was useless with the ledgers. She couldn't stay and pine after the loss of Grayson from her life.

She reached for her cloak and stepped outside.

The air was cold and damp as she made her way across the street toward the park. Her breath left puffs in the frigid air. Eliza inhaled the cold, felt it in her lungs. Last night's confrontation with Grayson flitted through her mind.

She refused to be his mistress. His position in society required he marry and produce an heir to the earldom. And his driving need for revenge toward her father would always be utmost in his mind. It would always come between them.

They could never be together. Their stations in life were as clearly drawn as lines in the sand.

Then why was it so painful? She'd had what she'd wanted, hadn't she? An incredible night with the Earl of Huntingdon. Memories to last her for many lonely nights. She'd known better than to expect more.

She reached the park. It was isolated as she knew it would be this time of year. The oak trees that would shade the walk in the summer months were barren and sleeping. She sat on a bench and pulled her cloak tight around her. A squirrel darted across the path in front of her bench.

A sound drew her attention. Almost like the scrape of booted feet on the stone path. She turned and saw nothing but a hedge of shrubs.

The wind? An animal?

Still, she had a weird sensation that she was being watched.

Her pulse quickened with unbidden excitement. Had Grayson followed her?

She scanned the park but saw nothing. She finally turned away. She must be bad off if she was imagining his presence.

She stood and quickly headed back to the shop.

• • •

The next day, Eliza was in the back workroom cataloging shelves of supplies as the shop's bells chimed. She needn't worry about seeing to any customers since Chloe was out front. But then she heard *his* voice.

"Good day, Miss Chloe."

"Good afternoon, my lord," Chloe said.

Eliza swept the curtain aside to see Grayson's tall, cloaked figure. He spotted her clutching the fabric and their gazes sizzled across the room. He removed his beaver hat, and her heart immediately gave a little jump.

Eliza stepped forward, the curtain closing behind her.

"I wanted to see the painting safely delivered," he said.

Chloe spoke first. "Thank you. Eliza will surely sleep better now."

"Oh? Has she had difficulty?" he asked, his eyes never leaving Eliza's face.

"Heavens, yes!" Chloe said.

"Chloe!" Eliza admonished.

Chloe's lips curled in a mischievous smile. "If you will pardon me, Lord Huntingdon. I told Amelia I would help her with her errands," she said as she fetched her cloak from a hook by the door and fled the shop.

Eliza stood still, a tumult of confused emotions racing through her. She wanted to scream at him. She wanted to kiss him.

"Is it true that you've had a hard time sleeping?" he asked softly.

"What does it matter?"

"It matters to me." He looked like he would take a step forward, then stopped. "The other night ended badly between us."

"Badly? Is that how you would describe it?"

His expression was somber, his eyes never leaving her face. "I never meant to hurt you. I care for you, Eliza. More than any other woman I've ever known."

She sucked in a breath. She wanted to believe him so badly. It was the closest he'd ever come to revealing his true feelings for her.

"It no longer matters. Our business together is at an end. I'm happy the Rembrandt is found and hope the duke keeps his promise and loans it to the museum."

"And us?"

"There is no us. There never was," she said sadly.

"Yes. There is. I see it in your eyes. Be my lover. You shall want for naught. A town house, a carriage, jewels. Whatever you desire shall be yours."

Was that what he thought of her? That she could be brought and bribed?

Just like her father?

She swallowed the despair in her throat. She loved him and he saw her only as mistress material. Worse yet, he still wanted her father's head.

He may care for her, but was it enough to change his ways? There was one last test.

"I don't want monetary things. Instead, let your need for vengeance go so there is nothing else between us. Cease your search for my father. Forget the past," she pled.

He was silent for so long she feared he wouldn't answer. "I cannot."

The words were crushing in their honesty. How unfair of fate to pair the man she loved with her dark and painful past. "I'm grateful for all you've done. And I shall never forget our night together." Reaching up on tiptoe, she kissed him one last time. "Good-bye, my lord."

She quickly stepped back, afraid he would pull her to him, and even more afraid of her response if he did.

Chapter Twenty-Five

Grayson raised the crystal decanter and filled his glass to the brim. He was well on his way to becoming drunk. He sat in an armchair in his study and had left strict instructions for his servants not to disturb him. He'd spent the week sulking and drinking; even Brandon hadn't been successful in luring him out for long.

Grayson reached for the glass, took a swallow of whiskey, and watched the fire in the grate.

A knock sounded on the door.

Damn. Who would dare?

"Leave me," he growled, barely recognizing his own voice.

The door opened. He swung around, fully intending to deliver a tongue-lashing to the servant.

Sara stood there instead. "What's wrong with you?"

Had she really asked him that? She was old enough to know when a man was drunk, wasn't she?

He scowled at her. "It's not a good time. Leave me be, Sara."

She ignored his command, entered the room, and closed

the door behind her.

Grayson nearly growled in disapproval. Apparently she didn't recognize a drunken man. She came forward and stopped in front of him. Her dark eyes darted from the half full decanter to his glass before focusing on his face.

"What did you say to Mrs. Somerton?" she asked.

"You're too young to ask me that." He kept his attention on the fire. Maybe if he ignored her, she'd leave.

"I may be young, but I've more sense than you," Sara said tersely.

His gaze snapped to his sister.

"Sara," he said, a note of warning in his voice.

"Please don't shut me out, Grayson. I won't leave until you tell me what happened between you and Eliza."

He waved his glass. "She won't have me."

"You proposed to her?"

He scowled. "Of course not."

"Then what do you mean she won't have you?"

He must be truly inebriated to have mentioned anything to his sister about his personal relationships. But he saw the moment that enlightenment dawned on Sara's face.

"Oh, I see. You want her to be your paramour."

Holy hell. He sat up. "Where did you even hear that word?"

"I'm not completely naive. I know what went on between you and Leticia when she visited late evenings."

"Sara," he growled. "We are not having this conversation."

"Why not? It's a perfectly good conversation."

He set his crystal glass down with a loud chink. "You have been raised far too leniently. I'm hiring a strict governess for you first thing tomorrow."

She didn't appear at all frightened which confirmed he'd been too lax with her upbringing.

"No wonder Eliza refused you. You should propose to

her. Get down on your knee and offer her our mama's ring. She may not bear a title, but she is a lady."

He stood and ran his fingers through his hair. "You don't know what you're saying. Reality is far from one of your childhood storybooks."

"Why? Because she is a shopkeeper? She's the best thing that's ever happened to you. You're happy when you're with her. I saw the way you looked at her when we went to Gunter's."

Sara's words hit a spot deep in his gut. Feeling restless and caged, he started pacing.

"I also know you are drinking yourself silly because you miss her," Sara continued.

He did. He missed Eliza terribly. But he'd never admit it out loud to Sara.

He stopped pacing and glared at Sara. "Marriage is out of the question. What kind of example would I set for you?"

Two bright spots stained Sara's cheeks and her lips thinned. "For me? Don't you dare tell me you are doing this for me! You love her, you idiot."

His jaw gaped. "What did you call me?" He stared at her in shock. His beautiful sister may be stubborn and willful, but she never, ever spoke to him that way.

Sara let out an exasperated sigh. "I think marrying Eliza would set a wonderful example."

A sudden thought occurred to him. "Eliza spoke to me at Gunter's about you. I didn't fully understand what she meant then, but now I have a suspicion."

A streak of unease crossed Sara's face. "She spoke to you about—"

"The Duke of Trent's son. You don't fancy him, do you?" Grayson asked.

Sara's shoulder's eased a notch. "Eliza spoke to you about the duke's son?"

"Yes. Answer me."

"No. I don't fancy him at all. He doesn't listen to a word I say and he cares only for himself."

Grayson shook his head. "Then he won't do at all. Not for my sister. I apologize for not seeing it."

Sara hesitated and worried her lip. "Eliza said I should confide in you. That I can trust you. That you want only my happiness."

"She said that?"

"She did."

His heart did a leap. Somewhere deep inside Eliza *must* trust him. He had only to convince her that he cared for her, truly cared.

"There's someone I do fancy. He's smart, hardworking, and"—Sara touched her heart—"he makes me feel special."

"Who?"

"Mr. Samuel Neal."

Grayson remembered the young man. The father and son had attended Lady Belmont's ball last year and the son had struck him as an upstanding man. Grayson had thought the father was fortunate to have a solid heir for his business.

"He's not titled," Grayson pointed out.

"Neither is Eliza, but she makes you feel alive, doesn't she?"

Yes, she did. A sudden thought clicked in his mind. It may have taken half a decanter of whiskey and a surprising talk from his sister, but he realized it just the same.

He was in love with Eliza Somerton.

Stark, raving love. His whole being tightened, and he knew it was true. He couldn't imagine his life without her in it. Without making Eliza his own. Nothing else mattered but her.

Not even the need for justice for her father's crimes.

He blinked and found Sara studying him expectantly. "If you still feel the same for Mr. Neal after you have your first Season, then I will seriously consider his request to court you," he said.

"Oh, truly!"

Grayson held up a hand. "But first he will have to impress me that he truly loves you and will provide for you."

"I'll agree to that." She hugged him tightly. "Promise you'll do the same. Why not seek the same happiness for yourself? For us? Eliza would make a wonderful sister-in-law. And if it wasn't for her, we'd never have had this talk."

Sara kissed his cheek and slipped from the room leaving Grayson alone with his whiskey once again.

He returned to his chair and stared at his glass. He had no doubt Eliza would make a wonderful sister-in-law for Sara. She would also make a wonderful mother and the thought of her carrying his child didn't scare him, but rather filled him with joy.

If she wouldn't be his mistress would she agree to be his wife?

What had he offered her except a position as his mistress and a promise to continue to pursue her father?

The need for justice that had burned so hotly and for so long in his gut seemed to diminish and evaporate.

From the first time he'd seen her, he'd threatened to turn her in to the constable if she didn't help him. He'd pursued her in his bed even knowing he still wanted Jonathan Miller hung. He'd told her as much.

Christ. Why *would* she have him?

He set the glass down. He could lose her forever. Had lost her. Not marrying her wasn't protecting Sara's interests. Having Eliza's influence and love would be the best thing for Sara.

And him.

He jumped to his feet and caught his reflection in a decorative silver mirror. He looked a fright with disheveled hair, sallow skin, bloodshot eyes, and wrinkled cravat and jacket.

It was late and he suspected it would take him until morning to sober and properly dress. He had a lot to do before then. He opened the door and shouted for his valet.

Chapter Twenty-Six

Eliza pulled the candle closer. Well past midnight, she had snuck downstairs, lit a candle, and sat at a table with her ledgers spread out before her, going over the shop's accounts. Her sisters were soundly asleep upstairs and the room was blessedly quiet.

It was no use returning upstairs to sleep. Immersing herself in dull figures was all that she could do to keep her sanity.

She missed Grayson terribly. It was ludicrous, really. She was made of sterner stuff than that of a lovesick female. She should be happy. Business was steadily improving. Whether it was due to Grayson's influence or the end of a bitter winter, she should be grateful. Chloe was healthy. Amelia had ceased talking of selling forgeries, and the concerning forged Jan Wildens was back beneath their roof where it belonged.

None of it helped. Her heart was breaking. She had wanted to go to Grayson a hundred times over the past week.

Yes, I'll be your lover. She imagined herself huskily speaking the words. *Teach me more about lovemaking. Show me everything.*

How easy it would be to forget their differences. To forget Lady Kinsdale's taunts. Forget that he still hunted her father.

To simply become Grayson's lover.

But for how long? How long before he tired of her and sought out another lover? How long before he married a titled lady of his station and had children? What would she be left with then?

Loneliness. Despair.

She'd given up dreams of ever marrying after her father left. She was a businesswoman. Her efforts went into the print shop and providing for her sisters. She wanted them to marry for love and security, but she'd never felt the urge to marry herself. If only he wasn't so tempting, if only she didn't want him so badly.

Her thoughts were disturbed by a scratching sound outside the shop's bay window.

Eliza froze, quill in hand.

What was that?

Perhaps it was a passerby in the street? Or a drunken neighbor finding his way home?

Or, heaven forbid, a burglar?

She glanced at the door, making sure it was bolted. She always locked the door at the end of the workday. Three unmarried women living upstairs required the utmost precaution.

The scratching sound repeated, this time followed by a low knock.

The hair on her nape stood on end. It was close to one o'clock in the morning. Who could it be?

She stood and grasped the candlestick. Her stockinged feet were silent on the wood floorboards. There were no lit street lamps this late outside her shop, and darkness met her gaze out the front bay window.

She pressed her ear to the door.

"Who's there?" she said.

"Eliza Somerton?" said a gruff-sounding voice.

She stiffened. The stranger knew her name, but that did not put her at ease. Anyone could learn the name of the proprietor of a shop. She wasn't foolish enough to open the door to a stranger in the dead of night.

"Go to the window," she said.

She went to the bay window and held up her candle. The stranger held up a lantern and the glow illuminated his face.

Air sucked from her lungs as pulse-pounding recognition struck her. It couldn't be! She felt like a bird flown into a stone wall.

"Father?" she whispered.

• • •

Fingers trembling, Eliza opened the shop door. A lone man stepped inside.

He was of average height and his face was illuminated by the lamp he carried. His pleasant, even features were as she recalled, but he looked older than his fifty-something years with more grey than brown in his hair and sideburns. His clothing was nondescript—plain trousers and a brown corduroy jacket. But the intensity in his green eyes was the same, sharp and assessing, as he looked at her.

"My God," she said. "It's really you, Father."

"Yes, Eliza. It's me."

She stood awkwardly, unsure whether her exhaustion was causing her to hallucinate. A part of her wanted to embrace him, another to strike him with the candlestick.

He set the lantern down on counter beside her ledgers. "It's good to finally see you. You look well."

"What are you doing here? We feared you were dead."

"I'm sorry for everything."

"Sorry! You left us." She was coming fully to her senses now, the blood pounding in her veins. She would have raised her voice, but she thought of her sleeping sisters.

She couldn't wake them, not yet…

"I had to run. The constable would have put me in jail," he said.

"But what about us? Chloe was so young. And Amelia not much older. We struggled to survive after you left."

Her father shifted from foot to foot as his gaze swept the interior of the shop. "But you have done well. I always knew you would, Eliza."

"But five years with no word from you. We feared the worst. You could have sent word that you were all right. Contacted us some way by—"

"I'm sorry," he cut her off. "But I couldn't risk it. Others were hunting me. Are still searching for me."

She thought of Grayson. How many others were wronged by her father? Dozens? A hundred if one considered the extent of his career.

"You hurt people," she said.

A wrinkle appeared between his brows. "It was only money from those that had ample."

After all these years he still held the same twisted beliefs. She felt as if she were thrown back in time and was a young girl standing beside him as he painted in his workroom. *The rich are filthy rich, Eliza. I'm just skimming a few pounds from them with none the wiser.*

She shook her head. "No. It wasn't just the money. You truly harmed others."

For an instant his glance sharpened. "Ah, you must be speaking specifically of Lord Huntingdon."

A terrible tenseness enveloped her body. Could he possible know about her relationship with Grayson?

Impossible.

He'd been away and they'd been discreet. She took a deep breath and tried to calm her racing heart. Her father was adept at reading people and she couldn't show the panic she was feeling. There was a rational explanation for his bringing up Huntingdon—an explanation that had nothing to do with her feelings. Grayson's humiliation was printed in the papers, and he'd been the one rallying the magistrate for a warrant for Jonathan Miller's arrest. It made sense that her father would mention him.

"There were others who were harmed. Dozens of them. You must know this as you painted many forgeries," she pointed out.

His eyes pierced the distance between them. "None as influential as Lord Huntingdon. Come now, daughter. I may be in hiding, but I'm not entirely ignorant of London events."

Wanting to change the subject, she decided to ask the question she'd wondered for five long years. "Where have you been all this time?"

"Not far. In town with different friends."

He'd been close, yet he couldn't send a letter or short note? She thought of all the times she'd wondered if he was ill and suffering in an alley. Or all the evenings she'd comforted Chloe after she'd woken from a nightmare. Or the days she'd caught Amelia painting feverishly, her brush almost battering the canvas in anger.

A sudden thin chill hung on the edge of Eliza's words. "Was Dorian Reed one of those friends?"

He looked at her questioningly. "Not recently. However did you learn of Mr. Reed?"

"It doesn't matter how I learned of him," she snapped. "What does matter is that you owe him a thousand pounds."

"An unfortunate business dealing gone sour."

"Unfortunate indeed! He wanted to take our livelihood.

You left us in a horrible position."

"But you handled it, no? I've heard Lord Huntingdon took care of you," he said.

"I don't know what you mean." Her unease rose as he mentioned Grayson's name once again.

He reached inside his coat pocket to pull out a newspaper and placed it on the counter. In the lantern light it was unmistakable.

The *Times* article.

"In fact, Lord Huntingdon has been taking care of you for quite a while now, hasn't he?" he said.

A coldness centered in her chest. "Why have you really returned?"

His gaze held her still. "I'm in need of funds. I don't need much. Just a few hundred pounds."

A knot formed in her stomach. "Five years and not a word and you return in the dead of the night to ask me for *money*?" she asked incredulously.

"Not you, Eliza. Lord Huntingdon."

"Huntingdon? How do you plan to achieve that?" she asked.

"You can use your feminine wiles to cajole it from him."

She stared at him in shock. "I cannot."

"Yes, you can. It's clear he's enamored of you. I don't hold it against you that you have become the mistress of the man who's hunted me with a vengeance and still wants my neck in the hangman's noose. But I do expect some loyalty."

If he took out a pistol and shot her, she couldn't have been more shocked. "Loyalty!" The notion was ridiculous coming from him.

"You're my eldest daughter. I'd say Huntingdon owes me for bedding you."

Eliza went suddenly still as anger welled in her chest. "I want you to leave." She'd never dreamed she'd say those words to her parent after she'd been so desperate to find him. She'd always known he was a fraud and forger, but now, as he stood before her, she saw him for who he truly was.

A master manipulator. A heartless man.

And she was to be the next victim of his schemes. He'd only returned because of her association with Grayson. She saw it now as clearly as if it had been branded on his forehead.

"What do you think Huntingdon will say if he learns who Mrs. Somerton truly is?" His lips curled mockingly.

She gave him a hostile glare. "You mean if he knew I was your daughter?"

He chuckled. "Yes. I can only imagine how humiliating that would be for the man. To be fooled twice by two members of the same family."

Clenching her teeth, she squared her shoulders as she faced him. Now that she knew why he'd returned, she wouldn't allow him to manipulate her further. "He knows the truth."

Surprise flashed across his face, but then the all too familiar avaricious gleam returned to his eyes. "Then Huntingdon must truly be smitten. It will be easy for you."

"You're wrong. My association with Huntingdon is at an end. You'll have to find some other way to steal your money."

"I should think it would be a simple task for you to make amends with the earl."

"Get out."

"What about Amelia? And Chloe? Don't you think they'd welcome a visit from me?" he asked.

The tension stretched tighter between them. "They will never learn of it," she swore.

He donned his hat and went the door. "I'll respect your wishes for now, but think about what I've said."

After her father left, Eliza stared at the door in disbelief. He was alive. After all these years, her father was alive.

And he was rotten.

Her gaze landed on the newspaper he'd left on the counter. She wanted to tear it into bits and scream.

She could not. She had to keep quiet, and she said a silent prayer of thanks that her sisters hadn't awakened to witness the scene. They'd both be devastated, but for different reasons. Although Amelia had ceased wanting to search for their father long ago, she understood his obsession for producing forgeries and struggled with the temptation of the artistic curse as well. Chloe had been much younger when he'd abandoned them, and her memories were of a father who was a hero to a young girl.

As for herself, Eliza had believed there was good in Jonathan Miller. She'd desperately wanted to believe.

She strode to the door and bolted it. He'd threatened to contact her sisters, but he would fail. She'd tell Amelia and Chloe the truth before she allowed him to hurt them more than they'd already suffered from his abandonment.

As for using Grayson, Eliza had no idea of her father's future intentions. Her mind spun with all the possible scenarios Jonathan Miller could act upon.

His motives were simple. He needed money. But she wouldn't fall into his trap. She loved Grayson too much to see him harmed. And Grayson *would* be harmed if she remained a part of his life. She didn't trust a word from her father's mouth. Even if she agreed to "use her wiles" to extort money from Grayson, her father wouldn't cease his efforts. He'd come calling again, for as long as he could use his eldest daughter to steal money from the Earl of Huntingdon.

But could her father still do harm? He could somehow let the press know that Mrs. Somerton, a close friend of Lord Huntingdon's, was the daughter of Jonathan Miller and a charlatan with a false name herself. Once again, Grayson would be humiliated. A laughingstock. She could just imagine what Viscount Pickens would say to the press. It would present the perfect opportunity for Pickens to gain his vengeance for the loss of the Rembrandt.

Yet she didn't think her father would reach out to the press for the simple reason that he couldn't profit from such an endeavor. He'd have nothing to gain, but would rouse Grayson's wrath even further and risk him renewing his search for the forger of the *ton* with vigor. It would be like waking a sleeping dragon with a hot poker, and her father was no fool.

No, if her father believed Eliza's relationship with Huntingdon was over and she refused to have any contact with him, then Grayson would be safe from scandal.

She loved Grayson with all her heart and would do everything in her power to protect him. Eliza swallowed the lump that lingered in her throat and rigidly held her tears in check. It was best that she had ended their relationship even if the only thing left was a raw and aching heart.

Her past had finally caught up with her.

Chapter Twenty-Seven

The following morning, Eliza woke exhausted. She'd finally fallen asleep on the couch by the bay window as the first light of dawn had touched the sky. She'd been afraid her father would return to bang on the front door and holler for her sisters.

She blinked in confusion as the bright morning sunlight streamed through the window. For an instant, she wondered if last night had been nothing more than a horrid nightmare.

She sat up, rubbed her eyes, and immediately noticed the *Times* article in the wastebasket where she'd thrown it the prior evening. She cringed. So much for it being just a bad dream.

Chloe and Amelia came downstairs smiling and carefree.

"Did you spend the entire night down here?" Amelia asked.

"I had to go over the ledgers," Eliza said.

Amelia placed her hands on her hips. "Well you look a fright. You work too hard." She came close and smoothed a frizzy curl on Eliza's forehead. "You should go upstairs and put on one of your new dresses. I like the blue one with the Brussels lace."

"It's my favorite as well," Chloe chimed in.

"Why bother? The shop will open in a few hours and one of my older dresses are sufficient," Eliza pointed out.

"A lady doesn't need a reason to look nice," Amelia pointed out.

At Eliza's quizzical look, Chloe chimed in. "We decided to go shopping today. Amelia needs supplies."

Eliza was exhausted and shopping held little appeal. "You two go without me."

Chloe nodded. "We'll buy you a bonnet while we're out."

Eliza frowned. "A bonnet? Whatever for?" She had several serviceable bonnets and her sisters knew it.

"For fun. The shop has been doing well, remember?" Amelia said, glancing out the bay window. "Chloe will hail a hackney while I help you change upstairs."

A moment of unease ran down Eliza's spine. Her sisters were acting strangely. Why the sudden need for supplies? And why insist she wear a new dress?

Had they seen their father last night? Did he throw stones at their bedroom window and speak to them?

"What's wrong with you two?" Eliza asked.

Two pairs of innocent eyes stared at her. If they had contact with their father, it didn't show.

Eliza let out a held in breath and the tension inside her eased. "Very well. We are short on supplies."

Eliza trudged upstairs to dress and Amelia made a valiant effort to fix her hair. Spending the night tossing and turning on the couch had left her ebony locks unruly and knotted.

By the time they made it downstairs, the hackney was waiting. "Doesn't she look much better?" Amelia asked Chloe.

Chloe smiled. "Absolutely."

He sisters donned their cloaks, anxious expressions on their faces as they looked at her as if she were a prize horse at a country fair. Eliza couldn't shake the feeling that they were behaving oddly.

"We won't be back until the afternoon," Amelia said on her way out.

Eliza closed the door and sighed. She was glad to have a few hours peace. She rarely had time alone. At least not since she opened the shop and her sisters lived upstairs. She needed time to think and knew menial labor would help calm her restless energy and focus her mind.

She started to dust the shelves of bric-a-brac decorations just as the shop's bells chimed and the door opened.

"Hello, Eliza."

Eliza whirled at the familiar masculine voice as Grayson stepped inside. Her heart did a little jolt at the sight of him, and she dropped the dust cloth in her hand. His chiseled features drew her gaze and she wanted him so badly.

"I thought Amelia and Chloe were acting strange. Did they know you were coming?" she asked.

He smiled mischievously. "I sent them a note yesterday."

"No wonder they were in such a rush to go shopping," she said to herself as much as to him. A sudden fear made her stomach clench tight. Eliza looked out the bay window. "This is a bad idea."

Was her father watching the shop? Did he know Grayson was inside? Could he see them now?

"I know you said you didn't want to see me anymore, but you must hear me out," he said.

"This really isn't a good idea, my lord. We shouldn't be seen together."

"You needn't worry. My carriage is down the street. Your reputation is secure."

It wasn't her reputation she was worried about but his, if

her father had seen him arrive here.

"Still, I—"

"Shh," he said, placing a finger on her lips.

She stiffened at the brief touch. Excitement tingled in her veins, and despite everything, she desperately wanted him to kiss her.

"I have something to ask you. Something very important," he said.

She glanced out the window. "Fine," she said quickly. "Let's go upstairs then." If he wouldn't leave, then she needed to be sure no one could see him inside the shop. Their living quarters didn't have a window facing the street.

If Grayson was confused by her request, he didn't show it. "Of course."

He followed her upstairs, and she motioned for him to sit at the table. He held a chair for her, but refused to sit himself. Then he did the most shockingly unexpected thing.

He knelt on one knee before her and cradled her hand in his. "Eliza, I want you to marry me."

She blinked. "Pardon?"

His eyes swept over her face. "Make me the happiest man in London and marry me."

Goodness. Of all the things she'd expected him to say, a marriage proposal wasn't one of them. She stared, dumbfounded, as myriad emotions flooded her.

Love. Happiness.

Despair.

He squeezed her hand. "I've been a complete fool. Nothing matters but how we feel for each other. From the moment we first met, I've acted abominably by coercing you into helping me. I also gave you nothing but promises to pursue your parent for his bad deeds. Crimes that no longer matter. I swear to give up my pursuit of him."

She swallowed. She wanted to toss caution aside and

throw herself into his arms. She wanted so badly to accept what he was offering. "What of your title?" she asked. "You are an earl."

"It doesn't matter to me. You will be accepted as my wife."

"But I've lied about my own past."

"I'll speak with Begley to ensure his silence. No one else will learn of it," he swore.

"What about your sister, Sara?"

"She adores you and wholeheartedly approves." He kissed the back of her hand, then held her gaze. "Will you have me?"

Love poured from her chest. Oh, how she wanted to say yes and confess her love. But her past had reared its ugliness in the form of her father. He'd returned and nothing could change the truth of her background. Not even Grayson's devotion.

How could she marry this wonderful man and expose him to the same humiliation that he'd already suffered? He'd never forgive her. She'd never forgive herself.

They could never keep her true identity a secret. Her father would see to it. If they married, they would be at Jonathan Miller's mercy. He would blackmail Grayson forever to prevent the truth from coming out.

And if Grayson refused to play her father's game, society would learn everything. Grayson would be ostracized and his reputation damaged beyond repair. Jealous men like Viscount Pickens would be ruthless. Could she selfishly put the man she loved through such pain?

"I…I'm sorry, but I cannot marry you." Her voice was a hoarse whisper.

He blinked. "You can't? Or you won't?"

Her eyes filled with tears, and she pulled her hand from his. "You don't understand."

His eyes searched her face, reaching into her thoughts.

"No. I don't. Is there someone else?"

"Yes, in a way. Someone I cannot escape from."

His brows drew downward. "What does that mean?"

"I don't want to hurt you. It's best for both of us. We're ill suited," she said.

"Ill suited? I've never met a woman who was such a perfect match for me. I'm complete with you, happy for the first time in my life. Look me in the eye and tell me you don't feel the same."

She couldn't meet his gaze. "Please! Don't make this harder. Please go," she said, a note of hysteria in her voice.

She was desperate. She needed him to leave before she threw herself into his arms and kissed him with all the pent up emotion that was whirling inside her. She knew she couldn't reach out and touch him. His nearness in the small room was taking its toll on her restraint.

"The hell I will," he growled.

He stood and pulled her into his arms. His mouth swooped down to capture hers. His fingers speared through her hair and held her captive as his tongue plundered her mouth. His kiss was raw and possessive, urging her to submit. Heat leaped between them, arousing a fiery need in her that begged to be quenched.

Any thought to resist him dissolved in a surge of desire. She was already fighting too many emotions—too many open wounds of her past—to battle this fierce lust as well. Her hands grasped his strong shoulders and she kissed him back in fierce abandon, desperate to know him one last time.

His hands worked at the buttons of her gown. She longed to feel her bare breasts against his hard chest. She gave a throaty moan of approval as the first few buttons came undone. His normally nimble fingers were impatient and the last remaining buttons popped and the silk tore. She didn't care, not when his dark eyes devoured her with savage need.

They shed their remaining clothes quickly.

His head lowered to kiss each of her breasts, and raw, sizzling sensations coursed through her. She clutched his shoulders for support. He picked her up and carried her to her bed.

His body covered hers and she felt the hot, hard flesh between her thighs. She arched forward until he slid in deep and moaned at the exquisite pleasure of the throbbing fullness of him. She watched him, as he began to move–all sleek muscle and sinew–and tried to burn the memory of him in her mind forever. He pumped inside her until the friction built to a fevered pitch. She threw back her head, crying out, as waves of exquisite pleasure rocked her. He shouted out hoarsely as he withdrew and spent on her belly.

They lay panting beside each other. His hands stroked her hair and back. He kissed the top of her head. "Do you still think we weren't meant to be together?"

Her heart ached. She was not for him, and no matter how painful, she must end whatever feelings he had for her. "I'm sorry. My answer is still no. We shouldn't have done this."

She tried to rise, but his arms tightened about her. "Nothing about this was a mistake," he said.

Now that the frenzied passion had passed, her unease returned. Lifting her head, she looked in his eyes. "Please. My sisters will return soon. We cannot let them find us here like this."

He nodded and loosened his grip. She rose quickly to pick up her dress only to realize it had torn. She yanked open the doors of her wardrobe and pulled out one of her older gowns. She turned when she was finished dressing to see him pull up his trousers. Her heart beat as his muscles flexed and his broad shoulders gleamed from a shaft of sunlight from the overhead window. He was magnificently built and she'd need to remember him to survive the lonely years ahead.

They descended the stairs together, and she opened the front door. She tried to glance outside to see if anyone was lurking about, but Grayson's broad shoulders blocked her view.

"I won't give up, Eliza," he said. "Not until you agree to be my wife."

"I'm sorry, but my mind is set."

Guilt stabbed her breast. Her misery was a steel weight as she looked up at him. How could she send away what she loved so much?

His expression was grim when he turned to leave. She closed the door behind him and sagged against the frame.

Only after she'd heard his carriage depart, did she cover her face with trembling hands and cry for the agony of her loss.

Chapter Twenty-Eight

Cradling a full glass of brandy, Grayson sat alone at a table in White's club. He swirled the amber colored liquor in the glass. He'd been here for two hours and hadn't drunk a drop. Acquaintances had passed by and nodded in greeting, but no one approached. Grayson's expression was that of a man who wanted to be left alone.

Something wasn't right in the world.

Eliza had refused him.

It wasn't just her refusal that alerted him, but the way she'd done it. He'd expected surprise, shock, and even hesitation. After all, he hadn't treated her with the respect she deserved by initially offering to make her his mistress, but he'd hoped that once he'd asked her to marry him and he swore to give up his search for her father, she'd realize how sincere he was... how hopelessly devoted.

He'd understood her hesitation, he'd even expected it. But not her rejection. Because at the last second—just before she'd turned away—he'd seen the longing in her eyes and the desperate yearning to say yes. Their passionate lovemaking had seared his heart and his body. She'd been desperate in her need, consuming in her passion, and he'd been so certain she'd accept him.

Something was wrong.

Devastatingly wrong.

Grayson set the full glass down and walked out of the club. It was a chilly evening and he pulled his coat collar up as he descended the club's stairs. He rounded the corner to where his coach was parked when he heard his name.

"Lord Huntingdon."

Grayson halted and spotted a man leaning against the side of the brick building. He stood in the shadows and could have easily been missed.

"A moment of your time, my lord," the man said.

Grayson's senses were alert. The club was located in a good part of town, but it wasn't unheard of for a gentleman to run into a pickpocket or thief.

"Who are you?" Grayson asked.

"Someone you've been looking for."

Grayson's gaze narrowed. Something about the man's stance and voice were vaguely familiar. "Your name, sir?"

"I dare not say it aloud, but you know who I am." The man stepped into the light of a nearby gas lamp and removed his cap.

Grayson froze, not believing his eyes. "Jonathan Miller. I'll be damned."

Miller put his hat back on and glanced from side to side before returning to look at Grayson. "I hear you've been searching for me, my lord."

Grayson's eyes narrowed. What the hell was Miller doing here seeking him out? The blackguard was too smart to willingly hand himself over to the authorities. "Shall I summon the constable?"

"I see you haven't forgotten the past."

"Did you think I would? You produced more forgeries than any other artist in the history of London."

"Am I that acclaimed?"

Grayson scoffed and stepped forward. "Let's not mince words. You should already be in jail."

Jonathan Miller took a quick step back and raised a hand. "Wait. I understand you've met my daughters."

Grayson's jaw clenched and he halted. He knew there was a reason behind Miller's sudden appearance. So what was his game? "You've seen them, haven't you?"

"Only Eliza, my eldest," Miller said.

In a flash, Grayson grabbed him by the throat. He threw him against the brick wall in the alley. Trying to get air, Miller clawed at Grayson's hand. For a split second Grayson imagined what it would be like to squeeze the life out of the bastard.

"What did you do to her?" Grayson snarled.

Miller's eyes bulged in his reddening face. "Nothing," he gasped. "I only asked her for what I need."

Grayson dropped his hand as understanding struck him. "You asked Eliza for money, didn't you?"

Miller nodded curtly and rubbed his throat.

"Things must be desperate for you to show your face to your daughter after you abandoned her and left her to care for her two younger sisters. No money, food, or shelter. Your forgery crimes pale in comparison."

Icy contempt flashed in Miller's eyes. "It's true then. You have fallen for Eliza. Does it bother you to know she's my daughter? That my blood runs in her veins? Or that she is just like me?"

"She's nothing like you," Grayson snapped. "She's hardworking, caring, and loyal. She must take after her mother."

Miller paled for an instant at the mention of his dead wife.

Grayson suddenly knew the truth. "You know she doesn't

have money so you asked her to get it from me, didn't you? You asked her to use me and she refused, didn't she?"

Things were starting to make perfect sense. The desperation he spotted in her gaze moments before she rejected him.

Her emotional words. *I don't want to hurt you.*

She was worried for him. Worried that her father would surface and the truth would come out that she was Jonathan Miller's daughter. She feared that his reputation would be harmed once again. Eliza wanted to protect him.

Grayson glared at his long-time nemesis. He saw it all clearly now. "You blackmailed your own daughter for money. And I thought you were a bastard before," Grayson hissed.

"I need to survive."

"I'll pay you," Grayson said.

A glint of greed lit Jonathan Miller's eyes.

"I'll pay you, but not to keep it a secret that I'm going to marry your daughter. I don't care if the world knows. Shout it from the rooftops if you want. I'll not let you ruin her future or her happiness any longer than you've tormented her in the past," Grayson said.

"You won't summon the constable or pursue me?"

"No. Despite everything I don't believe Eliza would want to see you hung. Amelia and Chloe, either. It would cause them pain, and I'd forgo revenge rather than see them suffer. So I'll pay you to disappear for good. But trust me when I say that after you take my money, you are never to trouble them again." His hand snaked out once again to wrap around Miller's throat and squeeze.

Miller coughed and sputtered, gasping for air.

"Understand?" Grayson's voice was edged with steel.

"Yes…yes."

...

Loud banging on the shop door woke Eliza and her sisters. The trio scrambled down the stairs.

"Good heavens! Who could it be at this time of night?" Amelia asked as she threw on a wrapper.

Eliza lit a lamp and handed it to Chloe. Her heart thumped madly in her chest like a drum. Had their father returned? She hurried down the stairs with Amelia and Chloe close behind her.

Eliza cracked the door. "Grayson! What in the world are you doing here? It's the middle of the night."

"Please pardon the late hour," he said as he stepped inside the shop. He glanced at Chloe and Eliza. "If you two don't mind, I need a moment of Eliza's time in private upstairs. I promise she'll be safe."

When both Chloe and Amelia nodded, Eliza protested.

"Come with me," he said. It was a demand, not a request.

"But I'm not dressed and I told you—"

He leaned down to whisper in her ear. "Your father paid me a visit this evening."

Her eyes widened and she felt the blood drain from her face. She was highly conscious of her sisters standing a few feet away. She opened her mouth to speak, but the words wouldn't come.

"Come with me," he urged.

He took her hand and led her toward the stairs leading up to their living quarters. She didn't protest. Her thoughts were a jumble of confusion and fear. She couldn't believe her father had contacted Grayson. She'd never believed he would be so reckless.

Grayson must be furious. Rightfully so.

She glanced at him as they went up the stairs. His profile was strong and proud and his hand was warm as it enveloped hers.

He pulled out a chair at their small kitchen table. "Sit."

Her pulse beat erratically, and she finally found her voice. "I'm so sorry my father approached you." She was ashamed and scared. Had he asked Grayson for money? Had he tried to blackmail him?

"No," Grayson said, lifting her chin to force her to meet his gaze. "Never apologize for him again. You have been wronged by him more than I have, more than any of his prior victims."

She sat stunned. "But he wanted me to get money from you! To use you."

"Shh. I don't care. None of it matters. I still want you as my wife."

She stared at him in shock. He wanted to marry her after all that had happened? "But he will ruin you. What if my true identity is revealed? What then? What of your reputation as an art critic? What about Sara?"

"I don't care what anyone else thinks. It's been years and my reputation as a critic is proven and secure. Besides it's more likely my fellow critics will be green with envy when they learn you are my wife. As for Sara, she will be thrilled to have you as a sister and mother figure. Her dowry will more than make up for any gossip."

She bit her lip. "What if he returns?"

"I don't believe Jonathan Miller will return and the truth is that I don't care if he does. In fact, I just may announce it at the next Academy Exhibition. The Earl of Huntingdon has married the daughter of the forger of the *ton*."

Her mouth gaped. "Are you crazed?"

"Only for you. My life would be hopelessly empty without you."

"What about justice. Now that Miller has returned, don't you want to see him held accountable for all his crimes? Even more so now that he tried to blackmail you?"

"I no longer care."

"What? Why?"

"As long as he cannot harm you, I don't care if he is never arrested and I no longer wish him ill-will. Let all the others who purchased his forgeries seek his arrest. I suspect he'll be on the run forever and die a lonely, hunted man. But the more important question is will *you* miss him?"

She met Grayson's gaze. His brow was furrowed and she reached out and smoothed the lines. "No. I will not. I'm now certain that our lives are better without him."

"And what of your sisters? What will you tell them?"

She bit her bottom lip. "I had initially thought to keep father's return from them, but now that I've had time to think, I believe Amelia and Chloe should know the truth. No more secrets."

Grayson smiled. "You're the most courageous woman I know. I love you. Completely and utterly."

Tears sprang to her eyes. "Oh, Grayson."

Reaching into his pocket, he pulled out a box and opened it to reveal a large emerald surrounded by diamonds nestled in black velvet. He knelt on a knee and took her hand in his. "This belonged to my mother, and I want to do this properly. Eliza Miller Somerton, will you do me the honor of becoming my wife?"

She stared at the magnificent ring, then met his gaze. Her heart swelled. "Oh, Grayson. I've loved you for so long now. But I never dared hope of a future together."

"Please say yes, Eliza. I'll be a happy man with you by my side. Will you be mine forever?"

"Yes, my love. Yes." She dropped to her knees and threw her arms around him.

She had what she wanted as he drew her into his arms and kissed her tenderly. Only an hour before she thought the future held nothing but loneliness and uncertainty. But now, the future looked very promising indeed.

Epilogue

THREE MONTHS LATER

"How long must I endure that satisfied grin on your face?" Brandon asked.

Grayson's smile widened as he glanced at his wife across the parlor. "Get used to it. Our honeymoon is far from over."

Grayson marveled at how much his life had changed over the past months. He'd obtained a special license and married Eliza. They'd returned from a honeymoon visiting his country estate in Lincolnshire, and he'd moved both Amelia and Chloe into his London home. Sara was thrilled to get not only one new sister, but two more, and the three had become fast friends.

As for the Peacock Print Shop, Eliza had been hesitant to sell the business since it had saved her and her sisters from the poorhouse. Grayson had understood her connection to the shop and together they'd found a partner to run the business on a daily basis. Meanwhile, Eliza had started a new part of her life as Lady Huntingdon.

Brandon stared at Amelia as she laughed at something Sara said. "Do you think she'll give me the time of day now that she's the sister-in-law of an earl?"

Grayson shrugged. "You're to be betrothed to a duke's daughter, remember?"

Brandon shook his head. "It hasn't happened yet. I cannot bring myself to even court her, let alone propose."

Grayson didn't envy his friend. The longing on Brandon's face was unmistakable every time he glanced at Amelia. Brandon had to either forget her or bed her and Grayson wondered which would eventually win out.

But that was his friend's dilemma. Grayson's thoughts returned to his beautiful wife as she approached carrying a glass of champagne. Eliza looked delectable in a sea foam gown that heightened her chestnut curls and the swell of her breasts above the tight bodice.

"Your dress is driving me to distraction. I can't wait to remove it tonight," he whispered in her ear.

She struck his hand lightly with her fan. "Tsk. Tsk," she said, but her emerald eyes said something else entirely.

"I'm happy to see that your sisters have adjusted well to living here," Grayson said.

"Yes. But I still can't believe no one has spoken ill of us after the truth has come out in the newspaper."

The reporter from the Royal Academy had reached out to Grayson for an interview for the opening of a new gallery. Grayson had granted the reporter an interview, but instead of commenting on the new gallery, he'd told the reporter that his new wife was the daughter of the forger of the *ton*. The reporter had dropped his pad twice before he'd furiously finished scribbling his notes.

As soon as the article appeared in the newspaper, the gossips had been in their glory. But rather than the malicious gossip Eliza had dreaded, the fervent drawing room whispers had been of how the love of art had brought together a powerful earl and a wronged woman. Of course, Viscount Pickens had been bitterly outspoken, but his criticism had been drowned out by the romanticism of the marriage.

"I told you not to worry, my love."

"But how did you manage to finally silence Viscount Pickens?" Eliza asked.

"I believe he discovered that he owned one of your father's forgeries in his own private gallery."

Her mouth gaped. "You told him?"

"I didn't, but the Duke of Desford did."

"How did you get the duke to agree?"

"He was very grateful for the return of his stolen Rembrandt. When I learned he was to attend a function Pickens was hosting, I stated in passing that I believed Pickens owned a forgery. Pickens stopped his tirade immediately thereafter."

She giggled. "I wish I'd seen it."

"Me, too."

The butler announced it was time for dinner and the guests headed into the dining room. Grayson pulled Eliza aside. "I cannot wait another second to tell you I love you."

Tears formed in Eliza's eyes. His arms closed around her and she pulled his mouth to hers. He kissed her tenderly as his heart thudded in his chest. He didn't regret the past. Not a single second. Without it, he never would have met the woman who had given him hope, love, and such a bright future.

Acknowledgements

Writing a book takes much support from family, writing partners, and professionals. I couldn't have done it without my wonderful husband, John. Thank you to all my wonderful friends at NJ Romance Writers and RWA.

Thank you also to my supportive agent, Stephany Evans, for her wonderful feedback on my books. A note of thanks to my editor, Alycia Tornetta, at Entangled Publishing as well.

I'm also eternally grateful for my readers. Without you there would be no books!

About the Author

Best-selling author Tina Gabrielle is an attorney and former mechanical engineer whose love of reading for pleasure helped her get through years of academia. She often picked up a romance and let her fantasies of knights in shining armor and lords and ladies carry her away.

She is the author of adventurous Regency historical romances, *A Spy Unmasked* and *At the Spy's Pleasure,* books *In The Crown's Secret Service* series. Tina has also written *In the Barrister's Bed, In the Barrister's Chambers, Lady of Scandal*, and *A Perfect Scandal* from Kensington Books. *An Artful Seduction* is the first book in the Infamous Somertons series, and the next two books will be released by Entangled Publishing soon!

Publisher's Weekly calls her Regency Barrister's series, "Well-matched lovers...witty comradely repartee." Tina's books have been Barnes & Noble top picks, and her first book, *Lady Of Scandal*, was nominated as best first historical by *Romantic Times Book Reviews*. Tina lives in New Jersey and is married to her own hero and is blessed with two daughters. She loves to hear from readers. Visit her website to learn about upcoming releases, join her newsletter, and enter free monthly contests at www.tinagabrielle.com

You can also find Tina on Twitter, Facebook, and Instagram.

Get Scandalous with these historical reads...

LADY SCANDAL
a *Furies* novel by Wendy LaCapra

Sophia Baneham exists outside of polite society's influence, holding gambling parties for London's most dangerous men. Then a man walks into one her soirees, a compelling mix of charisma and icy control. And he offers the lady of sin a wager she can't refuse. But when danger closes in, undercover spy Lord Randolph won't just have to protect Sophia from an intended killer. He'll have to protect her from herself...

LADY OF INTRIGUE
by Sabrina Darby

Lady Jane Langley's reason and logic gives way to terrible, icy fear when she finds herself in a devastating carriage accident where her companion is murdered. But this was no mere accident. This was an assassination. Spy Gerard Badeau takes Jane hostage. But if he doesn't kill her, he risks a fate that is far, far worse... falling in love with her.

DUELING WITH THE DUKE
a B*rotherhood of the Sword* novel by Robyn DeHart

Gabriel Campbell, Duke of Lynford never intended to carry that title, but when his reckless brother gets himself killed in a duel over a woman, Gabe has no choice. Now he's sworn off love, blaming the woman that broke his brother's heart and led to his untimely death. Gabriel's position in the Brotherhood of the Sword leads him directly to Lilith Crisp's door. Lilith is the one woman he's always wanted. A secret about Lilith's niece brings them together to face a danger that threatens not only their lives, but the fate of England's Crown. Resisting Lilith is getting difficult and Gabe finally recognizes that finding love means forgiving the past and that might be the one thing he simply can't do…

How to Beguile a Duke
by Ally Broadfield

Catherine Malboeuf wants to reclaim her ancestral home and valuable missing heirloom. Unwilling to sell the estate, however, the attractive Duke of Boulstridge makes her a wager. He'll sell Walsley Manor if--and only if--Catherine secures an offer of marriage from an eligible member of the ton. After all, no proper gentleman would ever marry a woman who conceals a cutlass in her skirts. Yet Catherine's unconventional disposition seems to ignite a need in the duke. One that won't just cost him the wager, but the very heart he swore never to give away…

More from Tina Gabrielle...
A SPY UNMASKED
AT THE SPY'S PLEASURE

CPSIA information can be obtained at www.ICGtesting.com
Printed in the USA
BVOW01s1331080816

458319BV00001B/5/P